<u>Did I Read This Already?</u>
Place your initials or unique symbol in
square as a reminder to you that you have
read this title.

R. M					Mw
					CM

FREEDOM'S LIGHT

This Large Print Book carries the
Seal of Approval of N.A.V.H.

FREEDOM'S LIGHT

COLLEEN COBLE

THORNDIKE PRESS
A part of Gale, a Cengage Company

GALE
A Cengage Company

Farmington Hills, Mich • San Francisco • New York • Waterville, Maine
Meriden, Conn • Mason, Ohio • Chicago

Copyright © 2018 by Colleen Coble.
Scripture quotations are taken from the King James Version. Public domain.
Thorndike Press, a part of Gale, a Cengage Company.

Thorndike Press® Large Print Christian Fiction.
The text of this Large Print edition is unabridged.
Other aspects of the book may vary from the original edition.
Set in 16 pt. Plantin.

LIBRARY OF CONGRESS CIP DATA ON FILE.
CATALOGUING IN PUBLICATION FOR THIS BOOK
IS AVAILABLE FROM THE LIBRARY OF CONGRESS

ISBN-13: 978-1-4328-5651-9 (hardcover)

Published in 2018 by arrangement with Thomas Nelson, Inc., a division of HarperCollins Publishing, Inc.

Printed in Mexico
1 2 3 4 5 6 7 22 21 20 19 18

*For my friend Kristin Billerbeck,
who always believed in this novel*

CHAPTER 1

August 2, 1776

"I forbid you to go, Hannah."

Hannah Thomas curled her nails into her palms, slick with perspiration. Her husband couldn't leave her here on this rocky Massachusetts coast. He just couldn't. Other wives followed the Continental Army troops. Why couldn't she?

John smiled down at her, but the strain in his eyes signaled that he was tired of her womanly vapors. He shifted his bulk and his shoulders strained the seams of his makeshift uniform, just breeches and an oversize navy coat topped by his battered cocked hat. She'd wanted to let out the seams, but he told her one good thing about war was he'd likely shed some of his corpulence. She couldn't imagine him suffering deprivation.

He put his large, calloused hand on her shoulder. "I'd not have you in harm's way,

7

Hannah. You are needed here. Keeping the light for the sailors will be your contribution to the War of Independence. The colonials must have supplies, but the British would like nothing better than to see our ships crash on the rocky shores. Ease my mind, Wife, and accept my provision for you. Promise me."

Her words of protest died on her lips. She was used to speaking her mind to her husband, though he was twenty years her senior, but today she could tell it would do no good. Hannah bit her lip in a vain attempt to keep the tears at bay. "I promise."

"General Washington has asked for all able-bodied men to agree to serve one year in the Continental Army. I must answer the call. I should have gone last year. I know you understand this and support it."

The Second Continental Congress had appointed George Washington as general over the newly formed army, and he needed men.

She nodded. "Of course. I would serve myself if I could." Hannah had heard Paul Revere's cry, "The regulars are coming. The regulars are coming," with her own ears the night of April 18 last year and had seen the two lanterns shining from the bell tower of the Old North Church. She'd thrilled to have witnessed that event in the struggle for independence.

The colonists could no longer endure the endless taxation from Britain. War had come, and with it, so had many deaths. Good men, friends in Charles Town and others all across the colonies, had gone off to fight and had never returned. John had been part of the Sons of Liberty ever since she'd known him.

Much as she favored the struggle, she didn't want to lose him.

Through the open window, she could see the glow from the four lamps in the twin-towered lighthouse. She had hated this lonely outcropping of land ever since John had brought her here a year ago after they were wed — the crash of the waves never left her ears and it sounded as if a storm was brewing today. Come night, she would be hard-pressed to keep the lamps lit in the lighthouse. The thought brought her no joy.

From that first night, the lighthouse had beckoned from the carriage window. At times she hated the light and the attention it received from John. He'd wanted a son, something his first wife had failed to accomplish before she died of smallpox twelve years ago, one of nearly twenty thousand.

So far Hannah had also failed to conceive a child.

With John gone, she'd be alone without the comfort of a child to hold. She didn't know how she would bear the isolation. His mother and sister lived over the crest of the hill, but they disapproved of everything about her. How would they treat her with John no longer around to defend her? She reached out and grasped his hand in a tight grip.

"Send me not with tears, Hannah," John whispered as he thumbed a tear from her cheek. "Bid me go with a smile and a kiss. As our fellow patriot Thomas Paine said in *Common Sense,* 'It is not in numbers, but in unity, that our great strength lies; yet our present numbers are sufficient to repel the force of all the world.' I believe him, and I shall return, my Hannah."

She attempted a watery smile. "When will you return?"

She knew the answer before she asked it. John didn't know how long he would be away, or even where the battles would lead. Though Washington had asked for a year, her husband would not abandon his duty any more than she would. The British would not relinquish their colonies easily, and this war could go on for years.

He draped his scarlet cloak over his shoulders. "God alone knows that answer, Hannah. But know that I hold you in prayer. Be strong and vigilant. When you trim our wicks, remember the ships you save bring food to our troops. Kiss me. I must be off. Harlis waits."

Hannah could see her brother-in-law's shadowy figure waiting by the gate but was still reluctant to let John go. What if he never returned to her? She suppressed the foreboding and raised her face for a final kiss, clinging to his stalwart form as she inhaled the scent of him. His masculine aroma was always overlaid with the scent of sharp brine. She breathed it in deep until he pulled away. He was eager to go, and it stung a bit.

She gave him a playful push. "Go you, then. I shall await your return."

John took his musket from its place under the kitchen window and strode toward the door. He cast one last glance her way, then he took his leave. Hannah ran to the window and watched him mount Reliance, his bay gelding, then follow his brother down the rocky trail toward Plymouth.

Tears trailed down her cheeks, and she lifted her chin. She'd faced worse than this and survived. Hannah strained to see through the mist one last time, but he was gone. Though they did not share an overwhelming passion, but one of gentleness and comfort, Hannah missed him already.

Several long moments hence she wiped the wetness from her cheeks and forced herself to go about her duties for the coming night. The Thomas family had served the light for many years, and she could do this for him.

Hannah pulled on her cloak and tugged the hood over her head. The light mist still hung in the air, coating the view with a milky veil. She paused for a moment outside the door and listened. The only sound the wind carried back to her ears was the roar of the waves. She sighed and picked her way along the rocks and the sand to the lighthouse.

Opening the door to the nearest tower, she flinched at the stinging smoke. Her eyes smarting, she climbed the steps to the light tower. She extinguished all four wicks on the first bucket lamp and picked up her rag to clean the glass. She hated the monotony of the job. She'd had to do very little of the actual work with John here, but now the entire dreary burden would fall on her shoulders.

Rubbing the glass briskly, she let her attention drift. She hadn't thought her life would be tending a light on a lonely coastline in Massachusetts. She still missed the hustle and bustle of Charles Town — parties and soirees with her sisters, Lydia and Abigail.

Her hand paused at her duties, and her heart gave a sudden thump in her chest. She could ask Lydia to join her! Her parents would never spare their baby, Abigail, but surely they would allow Lydia to come to her. Her younger sister would keep her from loneliness and bring a bit of the southern ways Hannah so missed. She rushed through her cleaning and hurried back to the house with a smile on her face.

Once the letter was composed, she resigned herself to making a duty call on her in-laws.

Roses bloomed at the front of the stately two-story home, and Hannah breathed in the sweet aroma. She caressed a soft bloom but didn't dare pick one. Beatrice would never stand for it. Her roses were her pride and joy.

Hannah lowered her hand. Enough dallying. Straightening her shoulders, she pushed open the heavy wooden door. She could hear the murmur of voices from the parlor, and her heart sank when she recognized the deep tones of Arthur Goodman, the minister at the Congregational church.

"Your daughter-in-law has fallen asleep in worship the past three Sundays, Mistress Thomas. The church must act on this."

"I am aware of this problem, Reverend Goodman. What my son ever saw in her, I will never understand. I suppose it was her pretty face, but I had hoped I had raised my son to know the difference between fluff and substance."

"You know, I am sure, mistress, the holy Scriptures command that an overseer must have his wife and children under control. I fear the church must act to remove your son from his duties as deacon until he is more able to control his wife."

Hannah clenched her jaw at the condemning tone of the man's voice, and her temper flared. John was always warning her how her temper needed bridling, but she longed to rush into the parlor and berate them both for gossip. She'd endured the disdain of her in-laws and the community for a year now. But the minister's harsh words tore at her heart. In her church in Charles Town, faith was real and vital, not this strict adherence to law. The entire town of Gurnet, Massachusetts, was governed by their narrow moral code. Their ancestors had fled England to seek freedom of worship. Why could they not accord that same courtesy to others?

Breathing deeply, she leaned against the wall as they went on about her shortcomings. She supposed she should have bowed to the stern faith this community held, but it quenched the life from her.

The inhabitants of the pristine parlor were still unaware of her presence as she stood in the doorway. Reverend Goodman's fleshy form looked ludicrous perched on the delicate imported sofa, his large feet firmly planted on the lustrous red tones of the Oriental rug. The teacup looked tiny in his massive hands.

Her mother-in-law, Beatrice Thomas, sat in the lady's chair opposite him by the fireplace. Her face flushed when she finally caught sight of Hannah standing by the door. She rose with a soft whisper of silk and gave Hannah a brittle smile. "My dear Hannah, there you are. We were just discussing you. Would you care for some tea?"

Hannah struggled against the hot words that threatened to spill from her tongue. For John's sake, she would be respectful. "I would not, Mother Thomas. I can see you are busy, and I have duties to attend to. I will return at a more convenient time." To her chagrin, tears spilled down her cheeks, and she turned and fled from the room. Now they would know she had heard their hurtful words.

Humiliation and anger choked her, and she stumbled along the path up the cliff toward home. She rushed into the saltbox house. She put her palms against her hot face, then dropped her hands to her sides and paced the rug. She wanted to march right back over there and give them both a piece of her mind. She'd tried her best to be a good wife to John, but it was never enough for Mother Thomas. Was it her youth or her failure to conceive? Both were beyond her control.

Hannah dearly longed for a baby — a child she could nurture and raise. She'd never mistreat or ignore her child, but the good Lord had not yet seen fit to bring life to her womb. She'd not yet given up hope.

Gradually her agitation eased as she thought of the verse she'd read this morning in Proverbs 15. *A soft answer turneth away wrath: but grievous words stir up anger.* That had always been her trouble. It was hard to answer softly when her anger burned so brightly at injustice. At least she'd managed to bridle her tongue today.

Hannah's trembling finally ceased, and

she was left with a deep sense of loneliness. The house echoed with silence. She had to get out of here, just for a little while. She hitched her eight-year-old mare Sally to the gig and set out for Gurnet.

The breeze washed the heat and humidity from her skin. Ominous black clouds gathered to the north, and the wind snatched at her mobcap and teased tendrils of black curls loose from the ribbon, so she finally took off her cap and pulled the ribbon from her hair.

Suppressing an irreverent grin, she pulled the gig to a stop outside the general store. She knew she looked like a fishwife, so she hastily dragged her fingers through her hair and plaited it. She climbed down and took her basket from the back.

Ephraim Baxter looked up from behind the counter when she stepped inside the store. He gave her a toothless smile, but Hannah could see his wife, Edna, assessing her appearance. She obviously found it wanting — her wrinkled mouth scrunched even tighter.

"Mistress Thomas." Ephraim wiped his wrinkled hands on his stained apron. "How may we help you today?"

Hannah smiled at both of them, in spite of Edna's disapproving look. Any company was better than her own. After giving Ephraim her order, she wandered along the battered wooden floor and looked at the notions. Everything from pots, birdcages, and baskets hung from the ceiling, while the floor space was crammed with barrels of pickles and displays of spices and sewing needs. The scent of cinnamon mingled with that of leather and mint.

She paused in front of the boiled hard-candy display. Why not indulge, just this once? The Thomas household usually frowned on such waste, but John wasn't here to scold her, and she felt a bit reckless and defiant after her confrontation with Beatrice.

"I shall take a bit of candy," she told Edna.

Edna's pinched expression became even more pronounced, but she didn't argue. She handed the candy to Hannah silently.

"Where be Mr. Thomas this morning, mistress?" Ephraim handed her full basket back to her.

"He and Harlis are off to join the Continental Army." Hannah took the basket and checked to see if anything had been forgotten.

Ephraim's face brightened. "Aye, they be good men. Soon the British will be running back to England with their tails tucked between their legs."

"Some call it treason." Hannah loved nothing more than a good discussion about something more interesting than tea and gardening.

"Ha!" Ephraim shook his grizzled head. " 'Twas worse than treason what King George has done. The paper said he has hired Hessians to help him win this war. He'll soon find that no mercenaries can overcome Yankee fortitude."

"Hush, Ephraim. Mrs. Thomas has errands to run." Edna looked at Hannah as if daring her to contradict her.

Hannah knew when she wasn't wanted, and she gave a reluctant nod. She'd been eager to hear what else Ephraim had to say. With a smile of thanks, she hurried back out into the sunshine. The clouds had billowed higher and more ominous. She'd best get home or she would get caught in the storm.

The wind was whipping the water into whitecaps by the time she stopped outside her saltbox home. Weathered to a soft gray, the house looked the way she felt — soft and worn with cares and griefs. Some days she felt eighty instead of eighteen.

She curried the horse, then took her basket of goods and went inside. Thunder rolled out over the ocean, and flickers of lightning illuminated the sky. The storm was almost here. Perhaps she should get the lamps ready now. She sighed and hurried down the path to the rocky coastline.

Hannah entered the first tower and started up. The stairs were steep, and she was out of breath by the time she reached the top. She stood for a moment and looked out over the roiling sea. A longing as sharp as a cramp gripped her. Oh, to be able to travel the world over instead of being stuck in a remote place like Gurnet Point. Far in the distance, a ship sailed south. If she could have changed into a bird and flown off to meet it, she would have done so. Pushing away the fanciful musings, she began her tasks.

She carefully filled the pots as John had shown her, trimmed the wicks, and made sure the glass was clean and smudge-free. After descending the steep spiral steps, she walked to the other tower and repeated the preparations.

By the time night fell, wind-driven rain lashed the house, and thunder shook the windows. Hannah watched anxiously from the window to make sure the lamps were still lit, but both towers beamed with a reassuring glow. At midnight she went out through the gale and refilled the oil, cleaned the glass, and trimmed the wicks again.

The night stretched before her like the black Atlantic Ocean she could only hear, endless and vast. It would be the first of many such nights.

Chapter 2

Lydia Huddleston leaned out the window of her coach and waved to the scarlet-clad British soldiers marching in formation beside the road.

"Mercy sakes, child, get back in here!" The older woman beside her tugged on Lydia's arm until she pulled her head back in with reluctance.

"I just love soldiers." Lydia sighed. "They look so dashing in their uniforms. Did you see the blond one blow me a kiss?"

Martha Nelson, Lydia's chaperone, gave a scandalized sniff. "Why I ever agreed to see you to Boston, I shall never know! You had best keep such sentiments to yourself once you reach Yankee soil. You shall find yourself tarred and feathered and run out of town."

Lydia smiled. "Hannah would not let them." She was eager to see her older sister. It had been over a year since they'd been together. She'd been only too happy to quit her job at the millinery shop and leave the angry home she was raised in when she received Hannah's letter. Father had not been inclined to allow her to go, but Mother had brought him around. Lydia had felt badly about leaving Abigail behind. The poor child had cried and begged to be allowed to come too, but their parents refused.

The hills rolled endlessly, and occasionally she caught glimpses of deep-blue water through the trees. She gave a contented sigh. Soon she would be living along the ocean and could watch the ships sail past. Mayhap she would even have an opportunity to talk with some soldiers. Massachusetts was crawling with redcoats. She dreamed of marrying a British soldier and living in England someday. And why couldn't she? Anything was possible with her beauty and nerve, so her mother had always told her.

The steeples of New York gleamed above the treetops, and Lydia leaned forward again. The last she'd heard, Galen was stationed in New York. His sister, Margaret, had stopped by the millinery shop just last week and said she thought he'd be there indefinitely. Wouldn't it be grand if she found him?

"How long shall we be in New York?" she asked Martha.

"Three days. You are to stay out of trouble, miss. Once you get on the coach and leave for Plymouth, you are my responsibility no longer, but until then, you must keep your nose clean. Do you understand me, me girl?" She fixed her steely gray gaze on Lydia.

"Of course," Lydia said airily. "But surely, Mistress Nelson, we must see something of New York."

Martha gave another disdainful sniff. "Just see that you stay by my side. A mercy it was for your dear mother that I agreed to look out for you. You would have disappeared with some soldier the first day had I not restrained you."

Lydia ignored her and stared out the window. Martha had been a necessary trial. If she had not agreed to be chaperoned, her father would not have allowed her to come. He was still bitter about Hannah running off with John and was not inclined to do her any favors.

Lydia had thought her older sister mad to reject Galen's offer for her. John was so much older than she, and so stern and sober when their father had invited him to dinner one night. A true Puritan. She remembered

24

how full of fun and laughter Hannah had been when they were growing up. One day, just days after Hannah's sixteenth birthday, that all changed, and Lydia had never understood why. But maybe this trip would bring them close again, and she would be able to find out just what had caused Hannah to disappear a few months after that fateful birthday, only to send them a letter two months later announcing her marriage to John Thomas. Lydia had been incredulous when she heard the news.

The coach stopped at a low-slung building with a large sign proclaiming it the Golden Lion. Lydia was eager to get out and stretch her stiff muscles. A young boy brought the steps, and moments later they alighted on firm ground. The scent of cabbage roiled from the dirty inn before them. Carriages lined the street, and Martha started toward them to ask for conveyance to their lodgings.

"Can we not go into the inn for some refreshment first?" Lydia begged. "My throat is full of dust."

Martha hesitated, then gave a reluctant nod. "Aye, a body could do with a cup of tea."

Lydia led the way inside, and they were soon seated at a battered wooden table with steaming cups of fragrant tea and a plate of biscuits before them.

Lydia stared around the room with eagerness. The inn was packed with British soldiers. Several saw her interested glance and returned the perusal. She must look a sight after so many days on the stage. Just one more week of travel, and she would be with Hannah. But in the meantime, she meant to make the most of the opportunities at her disposal.

After tea they hired a carriage and spent the night in comfortable lodgings three blocks away. The next morning while Martha was engaged in a spirited discussion with the proprietress of the establishment, Lydia slipped outside. Last night they'd passed the British headquarters just two blocks down the street. She was determined to take advantage of the opportunity to find Galen.

A young officer, his eyes drooping sleepily, looked up when she entered the building. "May I help you?" His gaze flickered over her, and he sat up a bit straighter.

"I do hope so," she said with her winningest smile. "I'm looking for Lieutenant Galen Wright. Please inform him his sister is here." She told the lie without an ounce of shame. She would have been his sister if

Hannah had not been so stubborn.

He wrote the name down. "I shall see about getting the message to him. His sister, you say?"

"That is right. His sister Lydia. If you would be so kind as to inform him that I am residing just down the street at Larson's Inn, I would be most grateful."

The soldier leered at her. "I will give him the message, miss."

"You are too kind." She deliberately showed her dimple. "My brother will be very surprised to find me here. I thank you for giving him the message." She gave him one last smoldering glance, then hurried back to Larson's. When she slipped back inside, she was relieved to find that Martha hadn't even missed her.

If fortune smiled on her, she would soon see Galen's blue eyes and blond hair.

Galen strode through the streets of New York, enjoying the snippets of loyalist conversations he heard. He had wasted no time in joining the British forces after the Continental Congress had passed the Declaration of Independence. Did those separatists really think a bunch of colonials could stand against the might of Great Britain?

He reached the headquarters and went

inside to see why he had been summoned. "Lieutenant Wright reporting as requested."

The man seated at the desk looked up. "You had a visitor this morning. A young woman who claimed to be your sister, but she did not resemble you." He leered and winked at Galen. "Lydia, she said her name was."

Galen raised his eyebrows. "Where is she?"

"Just down the street." The man handed him the piece of paper.

He took the note, perused it, then pocketed it. "My thanks, sir." He couldn't imagine why Lydia would be here. He hurried down the street toward Larson's. Maybe she had news of Hannah.

The old lady who answered the door obviously was a colonial. Her dislike shone in her eyes. He asked for Lydia, and she showed him to the parlor with reluctance.

Moments later he heard the sound of running feet in the hall, then Lydia burst into the room. He stood to his feet, and she rushed into his embrace. She'd grown up since he'd seen her last. A year ago she was a skinny blonde girl with windblown hair. She had turned into a very beautiful young woman. But she wasn't Hannah. Nevertheless, he enjoyed the press of her lithe young body and only grudgingly let her go. "What are you doing here?"

She pouted prettily, then sat on the sofa beside him. "Hannah sent for me. John has gone off to war — for the colonials, of course — and she wanted some company."

Galen was silent for a moment. John was in the war now — and vulnerable. He barely heard Lydia chattering beside him. This was his opportunity, and he didn't intend to miss it. Hannah would be his yet. The war had opened many doors for him. Here was one more.

CHAPTER 3

September 7, 1776

"I wanted to thank you personally." General George Washington stood from behind the desk in his tent and extended his hand.

Washington's senior aide, Captain Alexander Hamilton, stood quietly off to one side of the desk. Nicknamed "the Little Lion" because of his lean muscles and outstanding intelligence, Hamilton was in his early twenties with reddish-brown hair and deep-blue, almost violet eyes. Birch had seen the ladies swarming around him at dinner parties, and even men found his geniality compelling.

Captain Birch Meredith gripped the general's hand. "No need for thanks, sir. I did my duty only." The general appeared tired, and no wonder. The past months had been grueling. Birch had ridden hard through the night, and he had a feeling it would be hours before he was allowed to seek his bed.

Though he was twenty-five to his general's forty-four, Birch knew he had to look as exhausted as his commander.

The general indicated a seat. "You are the finest spy I have, Captain. Without your timely intervention last month, the assassination attempt might have succeeded. For that, I thank you. But your new duties will be even more arduous." He pushed a piece of paper across the table to Birch.

Birch tightened his jaw. Nothing was too arduous if it meant paying the British back for killing his brother. He would die for the privilege of purging his country of them. He picked the paper up and perused it. It was the drawing of an odd contraption. He had no notion of what it could be.

"This could win the war for us, Captain. But we need to get it into position. That is where you come in."

Birch frowned. "Sir?"

Hamilton stepped closer and stabbed a finger on the paper. "This is a drawing of the *Turtle*, David Bushnell's craft meant to detonate gunpowder underwater. We mean to test it on the HMS *Eagle*, General Howe's own flagship. The *Eagle* rests near Manhattan's South Ferry this night. Bushnell has readied the *Turtle* for a test tomorrow night. After the *Eagle* is destroyed, I

31

want you to transport the *Turtle* to a safe place until we have further need of it."

Birch had heard of this David Bushnell. "Yes, sir."

"Your expression betrays you, Captain. You think this balderdash, do you not?" The general smiled. "We shall use whatever means we have at our disposal to defeat the enemy."

Birch chose his words with care. "I cannot see how this will work, General. It looks an awkward, cumbersome thing." He turned the paper the other way. He could make neither heads nor tails of it.

Washington sighed. "We can only try. The British harass us at every turn in New York. I would wish we had more loyal citizens in that region. Spies abound, but we trust our success to Providence. We have right on our side, Captain. Never forget that." He paused and stared at his paper. "After the *Turtle* is safely to her harbor, you are to go back to New York. Major Tallmadge has a vital shipment of arms to send to Massachusetts, but the British patrol the waters around New York like sharks."

At last a chance to really engage the enemy. Secretly, of course. He smiled in satisfaction, and Washington shook his head.

"I use your bitterness and hatred now,

Captain, but someday you must throw off that animosity you bear. I say this for your own sake." He dismissed Birch with a wave of his hand.

Birch gladly escaped the closeness of the tent with its foul-smelling oil lanterns and hurried through the dark night to the ship's tender. He could see the faint outline of the *Temptation* in the moonlight as she rocked on her moorings just offshore. Her cargo, hidden in a secret hull, would already have been safely delivered to the Continental Army, and Birch breathed a sigh of relief.

He rowed the boat with swift strokes, his muscles used to the motion. The oars dipped nearly silent in the gentle waves. After climbing the rope ladder, he left his crew to lift and secure the ship's boat to the side and hurried to his cabin. Only his first mate and bosun knew of his activities on behalf of the revolution. He carried just enough goods to British troops to maintain his cover as a British privateer.

His bosun was placing a tray with a bowl of stew on the desk when Birch entered his cabin.

"Smells good, Turley." Birch threw his hat onto the bunk, then poured water over his hands from the tin pitcher on a stand near the door. "I could eat a bear."

"Only fish stew tonight, Cap'n." A slight, spare man of about forty, Turley never smiled.

His long, slightly jowly expression always reminded Birch of his father's basset hound, Rolf. His expression grew bleak at the thought of Rolf's devotion to his brother, Charles. "Send Mick in please. We shove off immediately." He expected questions from Turley, but the older man simply offered a solemn nod and went to find the first mate.

Birch sighed and scarfed down his supper. The hot food revitalized him, and he pulled the strange drawing out of his pocket and stared at it again. What an odd little vessel. The morrow would tell if the thing would work.

The men crept through the marsh grass to the edge of the water. The lights of Manhattan glowed along the shore, but Birch knew the darkness would hide them. It would be dawn soon, so they must move with all haste. He motioned his men to bring their burden to the water.

They carried the *Turtle,* a round vessel made of two hulls that looked like giant tortoise shells. The two sides were held together with iron bands, and pitch sealed the juncture. One section had a hatch with small portholes the size of half dollars on it.

The group set their burden on the beach. Moving in silence, a short, stocky man slipped inside the hatch and another man locked him inside. Once he gave them a thumbs-up through the porthole, the men strapped a cask of gunpowder to the oak hull.

Birch turned to David Bushnell. "You're sure the firing mechanism and clock are both operating properly?"

"I checked it myself."

Birch returned his attention to the *Turtle.* Inside, Sergeant Ezra Lee stared at his controls. Bushnell explained the way the craft worked, and Birch could finally see how this vehicle might actually do all it was supposed to do. A smile crept across his face. This good old Yankee ingenuity should shock the British.

The *Turtle* could sink beneath the waves by taking on water in her ballast tanks, then move toward the target — underwater and undetected — by a propeller Sergeant Lee cranked from inside. Once in position, Lee would maneuver under Howe's flagship and attach the explosive with a screw on top of the craft. Thirty minutes. Not long, but long enough, Birch hoped. That explosion would take Howe's precious *Eagle* to the bottom of the Atlantic where it belonged.

Birch would pay all the coin in his coffers to see the look on Howe's face when that ship exploded and sank. The only way it could be better would be if Major Montgomery were on board. On second thought, Birch hoped that was not the way it transpired.

He wanted to kill Montgomery with his own hands. Drowning was too good for him.

Bushnell slapped the side of the craft. "Get her in the water, men."

The men waded into the water and dropped the craft. She floated a few moments, then began to sink beneath the gentle waves. Birch watched with bated breath. They only had a half hour before Lee would have to surface for air. The target was about an eighth of a mile out. At three knots an hour, Lee would be there in minutes. The *Temptation* was to push off farther out to sea and wait to pick up the *Turtle.* He motioned for the men to join him in the ship's boat. They silently piled in, and the men rowed out to the ship.

Once aboard the *Temptation* Bushnell shook his head. "I hope he can operate her. Sergeant Lee had mere hours to train. I should have done it myself."

"We had our orders. You were too valuable to risk." Birch held a spyglass to his eye and tried to determine the location of the craft, but not a ripple betrayed her movement. He motioned for Mick to weigh anchor and shove off.

Minutes later the canvas above them caught the wind, and they sailed out into the dark water just as dawn colored the sky pink. Birch kept his spyglass trained on the HMS *Eagle.* Suddenly a shape bobbed to the surface. Shouts from the *Eagle* echoed distantly over the water.

"They've spotted her!" Birch shouted. "Ready your guns. We may need to go to her assistance."

Bushnell leaned over the railing. "What is he doing? He should still be underwater. The fool! I should have made sure he was better trained."

The *Eagle* gave pursuit, but the little craft was fast. Moments later a muffled roar shook the deck, and a great plume of water shot into the air halfway between the *Eagle* and the *Turtle.* Birch winced. They'd failed. Lee obviously had not planted the cask and was detonating it in an attempt to rattle the British and escape. The vibration knocked a crewman from the rigging, and even Birch had to grip the railing to keep his balance. Shrieks from shore and the *Eagle* carried to them, then the British ship backed away from its pursuit of the craft.

"Come on, come on," Birch muttered. The *Turtle* seemed to approach at a glacial pace.

The men crowded to the rail. They were all rooting for the strange little craft to make it to safety. Then the *Turtle* was alongside them, and his men hurried to haul her to the deck. Once she was out of the water, the *Temptation* lifted her sails and sped away before the British ships had time to muster their courage and follow.

Bushnell opened the hatch and helped Sergeant Lee out. "What happened, man?"

Lee was white with shock. "The screw on top of her that was supposed to secure the cask bumped on something. It was surely the iron bar between the rudder hinge and the stern. I couldn't attach it to the ship."

"Why didn't you try again? You must have mishandled the ballast to come shooting up out of the water like that." Bushnell turned to Birch. "I told you we should have waited!"

Birch saw Sergeant Lee's shame and put a hand on his shoulder. "We'll try again at a more opportune time. You've all done a good job here today. The British know we are not the ignorant colonials they think us.

They shall wonder what new weapon of war we have." He grinned. "The explosion will linger in their memories. That was smart thinking to cut it loose, Sergeant."

Bushnell was mollified at the *Turtle*'s praise and smiled. "I will take her out next. Then you shall see what she is truly capable of. The British will turn tail and run." He smiled and turned away to see to his pride and joy.

Birch strode back to his cabin. The men should not see his disappointment. He would have given his inheritance to see the HMS *Eagle* at the bottom of the sea. But the British would pay. And one man in particular. Major Hugh Montgomery.

September 21, 1776

Galen strode the muddy streets with a satisfied grin on his face. New York still smoldered from the fires of yesterday, and the acrid odor stung his throat. The Americans had burned a quarter of the city, nearly six hundred homes. Howe had his answer to his appeal to establish a permanent union between England and America. Galen couldn't be sorry for that answer. It suited his purposes very well this day.

He stopped outside the mansion General Howe had commandeered for his headquarters and knocked on the door. Quickly ushered into Montgomery's office, he saluted to the man sitting at the desk. Major Montgomery looked as though he wore a perpetual frown.

"I did not expect you until next week, Galen." Montgomery pushed his papers away and leaned back in his chair.

"I have news that could not wait, Major." He had to force himself not to smile. "I bring you spies and arsonists taken in the woods."

A fire smoldered in Montgomery's eyes. "Quick work, Wright. They will hang at sundown." He motioned to the chair. "Sit. Refreshments will be in shortly. Tell me all about catching the spies."

Galen smiled and did as he was bid, with a few stretches of the truth. The major did not have to know that he had arranged for one of his men to be watching one particular private. At an opportune time John Thomas had been captured. He would hang with the others simply because he had made the mistake of marrying the woman Galen intended to have. He would have the satisfaction of explaining his fate to John.

The gibbet had been thrown together, but it would serve its purpose for the three spies lined up at its base. Galen smiled when he spotted John Thomas last in line. He'd planned it that way purposefully so the man who had taken his Hannah would suffer as he watched what would soon befall his own neck.

The sun was low in the sky when Galen pushed past the guards and stopped in front of John and surveyed him from head to toe. Hannah had chosen *this man* instead of him? Heavy jowled and aging, the man was nearly old enough to be her father.

The blood pounded in Galen's ears, and he clenched his fists before he could calm himself enough to speak. "You will die today, John Thomas."

John met his gaze. "I am no spy."

"No, you're not. Your crime is much more serious. You stole Hannah from me."

John's eyes widened. "You are Galen Wright, are you not?"

"She spoke of me?"

John narrowed his eyes. "Only that she was glad to escape your attentions."

Heat roared up Galen's neck to his face, and he wished for a knife to dispatch the man himself. He took several deep breaths, then stepped back. "You will die, and Hannah will be mine. She cannot escape her destiny."

John's color waned, but his gaze never left Galen's. "I will not be able to protect her, but God will. You will not prevail."

"God!" Galen sneered. "Where is God today, John? He's unable to keep you from swinging on yon gibbet with your friends."

John shrugged. " 'It is appointed unto man once to die.' I do not fear death. Or you, Galen Wright. You can only destroy this aging body, but you can't touch what really matters."

Galen clenched his jaw and stepped back. "Hang him."

Hours later he returned to his boarding-house with a sense of accomplishment. Things had gone exactly as planned. Hannah's husband now swung from a gibbet until morning when his body would be cut down and thrown into a mass grave. Galen would make sure Hannah was notified promptly of her widowhood. Perhaps then she would welcome help when he offered it.

A smile eased across his face. His only regret was that John had refused to beg for his life and had talked only of God. Galen snorted. Typical colonial propaganda.

CHAPTER 4

"Hannah, how do you bear this place day after day?" Lydia threw her hands out in an expansive gesture that encompassed the gray sea and even grayer sky. "I shall go quite mad, and I've only been here three weeks."

Hannah sighed. What had she been thinking to invite Lydia to keep her company? She had forgotten her younger sister's easy boredom and high spirits. There were no parties or people to keep her busy. Her mother-in-law had quickly shown her contempt, as had Olive, John's spinster sister. Hannah was running out of ideas. They had gone for strolls along the beach every day, but that took up little time. She had her duties to the lighthouse to attend to as well as the usual drudgery in the house. Lydia had very little tolerance for either.

Before she could answer Lydia, she heard a cart rattle up the hill to the house. Relieved at the distraction, Hannah turned to see who would brave her mother-in-law's displeasure by consorting with her. Her heart leapt at the sight of her brother-in-law. John was surely with Harlis. She darted her gaze around but saw no sign of her husband's burly form. She hurried to greet Harlis. Lydia followed her.

"Hannah." He gripped her hand.

What was that in his face? The breath left her lungs. She laid a hand to her throat. "Where is my husband, Harlis? Isn't he with you?"

"Hannah." He swallowed and his throat made a clicking noise. "I do not know how to tell you this."

A terrible foreboding shook her. The mournful cry of a seagull overhead deepened her apprehension. "It cannot be." She backed away from his agonized face. "You are mistaken!" The last word was a wail. Lydia took her hand and squeezed it. Hannah wanted to clap her hands over her ears and refuse to hear the terrible words on Harlis's lips.

"I fear my brother is no more, Hannah. He was hanged in New York two weeks ago as a spy, one of those who set New York ablaze." Harlis dropped his head.

Beside her, Lydia gasped at the starkness

of the pronouncement, but Hannah felt nothing for long moments. John, a spy? The thought was ludicrous. Even more ludicrous was the thought that her John could be dead these two weeks and she didn't know it, didn't sense it in her soul.

"I do not know how we shall bear this blow," Harlis said brokenly. "I must tell Mother and Olive." He paused a moment and stared at her.

It must be real if he intended to tell his mother. Hannah whimpered. "You must be mistaken, Harlis. Did you see this hanging with your own eyes?" Desperately, she tried to hold on to her hope.

He shook his head. "I buried his body." His words were low, but he held her gaze without flinching. "There is no mistake, Hannah. Do you think I would not recognize my own brother?"

It was true then. Harlis's anxious face wavered, then everything went black.

October 14, 1776
Widow. Hannah had thought the name would be hers someday, but not for many more years. Married one year and already alone. Except for Lydia who had been a comfort this past week.

"The weather is warmer today, Lydia.

45

Shall we walk along the beach?"

Lydia's face brightened at her sister's invitation. "I am glad to see you coming out of your doldrums, Sister." She wrapped her shawl around her shoulders and followed Hannah to the door.

For a moment Hannah felt a twinge of guilt at Lydia's careless remark. While it was true that the last few days had finally brought calmness to her soul, she still missed John's solid presence and reassuring manner. He had always taken care of everything for her before he left, even to arranging for the lightkeeper's yearly stipend of two hundred pounds to come to her. Now it all rested on her shoulders.

And John would not have wanted her to grieve long. He was a practical man, and an overwhelming love and passion had never been on either side of the marriage. He would want her to go on with her life, even to remarry someday. Although that thought was far from her mind.

She studied Lydia. Her sister looked lovely with the golden sunshine illuminating her hair as they strolled along the beach. They were like sunshine and shadow, Lydia with her hair so fair and Hannah's own as dark as midnight. "I would be lost without the comfort of your company. Are you settling into the isolation now?"

Lydia shrugged. "Do I have a choice? I have to say I am disappointed, though. I had thought to see some British soldiers around here, but the only ones I saw were in New York."

Hannah frowned. "What is this preoccupation with the British, Sister? Such talk is treasonous here. You must put such notions from your mind. Have you forgotten the British killed my husband?"

Lydia tossed her golden head. "I sorrow for your loss, but don't blame the British that John went to war against his country. I never understood why you married the man when you could have wed Galen. I want a man who is dashing and handsome, not some dry stick many years my senior."

At the mention of Galen's name, Hannah stared at her. She'd hoped never to hear that name again, and a shudder passed over her. Lydia's smile faltered at the fierce look Hannah gave her. "If you knew the evil in that man's soul, you would not utter his name in my presence, Sister. Do you never look beneath the surface of good looks and a ready smile?"

Hannah shook her head. "I despair what will become of you, Lydia. Though he was older, John was twice the man Galen is. He cared for me when I needed someone more than you know."

Lydia's blue eyes seemed guileless as a babe's. "You cannot dissuade me, Hannah. I refuse to believe ill of Galen. And I mean to marry an Englishman and live in England one day." She smiled dreamily. "Grandmother spoke so often of the balls and fetes, of being presented at court. Someday I will have that life."

Hannah gave a quick look around her and lowered her voice. "You must not say such things. If someone overheard you, you would be tarred and feathered and set on the road to New York."

"Well, it would be better than this place of crushing boredom." Lydia stared out over the ocean. "Just think, Hannah. Over this water lies England." She drew out the last word in a breath of awe.

The longing on her sister's face shook Hannah. This was no passing fancy of a young girl. Their grandmother's stories of her young years in England had clearly turned Lydia's head.

Hannah squinted up at the darkening sky. "I shall have a hard time of it tonight. Yonder comes a storm." The wind blew the salty tang of moisture into her face.

By the middle of the afternoon a

nor'easter roared down upon them. The wind and waves lashed the shore, and Hannah had to stay in constant attendance on her lights. The gale extinguished them twice through the long night. When morning broke, she looked out from the top of the lighthouse and saw the wreckage of a ship floating in the turbulent waters.

She rushed down the steps of the tower, then ran to the shore and fixed her gaze along the shoreline, trying to hold her panic at bay. Were there any survivors? Her feet made sucking sounds in the muck as she picked her way through the seaweed and debris left by the crashing waves. Pausing occasionally to scan the sea for bodies, she had gone nearly to the tip of Gurnet Point before she saw the first man, tossed onto the shore as flotsam.

He was dressed in a British uniform. It must have been an enemy ship that had crashed on the rocks. She knelt and touched him. Dead. She continued on her search and found five more bodies. The final man was still half submerged in the water.

Gasping at the shock of the cold water, she plunged up to her knees in the waves and dragged him to shore. He seemed different from the others, more pliant. Kneeling, she put her ear to his chest. He was still alive!

Lydia would never hear her above the howling wind. Hannah hesitated a moment, then knelt again. He must be kept warm. She pulled her shawl from under the rain slicker she wore and laid it over him, then hurried to the house to fetch assistance from Lydia.

By the time they managed to half-drag, half-carry him to the house, he was muttering and floating in and out of consciousness.

Hannah took off her wet outer clothing. "Get the fire going, Lydia, while I make some hot tea." She had to repeat her request. Lydia stood staring in wonder at the young man.

"He's so handsome. Poor man. Will he live, Hannah?"

"We shall try our best. But if God calls, he will not tarry." She dragged the man as close to the fireplace as she dared. "One of us needs to fetch the doctor. He is very poorly."

Lydia shivered. "I am still unfamiliar with the area, but I shall try if you like." She tucked the blanket more tightly around him.

Hannah gazed out the window. Sheets of rain sluiced over the glass, and the wind still howled. Although it was nearly nine o'clock in the morning, it was as dark as twilight. The beacons were still shining, though. The wind was beginning to die down. A ride to town would not be pleasant in this weather.

She sighed and turned to don her rain slicker. It was kind of Lydia to offer, but it wouldn't do. "No, I must go myself. You would be lost before you reached town, and you don't even know where the doctor resides."

Lydia nodded. "I shall stay by his side."

The man moaned, then muttered. "Water."

Hannah poured water into a tin cup and knelt beside him. He feebly tried to drink, but more dribbled down his chin than reached his throat.

"My thanks," he whispered. He stared at her with suddenly lucid eyes. "Where am I?"

"Gurnet Point lighthouse. Your ship was destroyed in the storm."

Alarm showed in his brown eyes for a moment. "Then the lighthouse still stands?"

Hannah frowned. "Of course." What did he mean? A vague uneasiness enveloped her.

"We must destroy the light." His eyes turned unfocused again. "It shall not stand come the morrow. It is crucial."

Her breath caught in her throat, the cup slipped out of her fingers and clattered on the floor. The cold water soaked the hem of her dress. Destroy her lighthouse?

"Tend to him," she told Lydia. "I must extinguish my lights before I fetch the doctor." Her heart pounded. Was an invasion imminent or just an attack on her lighthouse? Either one was a terrifying thought. She hated to let her lights go dark. What if a friendly ship needed guidance? But the danger was too great.

Lydia nodded and smoothed the man's hair back from his forehead. "I shall stay here."

Hannah sighed at her sister's dreamy tone and exited the house. Pelting through the mud puddles, she ran to the nearest tower and climbed the wooden steps to the top. The glass was black with soot. She extinguished the flame, then hurried to the other tower and did the same. Gazing through the window, she strained to see if any other ships navigated the storm-lashed sea, but it was impossible to tell.

She had done all she could. Now she must summon the doctor. The rain began to die down, and the wind quieted as she exited the tower nearest the house. Lydia waved frantically from the door.

"What is it?" she called when she neared the house.

"I think he is dead." Lydia's face was white. "You must see."

Hannah brushed by her and knelt by the sailor. She touched his cheek. Cold. Putting her ear to his chest again, she could detect no heartbeat, no rise and fall of his breath. "He has expired," she said softly. "May God have mercy on his soul." She sighed. They had all died, in spite of her work through the night to keep the lights burning. At times like this it seemed she labored in vain.

"We must bury this one and the others still on the beach," she told Lydia. "The men from the village will be arriving soon to scavenge among the wreckage. I shall ask them to dig the graves."

By the time the men arrived, only a gray drizzle fell from the equally dull sky. Elated by their finds along the beach, the men dug the graves in the little graveyard behind the house without grumbling. Several casks of beer and whiskey, a cask of gunpowder, various tools, and articles of clothing sweetened their tempers.

Hannah paced the hill overlooking the ocean. She chewed on a hangnail. Was a British frigate even now heading her way? The crisp air, cooler since the passing of the storm, touched her face with a caress that left her shivering, and not just from the temperature. Soon winter would be here. She dreaded tending the light with the biting wind tearing through her clothing.

Her stomach growled, and she realized she'd eaten nothing all day. Lydia would likely be famished as well. Wrapping her rain slicker more closely about her, Hannah forced herself to turn and walk back to the house. There was no recourse — tonight she must leave the lamp out. Knowing the plot, she dare not risk her lights.

Lydia had prepared a stew for supper. The stockpot on the trivet bubbled out a delicious aroma of beef and potatoes, and Hannah's stomach rumbled. Fresh bread was on the table and a kettle of hot tea.

She laid a hand on Lydia's shoulder where she sat on a stool tending the stew. "You are a blessing. That stew smells lovely."

Lydia gave her a warm smile. "Sit down and eat while 'tis hot." She poured the tea into mugs and set one in front of Hannah's place.

Hannah sank gratefully into her chair and gulped the hot tea laced with sugar. Lydia sat across from her. Hannah said grace, then they ate their meal in silence. "It's good, Lydia." Sometimes her sister seemed so selfish, then she turned around and did something considerate like this, almost sensing when Hannah needed a bit of extra care.

After supper Lydia washed the dishes while Hannah went to the beach to look over the dark water again. What else could she do to foil the British? She should have asked the men from the village to come back with their guns. But what good would they be against cannons? No, her best option was to keep the lighthouse dark this night. The British would soon prowl on to fresher targets.

Such a day it had been. Every muscle ached from lack of sleep and carrying the sailor to the house. She would welcome her bed this night. But she couldn't rest until she was certain the lighthouse was safe.

Peering through the darkness, she prayed for the British to miss her little lighthouse. She saw a blink of light. Was that a ship? She grabbed her spyglass and focused on the dim light. The moon appeared from behind a cloud and illuminated the water. It was a ship! The dark shape lumbered through the waves off to the north of her post and came closer to the dangerous shoals.

"It's too close," she whispered. If it did

not veer soon, the ship would crash on the rocks.

She held her breath. She bore no wish to see even a British frigate crash on the rocks. Should she light her lamps? Torn with indecision, she hesitated, then let out her breath. No, she could not run the risk. It could be the ship that sought to destroy her lighthouse. If so, it well deserved to run aground.

She kept her glass trained on the dim shape. It came closer yet. "Move away," she whispered. But still it approached. Then shouts echoed over the water. The sailors had seen the danger. It was surely too late. The ship began to turn but not fast enough. Hannah gripped the glass so tightly it cut into her palms. With a last majestic heave, the ship struck the rocks. The shouts turned to shrieks, and the ship began to break apart.

"Lydia!" Hannah ran down the steps. "Lydia, I need you!"

Her sister came to the door of the house and looked out.

"A ship is on the rocks. I must go to the rescue. Ready some hot tea and find all the blankets we have. Ring the bell to notify the village."

Lydia nodded and disappeared back inside. Hannah ran to the beach and dragged her dinghy into the water. Two shipwrecks in as many days. It promised to be a hard season.

The waves sucked at her skirt, but she gathered them in her hands and climbed into the small boat John called a coble. Leaning into the oars, she rowed with haste toward the sinking ship. The screams intensified as she neared the disabled craft. Bodies were tossed in the waves, and she reached an oar out toward the nearest one. The wild-eyed man made a grab for it and missed, then the waves hurled him into the rocks. He sank under the foam and never surfaced.

Soon men from the village would be here to comb for wreckage and survivors, but these men couldn't wait. A man clinging to a bit of detritus floated by, and she managed to get him into the boat. He was barely conscious, his dark hair hanging in wet hanks over his eyes. He wore breeches with a patterned waistcoat covered by a navy coat.

This must have been a merchant ship. Hannah's heart sank. Her decision had cost this crew their ship and livelihood. She could see the name *Temptation* on a part of the ship that was still intact.

Shouts rang out behind her and she turned to see several dinghies cutting through the waves toward her. Thankfully, she waved to them. They could see to the rest of the survivors, if there were any. She simply had no strength left. She would take this man home, then seek her own bed.

She fought the waves to shore, then jumped into the foam and pulled the coble ashore. How was she to get him to the house? Fatigue slowed her limbs. She might have to wait until some of the men came ashore. His leg, obviously broken, lay at an odd angle. Even if he were conscious, he would not be able to walk.

She leaned over and set her hand on his shoulder. He stirred and opened his eyes. As black as the night, his gaze caught and held her own. She felt as if she should know him, but there was nothing familiar about his features. Black hair and eyes, he reminded her of a pirate. She knew no one with that air of danger. Then why did she feel this connection between them?

She quelled the unease and smiled encouragingly. "You're safe now."

He frowned and sat up. "Who are you?" He tried to move and groaned. "My leg is broken, methinks."

"Yes, I believe it is. I am Hannah Thomas,

keeper of Gurnet Lighthouse. Your ship struck the shoals offshore."

He frowned more fiercely. "Lighthouse? I saw no light. If I had, we would have avoided this godforsaken place."

"God has not forsaken Gurnet Point," she said sharply. "Mind your tongue, sir."

He scowled. "Did you neglect your post, mistress? If so, I shall report your dereliction to the authorities. I carry important cargo for Great Britain. You shall pay dearly."

He shivered and she bit back the words of denial. This argument would get them nowhere. "I shall call the doctor to tend you. But I cannot carry you to the house by myself. Rest while I summon aid."

He shook his head. "If I may be so bold as to lean on your shoulder and you can find a stick as well, I believe I can walk."

"Not on a broken leg, surely."

He glowered. "If you would fetch a stick, I would show you."

Sighing at his stubbornness and pride, she found a thin, stout board left from yesterday's shipwreck and brought it to him.

He nodded. " 'Twill do," he said. He braced himself on the stick and slung an arm around her shoulders. With the man hopping on one leg and supported by Hannah and the stick, they made their way to the house. Their progress was slow and laborious, but eventually they were at the front stoop.

Hannah opened the door and helped him into the house. In the light of the lamp, his face was pale and sweat dotted his forehead and upper lip. She pushed the chair to him, and he collapsed into it.

Breathing heavily, he shuddered and gasped. "Methinks I need your help again, lightkeeper," he said in a mere whisper. Then he fainted.

CHAPTER 5

Pain. Birch Meredith cried out. His own voice woke him, and he opened one gummy eye, then quickly closed it at the piercing sunshine. Where was he? Groaning, he tried to move and found his right leg immobilized. He forced his eyes open and winced again at the sun's glare. Sitting up, he stared at his leg. Strips of cotton bound it to two pieces of wood. Broken.

The iron bed he lay in sat along the back wall of a small bedroom. The only other furnishings were a simple bedside commode and a small ragged rug on the floor.

Memory flooded back. The *Temptation,* his pride and joy, now lay at the bottom of the Atlantic Ocean. That thought hurt more than his leg. At least he had delivered the supplies for the revolution. But how was he to continue his espionage activities without a ship? He scowled. Thanks to that young woman who had let the light go out, his days as a privateer for the Continental Congress were over for now. If she were here now, he would throttle her.

As though his thoughts had summoned her, the woman opened the door to his small bedroom and entered. She carried a tray with a pot of tea and a plate of bread with jam. Her smile faltered at his scowl. She set the tray on the stand beside the bed. "You are awake."

"Obviously."

She bit her lip at his abrupt tone. She seemed nicely rounded with curly black hair and deep-green eyes. Dimples flashed in her cheeks, and she had full lips above a tiny pointed chin. Just his luck she would be wrapped in a nice package. But her looks wouldn't save her from his wrath. Did she realize what her negligence had cost him? He narrowed his eyes and stared at her silently.

Perhaps she had done it deliberately. Was she a loyalist? He meant to find out. It would be dangerous to have a keeper of the light not fully loyal to the new government. But he must do so with care. Rumor traveled on the wind these days. He couldn't afford to have anyone question his loyalty to the Crown or his value to Washington would be over.

"Perhaps your temper will improve with some refreshment." She poured the tea into a cup and handed it to him.

He took the tin cup, suddenly famished and thirsty. He wasn't sure when he'd last eaten. He didn't even know what day it was. He closed his fingers around the cup and took a gulp of the beverage. The heat of the tea warmed both his throat and his hands. "Thank you." He didn't want to owe her anything. It was her fault he was in this predicament.

She smiled, and the dimple in her left cheek flashed. "Those thanks did not pain you too much, now did they?"

He frowned to keep from smiling. "I thank you for the refreshment, but not for the circumstances in which I find myself. If you had attended to your duties, I would still have my ship. What was so important that you let your light extinguish? Now my cargo for the British troops in New York is scattered all over the bottom of the ocean." He hoped there was no trace of his true activities.

She looked away. "I am sorry for that."

"Sorry does not put food in the mouths of the troops. I shall have to report this, you know."

She shrugged her slim shoulders. "I care

63

not for what the British say."

"Oh, a revolutionary, eh?" He felt a wave of a relief, then scowled again. There was no guarantee she was telling the truth.

"I care not what label you put on it. But this country will be free, and pirates and money-mongers like yourself cannot stop liberty." Her lip curled in disdain.

Birch didn't much care for the contempt in her eyes, and he wasn't quite sure why. He'd seen plenty of it over the past two years posing as a loyalist. "Country? You think a piece of paper calling yourself a country will make it so? You are very naive, mistress."

Her green eyes flashed, and she took a step closer to him. "Your accent betrays you. You are from the South, are you not?"

What business was it of hers? "North Carolina," he admitted grudgingly.

"I am from South Carolina. In my colony, men were taught to hold women in respect. What would your mother say to the way you have spoken to me?"

He flushed at the reprimand, and he bowed, a bit awkwardly from the waist up, since he was lying in the bed with his leg bound. "It is my turn to apologize, Mrs. Thomas. My mother would have taken a switch to me had she heard our conversation."

She inclined her head stiffly. "I accept your apology."

She was a spunky little thing, but looks could be deceiving. He would reserve judgment. He forced himself to smile. Women usually softened when he tried to make himself agreeable. "Allow me to introduce myself. Captain Birch Meredith. It appears I shall have to avail myself of your mercy while this busted leg heals."

She curtsied. "I'll do my best to attend to your injuries, Captain."

It was easy to pretend to be a colonial and hide loyalist activities, especially in freedom-mad Massachusetts. "How came you to be caring for the lights yourself?"

A shadow darkened her extraordinary eyes. "My husband, John, was the keeper. His family donated the ground this light stands upon. When he went to join the Continental Army, I was left in charge."

She was married. Some women married young, but she couldn't be more than eighteen. He frowned at his own shaft of disappointment. It was nothing to him. "A large job for a small woman. It may be many years before your husband returns."

She shook her head, and the shadow in

her eyes deepened. "He shall never return, Captain Meredith. He was hung as a spy in New York over three weeks ago."

A shock ran through him. A spy! Did he know him? Quickly, his mind ran through the men he knew from New York. The name John Thomas did not sound familiar, but perhaps he used an alias.

"It is a most cruel lie," she continued. "John would never have been a spy. He was much too honest and straightforward for anyone to put him in such a position. I know not how this tragedy occurred, but the full story has not been told."

"I am sorry for your loss." He would have to check with his contacts in New York.

"More tea?"

"No, I thank you, but I would take some of that bread now."

Only after she left him did he realize she'd never answered his question about how she had let the light go out.

Lydia wrapped her shawl more tightly around her shoulders. The October wind was cold, and she was beginning to regret coming north. The wind blew through the cracks in the house, and even maintaining a blazing fire did not keep the chill away. She couldn't imagine what it would be like in full winter. South Carolina weather would still be warm.

"Would you mind going to Gurnet for supplies, Lydia?" Hannah called from her post at the fireplace. "I shall need to mind these roasting pigeons most of the afternoon."

"I should love it above all things." Lydia longed to get out of the house. She wanted to find a way to get a message to Galen. Did he know Hannah was free now? The thought caused her some discomfiture. She knew how he had always felt about her sister. But Lydia was determined to make him see how much more fit she would be as the wife of a British officer. Hannah would never do. She was a fervent colonial. Lydia had heard her arguing politics with Captain Meredith nearly every evening in the week the man had been here. She would be heartily glad for his leg to mend and him to be gone.

Still, he was an attractive man. Tall, broad shouldered with dark hair and even darker eyes. Hannah said he looked like a pirate. Lydia shivered at the thought of those eyes. They seemed to size her up and find her wanting. Why was that? She was beautiful. She and Hannah looked much alike except her hair was fair while Hannah's was dark.

Their features and figures were similar. He seemed to find Hannah attractive enough. Why was it men always seemed to notice Hannah first?

"There is a list of my needs on the table," Hannah said.

Lydia glanced at her sister on her stool near the fireplace. Her cheeks were pink with the heat, and the glow of the fire cast glimmers of light on her black hair. Normally, blonde hair attracted more attention. What was it about Hannah that men found so appealing? She shrugged. She wasn't a man, so she couldn't decipher it.

"May I borrow your cloak? It's so much warmer than my own."

"It's on the hook by the door."

Lydia picked up the list, threw the cloak about her shoulders, and went to hitch the pony to the wagon. The crisp, clear air was invigorating. It was colder than it looked, and she snuggled deeper into the wool cloak. The sunshine cast dappled patterns on the brilliant display of gold-and-red leaves that had fallen from the maple trees. She paused and looked toward the twin towers that held the light and on out to sea. England lay across the water. Would she ever get there? Sometimes she almost gave up hope.

When she got to town, she went to the mercantile and gave the list to Edna Baxter. While Edna filled her order, Lydia browsed the buckets of ribbon. A dashing British soldier eyed her with interest. When he saw he held her attention, he sauntered over with his hands in his pockets.

She did so love that red uniform. She smiled at him in a way that made her dimples show and was gratified at his flush.

He bowed. "Mistress. Major Hugh Montgomery at your disposal. You know, it is not safe for such a lovely young woman to wander about unescorted."

She curtsied. "Lydia Huddleston. I think I'm quite safe here, Major." He was a most attractive man. Not like Galen, of course. No one compared to Galen. But the major was medium height with sandy-blond hair and pale-blue eyes. She liked him instantly.

"In that case, might I interest you in refreshments at the tavern? You have to sup, do you not?"

Lydia was conscious of Mrs. Baxter's glare of disapproval, but she took the major's arm in defiance. The old baggage had no right to judge her. Just because she was a traitor to the mother country gave her no right to look down her nose at those who remained loyal. "I would be delighted, Major." She allowed him to lead her to the door. Pausing, she looked back with a triumphant smile. "I shall be back later to gather my supplies, Mrs. Baxter." She ignored the woman's glare and sauntered across the walk with the handsome major.

The Lion's Paw was nearly empty this early. In spite of the major's blandishments, it was much too soon for most residents to be thinking of dinner. The serving lass, glowering with disapproval, seated them at a table in a corner. The chit was simply jealous. And if Lydia had missed out on meeting a man as attractive as Major Montgomery, she might have been jealous too.

Major Montgomery ordered them kidney pie and tea, then stared into her eyes. "Now tell me all about yourself."

As Lydia told him about her childhood and her dream of going to England someday, his blue eyes never left her face. "So your sister is keeper of Gurnet Light? How would you like to help the mother country?"

Her heart pounded so hard, she thought she might suffocate. Wouldn't Galen be proud of her if she were able to strike a blow against the Continental Army? "How?"

"Just keep your eyes and ears open and report back to me. I have a contact here who will see that I receive your messages.

You can tell me if you see rebel ships offshore or smuggling supplies." He flashed his winsome smile. "And since we're going to be partners, would you call me Hugh?"

"I should like that." A harmless flirtation would be good for her ego. She smiled. "Could you deliver a letter to Lieutenant Galen Wright in New York? He is attached to General Howe's office."

Hugh frowned. "Who is he to you?"

"My sister's fiancé." Lydia lied without a trace of guilt. He should have been. She was still no closer to discovering what had happened between the two of them. Every time she asked Hannah, her face had clouded and she changed the subject. A mystery Lydia was determined to solve.

His face cleared. "I should be glad to do you this service when I return to New York tomorrow. I have heard it said that the keeper of the lights at Gurnet Point is a staunch colonial. How is it that she is engaged to a loyalist?"

"They were childhood friends. Right now relations are strained, but when England has won the war, they will soon be made right again." But only when Galen was wed to Lydia and they were both in England.

He nodded. "The conflict has split many families."

She pulled the sealed letter from the basket at her feet. "My sister will be grateful to you, and so am I." His besotted expression soothed her bruised ego. Maybe life in this backwater wouldn't be so bad after all.

The only thing she hated was betraying her sister. She loved Hannah, truly she did. Someday Hannah would thank her.

CHAPTER 6

October 28, 1776
The hills of White Plains beckoned in the distance. Galen pulled his horse to a halt and surveyed the battle arena. He hated battle. He was much more comfortable in the drawing rooms planning strategy. But Howe had transferred him to Major Hugh Montgomery's entourage, and Montgomery had insisted he come to the front.

The Americans held Chatterton's Hill, and the British meant to take it. Looking at the masses of troops around him, Galen doubted it would be much of a battle. This might even be their opportunity to defeat the rebellious colonies once and for all. Spies had told them the American troops were disheartened and poorly equipped. It wouldn't take much to send them all scurrying home like rats.

He held back a bit when Montgomery ordered the charge. He wanted to live to fight another day. Within minutes it was clear the tide was with the overwhelming numbers of British troops. The Americans retreated, and Galen soon stood on top of the very hill he'd looked up at this morning.

"Cease fire! We're setting up camp." The cry echoed throughout the milling troops just when Galen thought they would pursue the retreating forces. Galen pushed his way through the ensuing melee and found Major Montgomery.

The man's face was red, and his eyes bulged from their sockets. "Howe's a fool!" he burst out. "We could have wiped them out today and taken Washington himself captive. Their entire flank was exposed to our cannon."

Treasonous words for an officer to say about his commander. Galen glanced around to make sure no one had noticed. He didn't want to be tarred with Montgomery's brush. "I thought it odd myself."

"I swear I wonder if it was deliberate. Mayhap our leader nurses some tenderness for the Yankees. I do not!" Spittle flew from his mouth. "In fact, I have ordered all the prisoners hanged."

Galen had long heard of the major's cruel streak, but he doubted even the slaughter of the prisoners would assuage his ire. Was Montgomery about to have an apoplectic fit? Galen placed a hand on his shoulder. "Calm down, sir. You might be overheard."

"I care not!" He paced like a caged lion. "Howe should be replaced as soon as possible. I mean to write England over this matter. It smacks of treason. Moderate peace, he wants. The man is a fool! A bloody fool!"

Galen was inclined to agree, but the safest course was to divert the major's rage. "Would you care to sup, sir? Your tent is ready."

"Fine," he snapped. "Bring it to my tent." He spun on his heels and stalked off to his quarters.

Galen sighed and went to find some food and drink for his superior. By the time he was told to enter with the food, he could tell Major Montgomery had calmed down. His face preoccupied, he sat at his desk scribbling quickly with his quill.

Montgomery folded the paper and stamped it with a wax seal. "I want you to take this to New York and personally see that it is sent to England."

Galen paused before reaching out to take the letter. He did not want to get involved in any court machinations. It was a good way to wind up in London Tower. "Yes, sir."

"Wait for me in New York. There is no sense in trying to find me with a madman as a commander. We could be anywhere."

Galen nodded and left immediately. This suited him very well. Major Montgomery wouldn't be back for days at least. Galen could take a short trip up the coast to see Hannah. The letter he'd received a week ago via Major Montgomery had assured him he would be most welcome.

Galen tossed his haversack on the bed and sat on a chair. He pulled off his boots and rang for the maid to bring some water for a bath. Riffling through his things, he reread Lydia's letter. He smiled slowly at her request for him to visit soon. She would have her wish.

Hannah cleaned the last reflector, then sighed and pressed her hand on the ache in the small of her back. Staring out over the blue water, she thought she saw the white dot of a ship's sail on the horizon. Friend or foe? There was no way to tell until it came near enough to see the flag it flew, and it would be too late by then. The strain of always worrying about those ships out there was beginning to wear on her.

"What are you looking at?" Lydia had

climbed the steps behind her almost noise-lessly.

"Just the sea." What was ailing Lydia lately? She seemed to follow her everywhere, almost as though she was watching for something. "What is our guest doing?"

"Winding your yarn. Can you believe a man would do something like that?" Lydia raised her voice indignantly.

"He is not used to inactivity." Birch was mending fast. He planned to leave after the harvest feast. She wasn't sure how she felt about that. Against her will she found she nursed a powerful attraction to him, which shamed her since John was so lately in his grave. Though theirs had been no great passion, she owed him a sense of loyalty. She had no idea if Birch felt the same about her, but she doubted it. He was a staunch loyalist, and she didn't want to care about him. They disagreed about everything.

"He's a strange man. Always watching and weighing everything."

"And a Tory." Hannah voiced her main objection.

"It's the one good thing about him." Lydia stared at her sister as though daring her to contradict her.

Hannah compressed her lips. "We are all invited to the big house for supper tonight."

"Oh no!" Lydia wailed. "Olive's sniping is more than I can take."

Hannah could sympathize. John's sister tried her nerves most grievously. "Even Birch is invited. I'm not sure what Mother Thomas wants, but methinks she has her reasons." Hannah was no more eager to attend than her sister. The times they were all together were strained and unpleasant. She had tried her best to keep the peace, but it was so difficult with the attitude they had toward her. If she had been able to present them with a grandson to take John's place, it might have been better. But God had not ordained that.

Lydia pouted prettily. "I shall stay home."

"You'll do no such thing. They are John's family and, by extension, ours as well. We will attend, be pleasant, and do our duty."

"*Duty.* Such a dreary word." Lydia sighed. "You speak too much of duty."

"And you practice it too little. I fear I have done you no service by bringing you here, Sister. Daily you grow more enamored of the British. What of your duty to your country?"

Lydia stared Hannah in the eye. "Our duty belongs to our mother country, Hannah. Our forefathers came from Sussex, and we are British in our bones. Why can you not see this?"

"We are Americans. Americans! Born and bred on the soil of this new land. Are you so blinded by the glamour of the fairy tales Grandmother wove that you miss the true miracle in front of you?"

"You will never understand." Lydia turned with a flounce and stalked to the steps.

Hannah watched her with tears in her eyes. The disagreements came daily and grew louder. Neither could give an inch in this battle. It was too fundamental. She had tried to understand her sister, but it was impossible. She knew Lydia felt the same way. She saw it in the frustration in her face when they talked. She needed to remember that her sister believed she was in the right. That was the problem with disagreements of this nature. Hannah strolled to the house and closed the door behind her.

Birch looked up with his hands full of wool. "What did you do to Lydia? She stomped through here like an angry wet hen."

She suppressed a smile at the sight of such a large, obviously masculine man winding wool. "Lydia told me what you were doing, but I had to see it to believe it." He was such a puzzle to her. Strong and virile with his pirate eyes and black hair, yet somehow gentle when you least expected it.

"Are you trying to change the subject?" He smiled and put down the yarn. "I used to do this for my mother when I was growing up. She didn't have any daughters, and I did not mind helping her. Although my brothers often objected to the indignity."

Birch had that closed look again. At any mention of his brothers, his nostrils flared and his mouth grew pinched. She assumed they were not on good terms. "I thank you kindly for your help, as I am sure your mother did as well."

The pinched, haunted expression left his eyes. "Now tell me what happened with Lydia."

Hannah sighed and sat in the chair opposite him. "The usual."

"You mean you fought again about who was right, the Americans or the British?"

She nodded. "I don't know why I bother talking to her. She is like old Sally with her bit between her teeth."

"You ever think you fit that description as well?" he asked with a sly grin.

"Sometimes."

"At least you admit it."

"You are that way as well. When it comes to this conflict, there is no gray area, no in-between meeting place."

He sobered and gave a slow nod. "But we shall find our way through this someday. Perhaps then you and I can be friends."

She smiled at the thought. "I think I would miss our disagreements."

He chuckled, a deep, warm sound that sent a tingle glowing in the pit of her stomach, a somehow frightening and exhilarating feeling. She was gratified when he laughed. He so rarely did, it was a joy to hear him.

"We should soon find areas of discord." He rubbed his leg absently.

Her smile faded at the major source of their discord. She could never truly care for a loyalist. "Does your leg pain you?"

"Only a bit. I will soon be able to walk on it. Another week and we can remove the splint and try it."

Another week. She nodded bleakly and avoided his gaze. "Would you care for some tea?"

"I should, indeed."

She was conscious of his gaze as she took the cube of tea and shaved slivers into the tea caddy, then dropped it into the teapot and poured hot water from the kettle over it. As the tea steeped, she gathered up the yarn and neatened the ball. "I am most heartily sorry for the ordeal you must face tonight."

He smiled. "I can handle Miss Olive. I have gotten rather good at it by now."

Hannah had been amazed at just how well he handled Olive. He treated her with cool courtesy and ignored her simpering gazes and flirtatious pats with her fan. But her advances were becoming more blatant. The last time they'd seen her, Hannah had been mortified at her sister-in-law's behavior. She never knew when she would come in from her duties at the lighthouse to find Olive, her horse face drawn into a semblance of a smile, seated in the parlor. Though part of a lightkeeper's duties was caring for injured sailors, this situation wasn't something her mother-in-law was likely to condone, and Olive's infatuation was likely the only reason Mother Thomas hadn't insisted Hannah find other accommodations for Birch.

"Well, I had best prepare for our evening. I want to look my best."

"It would be difficult for you to look anything else." An appreciative glow in his eyes belied the impersonal tone of his voice.

Heat flushed her cheeks and she turned away quickly to hide her discomfiture. He was polite and gallant, nothing more. Not that she wanted anything more. He was a Tory of the worst stripe. She hurried up the steps to her room.

Her bedroom faced south so the lights could be seen. They twinkled brightly in the approaching gloom of twilight. She just hoped they stayed that way. She turned away and stared at her reflection in the mirror. Her mother-in-law had always insisted any family dinners be attended in full formal dress, not casual undress. Hannah had only one such outfit. Today Hannah's undress consisted of the usual skirt and jumps with the pinafore over it. What would Mother Thomas do if she arrived like this? Hannah smiled at the thought.

She disrobed and put on her stays. Wouldn't Mother Thomas be shocked to know she did not wear them all the time? She would have said she was no better than a servant. And that is what Hannah felt like sometimes. A servant to the light. At first she had tried to always wear the stays as Mother Thomas expected but soon found it impossible to bend to clean and perform her daily duties. Her mother-in-law had servants to do her bidding.

She opened her wardrobe and pulled out her green sacque. It was much too grand for the evening, but John had insisted on buying it for her right after they were wed. She only wore it to the big house. John had seen her in it but a few times. The gray-green color enhanced the green of her eyes, and she loved the gown. But she always felt like an imposter in it. She pulled tendrils of hair down and curled them with the hot tongs, then reddened her cheeks and lips slightly with rouge. She glanced in the mirror once more, then nodded. She would not disgrace herself.

Lydia and Birch were waiting in the hall beside the fireplace when she descended the stairs. Lydia looked lovely. Her golden hair was a riot of curls, and her blue caraco gown deepened her blue eyes to indigo. Birch looked splendid. Hannah had cut apart some of John's clothes and stitched them to fit him. The dark-blue frock coat over his breeches and waistcoat fit his broad shoulders to perfection. She'd cut a slit in the leg of the breeches for his splinted leg.

Lydia tapped Hannah's arm with her fan. "Shall we get this over with?"

Birch picked up his crutches and waved one in the air. "I think the carriage is outside. I heard it a few minutes ago."

It was kind of Mother Thomas to send the carriage for them. Olive probably had something to do with it. Birch hopped along with the aid of his crutches through the doorway and to the door of the carriage where Nate, the driver, helped him ascend, then assisted the ladies.

Candles shone from the windows as Nate helped them down. Hannah led the way inside. The aroma of roast pork made her mouth water, and she realized how hungry she was.

"Ah, my dear daughter. How lovely you look." Mother Thomas came toward her with outstretched arms.

Hannah allowed the kiss and placed one of her own on her mother-in-law's powdered cheek. Olive, already beginning to simper, approached Birch. What would they say if she announced that he was a Tory? She had kept quiet on that point as she wanted to avoid as much conflict as possible. But Olive would never be allowed to pursue a loyalist. One mention of Birch's true political views, and her mother would order a halt to her flirtation.

The maid ushered them into the parlor where they had tea before supper. Olive sat much too close to Birch, and even the dim candlelight did not hide the overzealous use of rouge or the gleam in her eyes. Hannah suppressed a sigh. It was going to be a long night.

At supper they ate three courses of meat and several vegetables followed by cake. It was nearly nine by the time they finished eating. Hannah kept waiting for the reason for the invitation, but it did not come until they were back in the parlor.

"Olive, dear, take Lydia and Hannah to see the new kittens in your room," Mother Thomas said. "I have some business to discuss with Captain Meredith."

Hannah looked at her sharply but could do nothing but obey her edict. Olive appeared excited and flustered as she led them up the steps. Hannah wanted to ask Olive about the private interview but wasn't quite sure how to couch the question. She followed Olive's swishing skirts.

Lydia stopped at the top of the stairs and took Olive's arm. "What is going on? I refuse to go another step until you explain."

Olive smiled, and her plain face was almost attractive. "Mother is proposing a match between me and the captain."

Hannah's stomach clenched until she felt almost physically sick. With something akin to horror, she realized she'd come to think of the handsome captain as her own property. This wave of jealousy was unaccustomed and unwelcome. She had no business having any feelings for a Tory.

CHAPTER 7

Birch leaned against the back of the sofa and looked at his hostess with expectation. He had to admit he was a bit curious about the elder Mrs. Thomas's business. He could not think of any business venture she might propose. And truth to tell, he could not imagine any business that would entice him to enter a close relationship with this woman.

Pride and haughtiness emanated from her like the whiff of a rose sachet that came through when he was close to her. Her clothing was of the finest quality, and the furnishings of the home whispered money and privilege. He had no patience for such as her. Mrs. Thomas would be one who would not listen to a partner about anything. But he would do her the courtesy of listening before gracefully refusing her offer, though only for Hannah's sake.

"Tea, Captain?" His hostess smiled as

though she were an unwed maid of twenty instead of a dowager with sagging jowls and a body running quickly to corpulence.

Birch gave her a perfunctory smile and took the proffered cup of tea. He wanted to tell her to get to the point. His leg ached, and he desperately longed for the hearth of the lighthouse, which felt like home. Funny how the little saltbox home on the cliff had so quickly become a sanctuary for him. Because of Hannah.

Mrs. Thomas smiled and settled her considerable girth into the chair opposite him. "Tell me, Captain, have you thought of taking a wife? The proper maid could add a lot to your comfort." She spoke with confidence as though she knew he would never have the temerity to refuse her suggestions.

So that was where this was headed. He kept his expression impassive. He felt sorry for Olive, but if he ever wed it would be to someone with fire and a passion for adventure to match his own. He was no stay-at-home man, but an adventurer and soldier. He wanted no clinging violet to tie him down. He took another sip of tea and considered how best to extricate himself.

"I am not in a position to take a wife now, ma'am. My duties will soon call me away, and a merchant's wife endures a lonely life unless she is brave enough to travel the seas with her husband." He thought that would quickly rule out Olive as a life partner.

Mrs. Thomas dabbed her lips with her hanky. "All the more reason to choose someone of wealth and stature in the community, my dear Captain. With sound financial backing you could expand your ventures and soon be in a position to take your place with other leaders. I propose to bestow my daughter, Olive, upon you with a generous dowry to help you regain all that you lost when your ship was destroyed."

The woman didn't take no for an answer. Even a tempting dowry couldn't compensate for being tied to a woman who bored him. For a moment an image of Hannah with her flashing green eyes and dark curls blazed through his mind. Her eyes were nearly the color of the inlet along the shore. With her in his arms, a man wouldn't mind giving up the restless ocean.

Ridiculous. She made no secret of her contempt for him. Would she still feel that way if she knew he worked secretly for the revolution instead of for England? He would never know. Nothing would cause him to betray his secret.

He forced himself to smile at Mrs. Thomas. "I thank you kindly for the offer, ma'am, but I fear I must decline. I hold Miss Olive in the highest regard, but as I said, I am in no position to take a wife right now. My life is just too unsettled."

She frowned but then forced a smile. "I know Olive is not the most beautiful of ladies, but one should look at more than outward beauty. An alliance with the Thomas family would bring great advantages to an astute businessman. Think on my offer, Captain. You would find me a most generous mother-in-law."

"I will do that, ma'am. But I fear I shall not change my mind. No disrespect meant to you or Olive, of course. But a wife is simply not in my plans."

She set her jaw and nodded. "Very well then. I shall say no more of this matter."

He heard the noise of the returning group with a sense of relief. Olive came into the parlor first. Her face eager, she glanced at her mother, and her smile faded at the pinched expression on her mother's face. Hannah and Lydia quickly followed, and they both sent sharp glances his way. He dared a wink at Hannah, and she colored delicately.

"I must be going soon, Mother Thomas," Hannah said. "The light calls for my attention."

Before her mother-in-law could respond, a strange whistling sound pierced the silence. "Get down!" Birch launched his body at Hannah and bore her to the ground. A strange thunder pealed out, and the earth shook. Olive and Lydia both screamed and dove behind the sofa while Mrs. Thomas struggled to get out of her chair.

"The light! They're firing the cannon at the light." Hannah tried to get up.

Birch refused to release her. "There is nothing you can do. Getting yourself killed will serve no purpose." Conscious of the softness of Hannah beneath him, he longed to release her and escape the emotions her closeness brought. To her credit, she lay quietly, her breath fanning his neck.

The bombardment continued for several long minutes, then silence fell. Even from here, Birch could smell the hot gunpowder. He cautiously raised his head, then rolled off Hannah. Her cheeks pink, she scrambled to her feet. His crutches lay cast aside a few feet away, and she gathered them up, then helped him to his feet. He took the crutches from her hand, and they exchanged a long look. Hannah was the first to look away. She turned and hurried to the door.

As soon as she opened the door, she gasped. "I can see the light from here —

the lighthouse is safe! The cannonballs missed their mark." The joy in her eyes as she glanced back at Birch warmed him. He'd never met such a brave woman. Her first thought was of the light, not her own safety. He wished General Washington knew of the dedication of this one lightkeeper. Mayhap he could tell him some day.

He and Lydia followed her outside. The smell of gunpowder was heavy in the autumn air. Olive cried and cowered still behind the sofa in spite of her mother's commands to quit being such a ninny. Birch gladly shut the door behind him and made his way down to the shore with Lydia and Hannah. Offshore he could see the lights from two ships. One seemed to be driving off the other. Something did not seem right to him. Why didn't the victorious ship fire on the fleeing one? He frowned.

"They are leaving."

He squinted in the darkness. "A boat seems to be coming ashore. You will have the opportunity to thank the crew who saved your lighthouse." He could just make out the outline of three men in the boat. Their tricorn hats pulled low on their heads, two of the men rowed against the surf while the third, seemingly impervious to the salty spray that drenched him, sat imperiously in the bow of the boat.

As soon as the boat was dragged ashore, the man in the bow stepped out and approached. Birch had just begun to make out rugged features with a square jaw and Roman nose when Lydia uttered a little shriek.

"Galen!" Lydia rushed toward the figure and threw herself into his arms.

Birch felt, rather than heard, Hannah's soft inhalation. Tenseness emanated from her slim shoulders, and she took a step backward. He wanted to take her hand, but he knew she would never allow such familiarity.

She took a deep breath and stepped forward. "Galen. It seems I must thank you for your work this day. My lighthouse is safe."

She spoke the words grudgingly, and Birch wondered at her tone. He had never known her to be ungrateful. And it wasn't just ingratitude in her voice. She bit her lip and wouldn't meet Galen's gaze.

His arm still around Lydia's shoulders, Galen stepped nearer. "My dear Hannah. How good it is to see you again."

Birch felt his hackles rise at the proprietary expression on Galen's face. Who was this man? He didn't trust his smooth smile.

Galen raised Hannah's hand to his lips.

He lingered overmuch before releasing it, and Birch could sense Hannah's agitation. What was between her and this British officer? Was this hot knife in his belly jealousy? He didn't care much for the feeling.

Birch forced the anger down and nodded at Galen. The other man's amused gaze slid over him and sharpened. "Who might you be?"

Birch gave a stiff nod. "Captain Birch Meredith."

Galen's gaze flickered over him once more, taking in the splint and crutches. "Might we go inside, my Hannah? I have much to tell you."

My Hannah. Birch could tell she liked those words as little as he did, though she simply inclined her head and led them up the hillside path. The moon illuminated the rocky trail. When they reached the top, Mrs. Thomas and Olive were waiting.

When the older woman saw the uniform Galen wore, her eyes flashed. "What business do you have here on our land? We hold no love for the British."

Galen's face darkened, and his lip curled.

Lydia stepped forward. "Captain Meredith is a Tory as well, Mistress Thomas. You were only too eager to marry him off to Olive a few minutes ago. Galen is an old friend, and he has saved the lighthouse this day."

Hannah gasped. "Lydia, no!"

Lydia looked back at her sister in defiance. "It's time the truth be told, Hannah. I tire of Olive's simpers and warm glances. Her mother would not care for a Tory as a son-in-law."

Olive burst into tears, and Mrs. Thomas looked as though she might have apoplexy any moment. She glared at them all, but her gaze lingered on Hannah. "A Tory? You have harbored a snake in our bosom all this time? You shall not hear the end of this." She turned and followed her daughter into the house.

Galen took Hannah's arm to escort her down the path to her home, but she pulled away. Birch puzzled over their relationship. Galen seemed to have warmer regards for Hannah than she did for him. She seemed almost afraid of him. In the weeks he had known her, he had never seen her flinch from anything, but she seemed to almost cower in this man's presence. Birch vowed to stay as close to her side as possible. He would not allow the man to harass her.

Lydia chattered to Galen as they picked their way down the path. Birch wished for a lantern or even just a candle to illuminate the way. Several times he nearly stumbled and fell as he tried to keep up with the rest of them. Hannah would have stopped to help him, but he refused to ask for aid. Soon he would be rid of this splint, and he could show her he was no cripple.

Hannah lit the candle just inside the door and led them all to the kitchen where she lit the lantern and began to prepare tea. Her hands trembled as she shaved tea into the caddy. Was he the only one who noticed her agitation? Lydia was obviously enamored of Galen, who was just as obviously intent upon Hannah. A strange triangle.

Birch dropped into the chair closest to Hannah. Galen sat opposite him with Lydia beside him. Lydia leaned closer to him than propriety allowed, but Galen stared intently at Hannah and spared not a glance for her sister. Birch felt his hackles rise even more at the gleam in Galen's eyes when he stared at Hannah.

"I was on my way to visit you both when I saw your lighthouse being fired upon," Galen said. "Luckily I was there, for they would surely have destroyed it."

"I thought that was our goal," Birch said. "The last I heard, Howe wanted to take out all the lighthouses."

Galen smiled. "Any other lighthouse but

this one. I would not let my dear friends suffer in that way. I outranked the commander of the other ship and ordered him away." He glanced again at Hannah as though to see if she was impressed by his statement of rank.

Birch didn't believe the other man for a moment. The way he refused to look a man in the eye did not bode well for his integrity. "A fortuitous happenstance," he observed dryly.

"Quite," Galen said. "How are you, Hannah? It has been over a year since we last met."

Hannah blanched, and her hands shook even more. "Fi-fine," she stuttered. How could Galen be unaware of her agitation? Birch frowned. He would like to throw the man out on his ear.

Galen seemed to like the effect he had on Hannah, for his grin broadened. "You look much the same, Hannah. Mayhap more beautiful, if that is possible. I have not been home these past nine months myself. How fare your parents?"

"She would not know," Lydia put in with a toss of her golden head. "She has not been back to South Carolina since she married John."

"Ah yes. John. How is your husband?" A

knowing smirk played around Galen's mouth.

Hannah bit her lip. "He was hanged several months ago. I am a widow now."

Galen's eyes brightened. "I am sorry to hear these sad tidings."

Lydia laid a hand on his arm and pouted. "Enough talk of depressing things. Tell me how the war goes. Are the Yankees ready to surrender yet?"

"Soon." Galen inclined his head. "We hear they are nearly out of ammunition, their troops wear rags, and many have no shoes. With winter approaching, many of Washington's troops will desert and return home."

"I think not! You have not yet tested our mettle." Hannah flushed when they all stared at her.

Glad she seemed to have recovered her fire, Birch decided to stir it a bit. "Washington seems to be a bit inept at this war game."

She banged the teapot onto the table. "We are not beaten yet, and by God's grace, we will drive the British back across the seas."

Galen laughed. "You always were a dreamer, Hannah. It was one of your many charms."

"Why are you here, Galen?" Her green eyes had finally lost their haunted look, and anger took its place.

"To see you and Lydia, of course."

"I thank you most kindly for your intervention, but I must tell you that I have not changed my opinion of you since we last met. I must ask you to leave when you have finished your tea." She folded her arms across her chest and glared at him.

"Hannah!" Lydia gasped. "You must not treat our friend in so cavalier a fashion."

"He is not my friend, Lydia. Nor is he yours, if you but knew."

Galen glowered, then his face cleared and he laughed. "I always did admire your spirit, Hannah." He stood and bowed to her. Clapping his tricorn hat back on his head, he stepped closer to her and touched his fingers to Hannah's chin. "I'll be back. You can count on that."

She flinched as though the touch burned her, but Galen did not release her chin until her eyes met his. Then he smiled and turned away.

Lydia glared at her sister and hurried to see Galen out. She exited with him, and Hannah let out a long sigh.

"I think there is some mystery here, Mistress Hannah." Birch tendered a sad smile.

She flicked her green gaze over him and

shuddered. "I cannot speak of it, Captain."

He nodded. "I understand."

"Do you?" She studied him a moment, then turned away to clear the cups and saucers from the table.

"Lydia seems quite taken with him."

Hannah nodded. "It was ever so. I fear for my sister. She rushes headlong into danger and cares not for the consequences."

The front door slammed, and Lydia rushed through the room and up the stairs. Her face was scarlet from weeping. She glared at her sister as she passed, then the bedroom door upstairs slammed shut and the sound of bitter weeping echoed down the steps.

Birch exchanged a long look with Hannah. He didn't envy her the task of dealing with Lydia. That girl would bring nothing but trouble to Hannah.

CHAPTER 8

Lydia threw her cloak around her shoulders and tiptoed out of the house. Her heart hammered in her chest, and her mouth was dry from the storm of weeping she'd given into earlier. Her hopelessness was over now, and she would change the course of her own fate. If Hannah caught her, all would be lost. Tonight was her only chance to make Galen see that she was the one for him, not her sister. The warm gazes he cast over Hannah had burned Lydia like gall.

As for Hannah, how could she treat him in such a fashion? Galen was a hero. He faced danger every day to safeguard the colonial ties with England. And he had saved the lighthouse! Surely that should account for something to Hannah. But it hadn't seemed to soften her attitude at all. She'd seemed almost frightened of him until she turned like a rabid dog and practically bit him.

Lydia just didn't understand her sister. And she probably never would. England was their heritage. Their allegiance should be to them. Just as Galen's should be to her. Lydia was the only one who could ever love him as he deserved to be loved.

Galen had said he would be at the Lion's Paw tonight before rowing back to his ship in the morning. Lydia set out along the path to town at a brisk pace. The moonlight illuminated the pathway, but the night sounds around her were unsettling. She'd never been out so late before. What if she met soldiers or thieves? She wished she could have hitched the mare to the buggy, but she didn't dare make more noise. Hannah would be up several times cleaning the lighthouse lanterns and trimming the wicks. And Birch was a light sleeper.

The fear dissipated as she thought of her quest, and she smiled. Galen would be surprised to see her. She hadn't had a chance to tell him of her activities on behalf of England. Did he know Major Montgomery? She would have to ask him.

Her quick pace ate up the distance to town, and she was on the outskirts of the village within half an hour. The lights still spilled from the windows of the Lion's Paw, and she heard guffaws and voices raised in merriment from the open doorway. She hoped Galen had not retired for the night. It would be embarrassing to have to awaken him. But she was determined to see him, no matter what.

Lydia patted her hair to make sure it hadn't come loose in her walk and straightened her shoulders. Her mother had always told her the way she carried herself would determine how others treated her. Act confident and in charge, and people would defer to her. Her head high, she walked through the front door of the Lion's Paw.

The place was full, even though it must be nearly midnight. Smoke and the yeasty odor of beer hung in the air. Several men at the table in the corner peered intently at the cards in their hands while another group joked with two of the serving maids on the other side of the room. Two men at the nearest table stared at her, then one made a comment to the other, and they both burst into rude laughter. She blushed with mortification. She hadn't thought about others seeing her here.

She raised her nose in the air and ignored their leers. A broad-shouldered man in the back corner let out a chuckle, and she turned at the familiar sound. She felt faint at the sight of Galen with a woman in his lap. The woman's coarse laughter, naked shoulders, and nearly naked bosom told her occupation.

Lydia gritted her teeth and marched to the table. She had expected better of him. But she comforted herself with the thought that he had no idea she would welcome his attentions. That she would sacrifice her reputation for him. He would soon send the wench on her way when he knew she was here to offer her love and devotion to him.

"Give us a kiss, Mattie," Galen said coaxingly.

"Lieutenant, you have stolen more kisses now than ya deserve. I'll have to see some copper before ya get anything more." The woman laughed again.

Lydia winced at the piercing quality of the woman's voice and glared at her. Galen need not lower himself to consort with a woman like that. She cleared her throat, and the woman saw her.

Eyes narrowed, she snaked a plump arm around Galen's neck and stared at Lydia. "I was here first. Find your own bloke."

Galen's head swiveled at the exchange. He gave Lydia a slow smile. "Run along, Mattie." He shoved her off his lap and stood.

The woman landed on her backside on

the dirty floor and screeched at him. She swore and then scrambled to her feet and stomped off with an angry glare at Lydia.

He glanced at his two companions, both dressed in British uniforms. "Excuse me, gentlemen. The lady and I need to have some privacy."

The men leered at Lydia as they stood. "You have all the good fortune, Galen. Have fun." The tall, thin man closest to Galen clapped him on the back, then they both sauntered away.

Lydia shuddered at their lewd glances but refused to let any of her discomfort show on her face. Galen must not know she was fearful or uncertain about the course of action she'd chosen this night. She would stake her claim tonight, and Galen would be hers forevermore.

"Sit." He indicated the recently vacated chair closest to him.

She waited until he realized she expected him to pull out the chair. With a wry grin, he pulled it out and seated her at the table. The room seemed over warm, and she fidgeted in her chair. Licking her lips nervously, she waited for him to be seated. She'd carefully rehearsed what she wanted to say and just wanted to get it said before she lost her nerve.

He sat in his chair and lit a cheroot. "What are you doing here, Lydia? Does Hannah know where you are?"

"What do you think?" She smiled so her dimples would show, and the admiration on his face deepened. Relieved at his response, she leaned forward and slid her hand across the table.

He raised an eyebrow but closed his fingers around hers. His smile widened. "I think you snuck out of the house, and if Hannah finds out you have come to a tavern, she will take a switch to you." He shook his head. "I have never met a woman with more courage than this, Lydia. It must be something very important to bring you down a dark road at midnight."

Lydia's heart thrilled at his words. He admired her courage. She raised her eyes to meet his gaze. "It was very important," she said softly. "And for your ears alone."

Galen glanced around to make sure no one was listening. "Can you tell me here?"

She took her courage in both hands. "Can we go somewhere more private? I have news for Major Montgomery." That should pique his interest enough to take her to his room.

His eyes narrowed. "Montgomery?"

"He enlisted my help, and I have information he should know." She glanced around the room again. It would never do for them to be overheard. If word got back to Hannah, her sister would ship her home at once. Coming here was bad enough. If it became known she was a spy, she could hang, in spite of her sex.

He stared at her with a brow raised. "I have a room for the night."

Though her mouth was dry, she managed to get the words out. "I think it would be best to discuss this matter there."

He said nothing for a long moment, but a slow smile tilted his lips. Then his chair scraped on the floor, and he stood and offered her his arm.

What was she doing? She should run for the door as fast as she was able, but instead she smiled up at Galen and took his arm. As he escorted her down the dingy hallway to the bedchamber, her heart hammered in her ears so loudly she would not have been able to hear him if he spoke.

His accommodations consisted of a tiny room not much larger than a closet with a cracked bowl and pitcher on a table near the door and a small bed with linen that looked none too clean. She looked around and took off her cloak.

Galen's gaze skimmed her figure, and admiration glowed in his eyes. Good. She would make him forget all about Hannah. She would be a good wife to him. She'd always known they belonged together. She knew him better than anyone. She'd studied everything about him. Back home, she had pestered his younger sisters with questions, practiced making all his favorite foods, and cultivated ties with his cousins and friends.

"What is this about Major Montgomery?" Galen crossed his arms over his chest.

She lifted her head and smiled into his eyes. "Hugh enlisted my aid in keeping an eye on the lighthouse and Hannah."

His eyes dilated at the use of the major's first name. Was that jealousy burning in his gaze?

He stared at her. "You are spying for the British? What joke is this?"

"No joke, Galen. I have important information for Hugh. Can you carry it to him?"

A grudging admiration crept into his eyes, and he nodded. "Even now, he marches the men toward New York. Tell me your information, and I will make sure he hears it directly from me."

"Tell him the village plans to throw up an earthen dam as soon as they can muster enough men. If he intends to destroy the lighthouse, he must move quickly." She smiled. "Perhaps you had best not tell him that you drove off a ship trying to do just that. There's also a man in the village, Abraham Nettles, who is betraying all of you with information to the colonists. He appears to be a Tory, but he's not."

His cheeks reddened. "You would betray your sister?"

There was no condemnation in his tone, just curiosity and a touch of respect. Still, his use of the word *betray* stung a bit. She turned away and sat on the edge of the bed. "Hugh has assured me she shall not be hurt. I wish she would see the error of her folly in supporting the revolution, but she persists in her loyalty to the traitors."

"I cannot think where she got those views, unless from her husband. She has always seemed an amenable lady. Now she is much too independent." He frowned and stepped closer to Lydia. "She even performs a man's job at the lighthouse." The lines of disapproval deepened around his mouth.

She thrilled at the anger in his voice. Even now, he had seen the error of holding Hannah in too great an esteem. Maybe this would be easier than she had first suspected. "I didn't know John well, but I do not think theirs was a love match. Still, Massachusetts is a hotbed of independency, and my sister is too easily swayed." She dropped her gaze at the lie.

He wrapped one of her curls around his finger. "I think that is not the real reason you are here, sweet Lydia. That message could have been conveyed to one of my men. Hannah's lighthouse is not of great import." His warm fingers touched her chin and raised her gaze to meet his.

Her heart hammered in her throat and an inner voice screamed for her to leave before it was too late, but she pushed it away. She wouldn't go back without what she'd come for. She smiled and took his hand. "What do you think, Galen?"

Moments later his lips met hers, and she had all she wanted within her grasp.

Hours later that voice of conscience had been totally silenced. Sitting beside Galen as the buggy jounced over the potholes, she felt a sense of accomplishment. He was hers now. She had given him everything — everything important. He would never yearn after Hannah again. The moon had set, and dawn would be here soon. She was new, reborn as the woman Galen loved.

Galen kissed her one last time and helped her down from the buggy. The lighthouse still beamed, but the house was dark. Maybe she would escape detection yet. She had feared Hannah would be awake and demand to know where she had been.

Clinging to Galen, she wound her fingers through his rough blond hair. "When will I see you again?" She couldn't bear to let him go. She could smell his hair pomade on her skin, in her pores. She was part of him, and he was part of her, just as it was meant to be. Would Hannah see the difference in her?

He held her close. "I will be in touch, sweet Lydia. But I'll write when I get to New York. I might be moving from place to place, but I will send for you soon. In the meantime, you must watch Hannah and report any news to Major Montgomery."

She bit her lip and forced back the tears. Galen admired courage not weakness. "As you say, Galen."

He kissed her again. "Tell no one of our love, Lydia, not even Major Montgomery. He is a hard man, and if needed, you can use your beauty to convince him to show favor to me. If he knows of our love, he might not be so amenable."

She swelled with pride that he showed his vulnerability to her. He needed her. It was a heady thought. She kissed him lingeringly, then he thrust her away. Tears filled her eyes at his abrupt movement, but she understood. He was moved himself and thought he might show a womanly emotion.

"You must depart, or we will be discovered."

Lydia nodded and sniffed back her tears. "Take my love with you, Galen. I shall pray for you daily." She buried the sense of shame the thought of God brought to her. God would understand the necessity of giving herself to Galen. He would understand her great love for him. Society may frown on what she had done, but surely God would understand.

He vaulted back into the seat of the buggy. "Good morrow, my sweet. I must be off. We weigh anchor at dawn." A smile tilted the corners of his lips, and he touched his cocked hat and flicked the whip over the horse's head.

She watched him go with burning eyes, then turned and slipped into the house.

Galen gathered his cloak about him, but it did little to ward off the spray from the waves. Planting his feet against the rolling of the sea, he gazed back toward Gurnet Point. The lights from the towers still shone. Was Hannah in one of the light towers looking out toward him?

An ironic laugh escaped his lips. She would be horrified if she knew what her sister was up to. Cor, but she had surprised him. He had always intended to seduce her, but she had come willingly into his arms. She would be a useful tool. Her beauty could be used to snare other men to his advantage. His plans were shaping up nicely.

He scowled. Why couldn't Hannah look at him with the same adoration Lydia did? She baffled him. And that Captain Meredith in her house. He did not care for the man or the way his Hannah looked at him. The sooner he was out of there, the better. Lydia said he was a Tory. It seemed odd that Hannah would allow a loyalist to reside in her home with her strong pro-revolution views, but she had always had a strange sense of duty. All the more reason to get him out of there.

He was still a bit miffed that his ploy to drive off the "attacking" ship had not met with more success. He had genuinely thought Hannah would be so grateful she would forget past grievances. But some women held grudges. Look at his mother. She had never forgiven him for shooting his pony when he was twelve. Always hovering and demanding to know where he was and what he was doing. It had nearly driven him mad. But now he answered to no man. Or woman, even though Lydia might think differently.

CHAPTER 9

Hannah awoke with a start. Her heart pounded, but she wasn't quite sure why. Something had awakened her. She could see the glow from the lighthouse, so all was well there. She rolled over to go back to sleep and heard a sound. *Squeak, squeak.* It sounded like someone creeping up the steps. The footfalls paused, then continued stealthily up the stairs. Fear tightened her throat. Who could be sneaking up the steps at this hour? She had looked in on Lydia about two and seen her huddled shape beneath the blankets. Birch could not climb steps yet; he still slept in the small bedroom downstairs.

She slipped out of bed and tiptoed to the door. Putting her ear to the door, she listened intently. Was that breathing? Her mouth dry with dread, she seized the loaded musket propped beside the door. Easing the door open, she peered down the dark corridor. Nothing. She stepped into the hall, then slipped silently toward the stairs.

A figure nearly collided with her at the stop of the steps, and she barely managed to squelch the scream that bubbled up in her throat. The other person let out a shriek that clearly identified her.

Her fear was replaced with concern and a touch of anger. "Lydia, what are you doing?" Hannah took her sister's arm and dragged her back to the master bedroom. She rushed to light the candle on her bedside table. Holding it up, she turned to look at her sister.

It took a moment for her appearance to sink in. She was completely dressed. Although a cloak hid most of her attire, Hannah caught a glimpse of the blue satin gown she'd worn to Mother Thomas's. Her slippers were wet and muddy, and she avoided Hannah's gaze.

Rage and a sense of betrayal vied for Hannah's emotions. Rage won first. She took Lydia's arm and propelled her to her own room. She pushed open the door, went to the bed, and threw back the covers. A rolled-up quilt had simulated Lydia's form in the bed. No wonder she hadn't realized she'd been missing.

Hannah wanted to scream at her sister, to

tear her hair out by the roots. "You have been with Galen, have you not?"

Lydia dropped her head, then raised shining eyes to meet her gaze. "Yes, I have. I love him and he loves me, Hannah." She turned away and pulled off her cloak. "You need not look so shocked. You have always known how I felt about Galen. I have loved him since I was ten years old, but he was always too smitten with you to notice me. Mother thought if you married him, his money would lift us all from that ramshackle cottage. If not for that, he would have noticed me and not you. Well, he noticed me tonight." She gave a silvery laugh and began to take the hairpins from her hair.

Hannah shuddered at the triumph in her sister's voice. "Lydia, what have you done?" she whispered. She was afraid of the answer. Lydia looked different, more adult, somehow. Bile rose in Hannah's throat, and she struggled against the nausea. This couldn't be what it appeared. Surely Lydia had merely spoken with Galen. Just because she'd been gone for hours didn't mean something more had happened. But even as she tried to reassure herself, she knew the truth. She read it in Lydia's tousled hair and guilty air.

"I have done nothing but lay claim to the

116

man I love," Lydia said in a pleading voice. "Please try to understand. We shall be married when this war is over. Galen has promised that we will make our home in London. I shall be presented at court."

Hannah felt light-headed. How could something like this happen to her baby sister? "I forbid you to have anything to do with Galen Wright!" Hannah seized her sister by the arms and shook her. "I forbid it! Hear me well, Sister. If you disobey me in this, I shall send you back to Charles Town." Their parents would blame her, not Lydia. She was the elder. She should have watched over her better.

Lydia's gaze sharpened with anger. "You forbid? I am a woman grown, Hannah. I love whom I love, just as you did when you married John. What makes you think you can forbid me this love I bear?"

Hannah quivered with outrage and shame. "He is not honorable, Lydia." If her sister knew how dishonorable, she would never have allowed him to touch her.

The anger faded, with an expression of genuine curiosity taking its place. "You are always making comments about Galen. I do not understand your distrust. He has done nothing but treat you kindly. What kind of Christian are you that you would be so hateful to him?"

"You talk to me of Christ! A strumpet who comes from a rake's bed? Do not bother to deny it. I can see the truth in your face." The shock of that truth nearly broke her heart. "What do you think our Lord would say of what you have done this night?"

A flush traveled up her sister's neck and cheeks. She dropped her gaze. "He would surely understand my love."

"Fornication, the Bible calls it, Lydia. Real love does not seek out sin." She softened her tone. Lydia was still a child, only sixteen. Surely she did not understand the magnitude of her sin. "Real love seeks that which is good and helpful to the object of caring. Perhaps you sought to show your love to Galen, but if he truly loved you, he would not have taken the gift that should have been reserved for the marriage bed."

Lydia burst into tears. She threw herself into Hannah's arms. "I love him so much! I ache with this love I bear him. In truth, I knew it was wrong, but I could not help myself." Noisy sobs shook her shoulders.

Hannah held her while a slow anger burned inside. Galen had taken advantage of Lydia's childish infatuation. How could she salvage something of this mess? What if Lydia was with child? Hannah grew nauseated at the thought. *Please, Lord. Please make it not so.*

She patted Lydia's back until her sister finally pulled away and wiped her wet cheeks. "Bid me not give him up, Hannah. I cannot do it," she whispered.

What could she say? Nothing would change her sister's mind. Instead of answering, she went to the door. "I must check the lights. Go then to bed." She closed the door and went wearily down the hall to her own room. Somehow she must save Lydia from this obsession with an evil man.

She pulled on her brown linsey-woolsey dress and shoes. Slipping down the steps, she saw Birch through the open bedroom door. Their argument had not roused him from sleep. Good. It was her problem, not Birch's. He had intervened and defused Lydia's restless anger on more than one occasion, but this was something he couldn't fix.

The drying leaves crunched beneath her feet and released their fragrance as she hurried down the path to the lighthouse. Frost limned the rosebushes and grass, and her breath fogged the cold air. Winter crouched at the door, and she hated to see it come. Why did she stay here now that John was dead? Why did she put herself through the torment of facing her mother-in-law? She should go back to Charles Town, she and Lydia both. But the thought held no appeal either.

What was left in Charles Town for her? A drunken father and a distant mother, a younger sister she didn't really know. Her parents' poor example had instilled a fierce desire to be accountable, to stand when others would fall. She couldn't abandon her post.

She had a small inheritance from John, but it was too little to sustain her without the lighthouse-keeper salary. If he had lived, they would have inherited the family money, but that would now go to Olive and her husband, if Mother Thomas ever found someone willing to wed her daughter. She could do nothing but remain in this place.

Climbing the spiraling staircase, the cold metal of the handrail numbed her hand, and the windswept light tower was even colder. Hannah hugged her arms and stared out over the dark water. Would she ever have a chance to venture onto the ocean herself, or would she be forever condemned to scurry along the seashore like a misplaced crab? Why couldn't she have been born a man? Then she could have sought her fortune on board a ship as Birch did.

Lights twinkled offshore and she frowned. It was likely Galen's ship. When he had shown up last night, she thought it was a nightmare come to life. She often awoke trembling with his face in her mind. Once she had been like Lydia, blind to the corruption that lay under the surface of Galen's good looks. Hannah sighed.

She gave herself a mental shake and turned to polish the glass in the lantern. This was important work, though tedious. Only when she reached heaven would she know how many men had been saved by her light. She did not shine her spiritual light nearly as well. Was it her fault Lydia had fallen? If she had been a better example, perhaps Lydia could have resisted temptation. Hannah straightened her shoulders.

Birch was up and stirring porridge on the fire when she got back inside. He was dressed in his breeches and waistcoat, but he had not tied his hair back yet. With it loose on his shoulders, he looked even more the pirate she thought him.

She approached the welcome warmth of the fire and rubbed her hands together. "Good morrow, Captain."

He glanced up from his task. "Good morrow. How do you fare this morn?"

"Quite well. Does your leg pain you?"

"I shall take off the splint and see if it will support me."

Hannah frowned. "It has only been four weeks."

He nodded. "But it feels whole and strong. Your good food has mended it well."

Indeed, he did look manly and virile. It was time for him to be gone too. Daily she found herself more drawn to him. And that would never do, even if she waited a suitable time before remarrying. Their views would never mesh. He prowled the coast and brought supplies to help England. One day his ship might be asked to aid in destroying her lighthouse.

He was a hard man to read. His dark good looks drew her yet frightened her all at the same time. Black hair and eyes with that devil-may-care expression in them. Quiet and strong, but with many secrets he held close. In these past weeks she had learned little about him. What did his family think of his life? His expression became grim and forbidding whenever his family was mentioned.

"Was Lydia out in the night?"

How much had he heard? He obviously hadn't been asleep as she'd thought. "Yes." Shame caused her to drop her eyes. The blame was hers not Lydia's.

"That Galen fellow, I presume?"

She nodded and knelt to stir the porridge.

"I do not trust him."

Startled, she looked up. "You are perceptive, Captain. He is like a tree full of termites."

"Lydia doesn't see this?"

Hannah shook her head. "She thinks me too harsh in my assessment. I have good reasons."

"Have you told her of these reasons?"

Heat flushed her face and she bent her head again to hide it. She swung the iron pole that suspended the pot of porridge away from the fire and picked up the wooden ladle. "I have told no one. They are mine to bear and mine alone." She could never tell the full story. The shame would be too great.

"Sometimes troubles are lessened with the sharing."

She carried the bowls to the table and poured milk from the pitcher before answering. "Some troubles cannot be shared." His dark eyes softened at her admission. She was touched he seemed to care.

He dropped his gaze and hopped to the table with his crutches. "This I know well."

They ate in silence. Hannah kept stealing glances at his strong jaw. Tendrils of dark hair curled against his neck. What was he thinking? Was he offended she could not share her problems with him? He had told her so little of himself, he had no right to any offense at her own circumspection.

He scraped the last of the porridge from the bowl. "I will try the leg without the splint now."

"Let me help you." She went to her sewing basket and found scissors. He stretched his leg before him, and she carefully snipped the bindings holding the splint in place. He sighed when the bandage fell away.

Leaning forward, he kneaded the white and flaky flesh of his leg. "The itching has driven me nearly mad."

Hannah tilted her head and looked at his leg. It seemed to be straight and strong. "Can you stand?"

"Let me see." He gripped the edge of the table and pushed himself up.

She handed him the crutch. "Go lightly at first. Don't put your full weight on it until you see if it will support you."

He took the crutch and carefully leaned part of his weight on the healing leg. A grimace of pain marred his features, but he bit his lip and his expression became stoic once again. He limped back and forth across the kitchen. With every step Hannah could see the pain lessening.

"I think you should use the crutch or a cane for a few weeks."

He nodded. "Aye. 'Twill help." He dropped back into his chair and massaged his leg again. "You've been a good nurse, Mistress Hannah. But it's time I relinquish your hospitality and got back to New York."

"New York? I thought you would sail back to England and find another ship." A spreading dismay troubled her. She knew it was time for him to leave. He was becoming too important to her.

"I have a job in a merchant's office awaiting me in New York."

She could not imagine this darkly rugged man in an office. He belonged on the prow of a ship with the sea breeze in his face. "Surely you jest."

He shook his head. "I must serve where I am most needed."

"How can you serve England?" She could have bitten her tongue at the words. They'd been having such a pleasant morning. But she just didn't understand. He seemed so honorable, so strong and upright. How could he support the British cause to keep the colonies in bondage?

"There is a duty you do not understand, mistress."

His dark eyes probed her face, and their gazes locked. She knew she could not sway him from his purpose. For a moment Hannah felt as though she could look into his soul. There was a loneliness, a hunger there she recognized in herself as well. What was this connection she felt for him? She had no business feeling anything for him, not even compassion, let alone this yearning.

With a gasp she tore her gaze away and stood. "I cry you mercy for prying, Captain. What you do is your own business."

Was that disappointment on his face? She swallowed hard and gathered up the bowls and spoons to wash them.

"Will you miss me, Mistress Hannah? I will miss our sparring." Lazy amusement filled his voice.

Had he seen the longing she felt? Her cheeks burned with mortification. "You shall find another dog to kick. Others who despise loyalists will soon give you pause."

He limped closer and put his hands on her shoulders. At his touch she went rigid. The heat of his fingers soaked through the cloth of her gown and into her skin. He stood so closely, she could smell the scent of the soap he'd used in his morning wash. She curled her fingers around the bowls and kept her head down. If she looked at him, she knew she would fling herself against his broad chest and beg him to stay. He reached around and took the dishes from her, then turned her to face him.

"And do you despise me, Mistress Hannah?" His breath whispered across her face, and he tipped her chin up to search the depths of her eyes. Their gazes locked once again, and Hannah was lost. He rubbed his thumb across her jaw and bent his head. His lips barely brushed her own. Hannah closed her eyes and breathed in the male scent of his skin as his lips settled more firmly against her own.

He pulled away and searched her eyes again. "Hannah, I —"

"What are you doing with my sister?"

Hannah sprang away guiltily at Lydia's shrill voice. Her sister stood with her hands planted on her hips. Her accusing glare shamed Hannah. What had she been thinking to allow Birch to take such familiarities with her? Tears pricked the backs of her eyes.

She swallowed. "Would you like some breakfast, Lydia?"

Lydia was not about to be diverted. "It's a good thing I came down when I did."

"Lydia, mind yourself." Hannah sent a warning glance at her sister.

"Captain, I see you are no longer on crutches. I think it is time you were on your way."

"You are probably right, Miss Lydia," he said with an enigmatic glance at Hannah. "I seem to have overstayed my welcome."

CHAPTER 10

November 15, 1776

Their infant nation was four months old. Birch had managed to hear snippets of how the war was going from Hannah, but he wasn't sure how accurate her news was. He suspected she colored it with hope for the cause of the colonials, and he needed to know the full truth. Even with her rosy outlook, it appeared the Continental Army was faltering. Men from Plymouth said the British had taken control of New Jersey. If that was true, he needed to get to New York and do all he could.

There was no longer an excuse to stay on the outskirts of this small village. Then why was he so reluctant to leave? He refused to entertain the thought that Hannah's green eyes had anything to do with it. He had no time for a woman in his life. Not until this war was over and Major Hugh Montgomery hung from the nearest gibbet. Birch would have justice for his brother's death at the man's hand.

He pulled on his greatcoat and limped outside. This was a peaceful spot. Gurnet Point stuck out like a pointing finger into the water and seemed nearly an island with water on three sides. He stirred restlessly. He needed no peace right now. He had too much to do. Major Tallmadge would surely need his assistance. Birch hoped word had traveled down the coast about the loss of the *Temptation*. Otherwise, his superior may wonder if he'd turned traitor.

"It is surely strange to see you up and standing on your own two feet."

He hadn't heard Hannah come up behind him. "Aye, it feels strange as well."

"Dreaming of sailing off?"

She looked lovely today. A sea-green gown covered a white petticoat and deepened the color of her eyes. Her dark-blue cloak brought out the sheen of her hair. She had not bothered with a hat, and her black hair hung in ringlets down her back. How would it feel to twirl one of those curls around his finger? He would likely never find out.

He gave her a brusque nod. "I must be off on the morrow."

Her smile faltered and she looked away. "I'm not surprised. You have not really been

130

with us these past two days."

"Would you care to walk along the beach?" He offered her his arm. He should not be going anywhere with her. The warm feelings he held for her were dangerous.

She took his arm. "It's too cold to be gone long. And I must soon tend the lights. Dusk will be here."

"Do you ever think of leaving this place, Mistress Hannah? This is a lonely job for a woman."

"Sometimes. I would love to sail to exotic ports, to see how others live." She sighed. "Instead God has put me here on this rocky coast for some purpose." She paused and looked back toward the twin-towered lighthouse. "It will be even lonelier when you are gone." She bit her lip as though she wished she could call the words back.

Her admission warmed his heart. Perhaps she held him in some regard. But he must not encourage her affections. He was not likely to survive the war. Spies were caught and hanged every week. "Lydia will keep things interesting for you." He was careful to keep his tone light and amused. She must never know how hard leaving her would be.

She sighed. "I don't know what to do about her. If I thought I could do it, I would send her back to Charles Town. But the trip home would take her through New York, and she would be certain to disappear with Galen."

"The man needs a thrashing." And he would like to be the one to do it.

"He needs more than a thrashing. He needs God. But I hate him too much to ever tell him." Her eyes darkened with shame at her admission.

He frowned and felt a restlessness in his spirit. She'd been talking about God more and more lately. Or was it only that the references bothered him more? "I used to believe that twaddle. But then I grew up."

Her luminous green eyes widened. "How can you sail the seas and look at the sky and not know there is a God who loves you?"

He snorted. "Where was he then when my brother was pulled from his horse and made to run like a fox through the forest while men chased him? Where was he when my brother took a last look at the blue sky before soldiers cut his throat and strung him by the heels from a nearby tree? He was only fifteen!"

Birch clenched his fists and turned away before she could see the tears in his eyes. He had said too much already. A slip of the tongue such as this could get him killed.

What was there about her that had loosed his tongue in this way? He had sworn to tell no one of this until Montgomery paid for his crime.

Hannah gasped and stepped closer, touching his arm gently. "Our men did that? You said soldiers. Surely you would not be defending England if British soldiers had done such a thing."

She was perceptive. Too perceptive. He clenched his jaw. He must let her think it was colonials. "Speak to me no more of God. If he does exist, I want nothing to do with a God who would let such atrocity wreck a family."

Her fingers tightened on his arm, and he glanced down at her. Her expression was tender, and he had to resist the impulse to take her in his arms and forget all about the war. He shook her hand off, then thrust his hands in his pockets.

"You are not the only one to suffer loss and heartache," she said softly. "But bitterness hurts only you."

"You are only eighteen, Mistress Hannah. What do you know of real heartache and loss? Though you are a widow, you will marry again and life will go on. My brother's bones lie cold in his grave." He offered her his arm. "Shall we return to the house? I think your duties call you." He knew he was being unfair. Her husband also lay in a cold grave, but at least he had enjoyed a long life. Death hadn't claimed him until he was almost forty.

She opened her mouth as though to say more but then closed it again and took his arm. He felt a strange sense of regret as he escorted her to the base of the first tower. She was a closed book, in spite of her talk of God. Though something had caused that shadow in her eyes, and he didn't think it was the loss of her husband.

A cold rain soon changed to snow the next morning. Birch packed his few belongings in a valise salvaged from the wreck of the *Temptation.* After breakfast Lydia hitched the horse to the cart, and the three of them went to the village. Gurnet was quiet this early. The stores were not open yet, and few strolled the snowy streets.

At the livery he tossed his valise to the ground, then clambered down from the cart. "Don't bother to stay," he told Hannah and Lydia. "The sky looks as though this snow may stay awhile. I shall purchase a horse and get as far as I can by nightfall."

"I still wish you would take the stage or a ship." Hannah bit her lower lip and stared at him anxiously. "Your leg is not ready for a long trip by horseback."

"Perhaps you are right. But I need to make my way to New York as quickly as possible. I'll be fine. By the time the next ship stops, I should be to New York." Hannah's heart-shaped face looked pinched and wan. The words he wanted to say were on the tip of his tongue, but he dare not utter them. If they had been alone, though, he would have dared one more kiss. But a look at Lydia's glowering face convinced him not to push his luck. She had been curt and unfriendly ever since she caught her sister in his arms in the kitchen.

He took his valise and tipped his hat. "Many thanks for your kind hospitality, Mistress Hannah. Perhaps we will meet again one day." He tried not to look at her too closely, or she would see the longing in his eyes.

"Godspeed, Captain. I shall pray for you."

Were those tears on her lashes? He did not dare look closer. He found a woman's tears hard to bear. He gazed at Lydia. "Farewell, Miss Lydia."

"Farewell, Captain." Lydia curtsied.

Only then did he dare to look at Hannah closely. He fixed her image in his mind, the green eyes tipped with heavy black lashes, her luxuriant hair, black as midnight, the dimples that flashed in her cheeks. He would never forget her beauty or goodness. He executed a stiff bow, then pivoted on his heels to go.

"Captain!" She tossed the reins aside and scrambled from the cart.

He turned in time to catch her as she rushed into his arms. Her wet cheeks dampened his face, but he didn't care. He tightened his arms about her, and she raised her face to meet his. He heard Lydia's gasp of outrage, then the joy of holding Hannah eclipsed any thought of remorse. He bent his head and kissed her thoroughly.

When he pulled away, Hannah's eyes were still closed. She opened them slowly and smiled tenderly. "Now I can say farewell, Captain. I pray for a good life for you, and that you may find peace with God."

What could he say to that? "Farewell, Mistress Hannah," he said hoarsely.

She stepped away, and he had no choice but to release her. He felt bereft. Mayhap he would find her again when this war was over. Until then he must put her out of his mind. He touched his tricorn hat and approached the livery.

Plodding through the snow on the horse gave him plenty of time to think. Too much time. Every time he found his thoughts straying to Hannah, he resolutely turned them to the duties that lay before him. This would be a dangerous mission. What did he know of working for a merchant? How had Major Tallmadge come up with such a plan? But he could learn.

Where was Major Montgomery now? Birch hoped he was in New York, but it was not likely his luck would stretch that far. He had hoped to work with General Washington and so be on the front lines where his opportunities to seek his revenge would be greater. Thoughts of that sweet revenge kept him warm on the trip to New York.

When he reached the city, he was surprised to find many buildings still standing in charred ruins of the city. The British had not bothered to tear down the destroyed buildings. It was nearing nightfall, so he decided to find a tavern where he might sup and retire to a room for the night. On the morrow he would seek a boardinghouse.

He was more at home near the water, so he made his way to the quay. From several blocks away he could smell the sea brine, and he urged his horse as quickly as was safe. Chaucer's Tavern, the building weathered gray by the sea, crouched beneath a great sycamore tree a block from the water. He tethered his horse to the post and limped inside. His leg had pained him a great deal, and he was ready to rest it and warm his hands.

Though he sent a quick look around, no familiar faces were among the sailors swilling beer and ale. A bit disappointed, he paid for his room and hired a boy to care for his horse. The innkeeper showed him to his lodgings, a tiny room with a small cot in one corner that depressed him further. These accommodations were far inferior to Hannah's comfortable home. He pulled off his boots and lay back against the straw pillow. At least he could rest his leg and sleep.

The next morning he found his way to the offices of Samuel Rivers. Men hurried down the hall, and he passed several offices with men huddled over desks and shouting about political views. He finally found someone who told him where he might find Mr. Rivers, who was also a patriot masquerading as a loyalist. He wrote impassioned loyalist articles in the paper, and the English trusted him implicitly. Birch hoped to be as successful in his charade.

He rapped on the door, and a slight man with sandy-brown hair looked up from the great desk in the middle of the room. "Yes?" He frowned.

"Samuel Rivers?"

"If you are selling something, see yourself out. I have work to do."

Birch stepped into the room and shut the door behind him. "I am Captain Birch Meredith."

Mr. Rivers's scowl disappeared, and he came around the desk to shake Birch's hand. "Captain! I expected you weeks ago." He indicated a leather chair facing his desk. "I heard you had a bit of trouble near Plymouth. Lost your ship, did you?"

Birch grimaced. He made it sound like it was Birch's own negligence that caused the accident. "The lighthouse was expected to be attacked that night, and the keeper extinguished the lights."

Mr. Rivers stroked his chin. "Excellent idea. A lightkeeper who was on his toes."

"Her toes. It was a woman."

"A woman lighthouse keeper?" For a moment he looked surprised, then shrugged. "Well, I am glad you have finally arrived. We have many tasks ahead of us."

"I hope so. I wish to make a difference in this war, Mr. Rivers." It was the only reason he was here. That and his revenge.

"Call me Samuel. We shall be working closely together." His face brightened. "The British do not suspect me at all, and by extension, you should have no problem.

Major Howe's headquarters are here in New York City, and I have been able to uncover much intelligence from his officers. They love a good party, and my wife is an excellent hostess." He stared at Birch with approval. "She will be delighted to have an eligible bachelor to squire the young ladies."

Birch scowled. "That is not why I have come."

"Perhaps not, but the young ladies hear more than you might expect. The British officers strut and crow about their accomplishments, and we find out their plans right after they are made." He grinned. "We all have to make our sacrifices, Birch."

Birch compressed his lips. He had no intention of getting embroiled with flirtatious young women and fancy balls. He had come here to do a job, not play.

Samuel smiled again. "You look too gloomy, sir. Let me show you to your office, and I shall tell you what your other duties will be." He wagged a finger at Birch. "But make no mistake, young man. You will find the social life here will yield far more results than normal skullduggery."

"What of the British headquarters? Who mans them?" Birch asked as he followed Samuel down the hall to the small, dark cubicle that was Birch's new office.

Samuel snorted. "Howe leaves Major Hugh Montgomery much in charge as well as Montgomery's simpering assistant, Lieutenant Galen Wright."

Birch couldn't stop the quick intake of breath. Montgomery and Wright both here? What luck. His thoughts raced. Was there any chance Wright would be suspicious of him? He didn't see how that could be. Hannah and Lydia both thought he was a Tory. How fortunate he had never told them the truth, though he had oft been tempted.

"I know both men, Samuel."

He snorted again. "You do well to stay away from both of them. Two more unsavory rascals I have never met."

Birch narrowed his gaze. "Unfortunately, I don't think that will be possible."

CHAPTER 11

Lydia attacked the clothes in the washtub as if they were all the reasons keeping Galen from her side. Why had there been no word from him? A fortnight had come and gone and still she had no reassurances of his love. Hot tears rolled down her cheeks and dripped into the tub of water with gentle plops. She was just glad Hannah was tending the light this morning. She would blame Galen for the tears, and Lydia was too upset to put a good face on her hurt.

She loved her sister, but sometimes she wished Hannah wasn't so narrow. Her shocked expression when she'd realized Lydia had been with Galen had hurt. It wasn't wrong, not like Hannah thought. Neither one of them were married, so it wasn't adultery. God surely understood youthful passions. A prick of guilt made her bite her lip. She and Galen would be married soon, anyway. He said only the press of his duties postponed their marriage. Perhaps that was the sticking point.

Why did Hannah hate Galen so? It made no sense. The family had fully expected them to marry. They would all have welcomed him into the family with open arms with the hopes of turning around their bad fortunes. Lydia had given up trying to understand her sister.

She sniffled and wiped her face against her sleeve. There was no use in wallowing in self-pity. If she did not hear from Galen this week, she would steal away and go to New York to find him. She just hoped he was all right. Those Yankees were everywhere. Galen told her the danger was great. They must be circumspect and on their guard until the time was right. By then Hannah would just have to accept him.

She dumped the laundry in the basket and began to hang it over twine strung around the fire for that purpose. Lydia looked out the kitchen window at Hannah hurrying in from the lighthouse. The wind whipped her skirts and blew her black hair around her face. Lydia composed her face in a smile to greet her sister. She must not give Hannah more cause to hate Galen.

Hannah's cheeks were pink when she entered the kitchen. "Brr, I hate the cold!

143

Why could John not have owned property in South Carolina? I don't know how I shall endure the winter of tending the light."

"You could leave it, and we could go home." Lydia had no intention of going back to Charles Town, but she could not resist the impulse to poke her sister a bit.

Hannah took the teakettle from the stove and prepared a pot of tea. "And how would I live, pray tell?"

"You have nothing from John?"

"We had a bit of money set aside, but nothing to sustain me for long."

"What about Mother Thomas? She could give you John's inheritance."

Hannah gave her an incredulous look. "You have met my mother-in-law and still make that suggestion? Have you lost your wits, Lydia?"

Lydia smiled to show she jested only. "I would fear to even ask the dragon."

Hannah chuckled. "And you have seen only her good side."

"I think Birch escaped just in time. She would have found some way to snare him for Olive." It would have been a good thing. She had no desire to see her sister involved with the handsome captain. She wasn't quite sure why. He was a Tory, after all, and might actually be able to convince her sister of the error of supporting the revolution.

At the mention of Birch's name, Hannah's smile faded. "He would never have been taken in by Mother Thomas or Olive. Birch is much too wary — and intelligent."

"All men are tempted by money and power. Even a pretty face pales in comparison to what an advantageous union can bring them." Why was she goading Hannah? Was it because she wanted her sister as miserable as she?

Hannah gave her a long look. "Perhaps you should apply that to your own life, Lydia. You will have no dowry besides your own fair self. Galen is a man who likes power, especially power over women. I fear for your future. And he's cruel. Surely you heard of Abraham Nettles who was beheaded in the night this week? He was called a traitor, but I don't believe it. I suspect Galen's appearance here had something to do with it."

Guilt rose in Lydia's breast, but she struggled to tamp it down. She'd only passed along what she heard. And she was so tired of Hannah's cryptic remarks. "Why can you not say what it is you have against Galen? Why must you always talk in riddles?"

Hannah's face went white. Was her news

so terrifying? Hannah's hands shook as she poured the tea into cups. She slid one cup toward Lydia and took the other herself, then sat at the kitchen table. Her head bowed, she hunched her shoulders and two tears slid down her cheeks.

Lydia felt a sense of shame at her sister's distress but not too shamed to push further. "What did Galen do that was so terrible, Hannah?" She softened her voice to a gentle coax. "I really need to know."

Hannah sighed, a long exhalation of the breath she'd been holding. "Perhaps it is time you were told. It is a hard thing to speak of, Lydia. I have kept it to myself these past eighteen months, but the holding of it grows more wearisome daily." She took a long sip of tea and stared into space.

A sense of disquiet crept up Lydia's throat at the resignation on Hannah's face. Did she really want to know? What if it was worse than she thought? Was there anything Galen could do that would destroy her love for him? She thought not, but what if she was wrong? Her heart sped up, and she gripped her hands together in her lap. "I need to know, Hannah."

Hannah, her eyes full of misery, looked up and stared into Lydia's face. "I think you do." She cast her gaze down again, then

146

took a sip of tea. She set it back onto the saucer with a clatter. "Very well. Galen asked for my hand."

"I suspected he might have. You were keeping company, and he seemed very smitten. He did not ask Father, though, did he?" The thought of her beloved Galen even looking at another woman, even her sister, stung.

Hannah shook her head. "He would have if I had not refused him."

"Why did you refuse him? The other I surmised. There must be more to it than a simple proposal and refusal." Why could Hannah not get to the point? Why must she drag it out? Did she take pleasure in causing Lydia pain?

Hannah sighed again. "I had seen things, heard things that caused me some concern."

"Rumors? You turned down the most eligible bachelor in Charles Town on a whim? Where is that Christianity you tout so often? That is mere gossip."

Hannah was silent at this accusation but then raised her head and gazed at Lydia. "I had heard he took liberties with his slave girls, so I questioned him about it."

Lydia shrugged. "It is not an uncommon practice, Hannah. I would not condone it, of course, but once he was happily wed, it would surely have ceased."

Her sister's face whitened, and tears filled her green eyes again. "Hear me out, Sister. The story is not told yet."

Lydia sighed. "Pray continue."

"Galen not only admitted it, but did so proudly. He told me he had fathered three children already and thought it a fine way to increase the population and the quality of his slaves." She gave a bitter laugh. "He let me know in no uncertain terms that no man was content with one woman only. I told him I would marry no man who could not pledge himself to me only. When I asked him how he would feel if his wife were to take other lovers, he grew enraged. He said that I belonged to him, and no other man would have me." Hannah buried her face in her hands and burst into bitter sobs. "I cannot say more of it."

Lydia's relief left her light-headed. "Many men hold to his ideals."

"I would have killed myself before I married him." Hannah's eyes shone with determination. "Now do you understand why you must have nothing to do with him? He is not honorable."

Lydia's heart pounded, but she felt absolved. She still loved Galen. She was almost relieved to discover that fact. "He is a lusty man, I admit that. But he will not stray any longer now that he is mine." What exactly had Galen done? She couldn't bear not to know.

"You are mad." Hannah whispered the words. Her eyes were wide. "Can you not see the true man inside his handsome facade?"

Hannah would do anything, say anything to turn her love from Galen. It was all spite and hatred. "You have always preached mercy and forgiveness, Hannah. Where is your mercy now?"

"You think I want to feel this contempt for him? I have tried to forgive him and go on with my life. I married John so I would not ever have to see Galen again. I cannot have my sister married to such a man."

Lydia clenched her fists. Hannah was overreacting. Her sister was foolish to let something like this affect her so severely. Hannah had no right to dictate her life. Just because she was not wise with men and misled him did not mean everyone else had to suffer. She would not give up Galen, not even for her sister. She was sure Galen would have a different version of events.

"You must get used to the idea, Hannah. I mean to wed Galen as soon as possible. I suggest you fall on your knees and seek

God's face. He can surely give you the grace to forgive Galen's youthful indiscretions."

Hannah gasped, and her face went even whiter. She shook her head, and her mobcap slid to the back of her head. "What will be your excuse for your willful blindness?" She rose and rushed from the room.

Lydia could hear her sobs, then her bedroom door slammed, and the sound of weeping was muffled. She pushed away the stab of guilt. She was certain she was woman enough for any man. She would have no trouble with slaves and other women. Galen loved her. She was sure he did. They would travel to England and have a wonderful life. She refused to even contemplate anything else.

The muffled weeping soon stopped. Lydia felt a shaft of relief. She hated to cause her sister pain. Hannah had been good to her. When they were children, Hannah had always made sure Lydia had the larger share of their meager meals. She gave Lydia first pick of their few toys and often deliberately incited their father's anger if he seemed to be unduly harsh with Lydia. Her offer of a home had been an escape from the strained atmosphere at home and had been like a lifeline.

Lydia prepared supper. She took the salt

pork from the larder, cut off thin strips, and dropped them into a kettle of water. She cut up vegetables and added them to the pot, then put the lid on and swung the crane over the fire. When it began to bubble, she went to stir it. A stray spark flicked from the fire and landed on her skirt. It quickly began to smolder and the spot blackened.

She gasped and beat at the spot, but instead of dying, the fire licked eagerly at the fabric of her skirt and spread. Reaching frantically for the wooden bucket beside the fireplace, she nearly stumbled in her haste. Empty. She had emptied it into the pot for stew.

The skin of her legs could feel the heat of the flames now. Panicked, she beat at the fire with her bare hands. The flames had consumed the fabric of her skirt and started on her petticoat. The burning sensation intensified. "Hannah!" she screamed and turned to run.

Before she could get two steps, her sister was beside her beating at the flames. Hannah seized a rug on the sofa and threw Lydia to the floor. She wrapped the rug around Lydia, and the flames touched Lydia's legs.

"The fire! It hurts!" Lydia struggled to get up and continue her fight, but Hannah held her down.

"Lie still." Hannah panted, her arms pinning Lydia to the floor. "It's almost out." She lay across Lydia. If the fire ignited again, she would be consumed as well.

Gradually Lydia realized the fire was out. Her hands hurt and her legs felt as though they were still on fire. Was her face burned? Her hands flew to her cheeks, and she felt her face all over. The smooth skin soothed her fears even as the pain increased.

"Hannah, I'm still on fire!" She felt light-headed from the pain.

Her sister raised the rug and looked at her legs. "No, Sister, the fire is out. But I must put butter on the burns. Can you walk to the sofa?" Hannah helped Lydia to her feet.

The skin on Lydia's legs and hands felt tight, and she walked stiffly to the sofa. It had happened so quickly. She was fortunate, she knew. If Hannah had not been there, she would have burned to death. It was a grisly thought. She would have been like Martha, their older sister who had died in a fire when she was twelve.

The pain from the burns intensified, and Lydia wept. She could have died. Galen would have been devastated at her loss. She wept as her sister smoothed cool butter on her burns.

CHAPTER 12

Raised patches of red marred Lydia's legs, nearly all the way to her hips. Some spots were even blistered, but it could have been much worse. Hannah cringed at the sight of the burned flesh and thanked God for his protection of Lydia. Their sister Martha had lived only a few hours, but Hannah would never forget her agony. Her cries of anguish were a memory she had never been able to release. How could she have borne it if Lydia had suffered and died like that?

The near tragedy made Lydia even more precious to her, but she felt helpless to fix things between them. How could she stand by and watch her sister destroy her life, and do nothing? Yet her hands were tied. Her hands shook as she tried to keep her sister calm.

Lydia moaned and thrashed about on the sofa. "Hannah, it hurts."

"I know, Sister. I wish I could take the

sting for you." She did too. She had always been the strong one, the one who protected Lydia from their father and schoolyard bullies.

Lydia was pale, and beads of perspiration clung to her upper lip. She gritted her teeth with her determination not to cry out.

"Perhaps a cool bath would calm the burning." Hannah didn't know what else to try. Butter was the accepted treatment for burns, but it didn't seem to be helping.

"I cannot bear it, Hannah. Please, we must try something." Lydia moaned.

"I will fetch water and the hip bath." Hannah hurried to the kitchen and took the hip bath from the nail on the wall. She set it in front of the fireplace and poured hot water from the kettle over the relit fire, then went out the back door to the well and hauled in buckets of water. When it was filled, it was barely tepid. She would not have wanted to bathe in it, but she hoped it would sooth Lydia. She helped her sister undress to her shift, then supported her while she eased into the water.

"It's cold!" Lydia gasped. Her shift was quickly soaked and clung to her. "But the pain is easing." She shivered.

Hannah draped an old quilt about Lydia's shoulders to warm her upper body while the cool water soothed the burns. Lydia soaked in the water for nearly an hour before she could be persuaded to come out. Lips blue, she shivered almost uncontrollably, though Hannah dried her and dressed her in a warm flannel nightgown and helped her to bed.

Hannah was exhausted, but the lights needed to be lit. They should have been lit hours ago. It was nearly nine o'clock. She pulled on her cloak and hurried along the path to the lighthouse. Its dark form was becoming so very familiar to her. How many times had she walked this path in the four months since John had left? She wished she had a shilling for each step. She trudged up the steps to the first tower. She looked out over the dark water before she lit it, but she could see no lights, only blackness. The sound of the sea carried to her, but no creaking of masts or the flapping of sails. Mayhap she had lost no ships this night.

She quickly lit the lamp, went to the next tower and did the same, then walked wearily back down the steps. The cold wind pierced her clothing and she shivered but paused anyway to take a deep breath of salty air. Where was Birch now? Did he ever think of the lightkeeper who had cost him his ship? He would be too busy with his new job to spare a thought for her. She sighed and turned to go back to the house.

As she neared the front door, she saw a dark figure standing there, and her heart skipped a beat. She bit back a cry, then relaxed. "Olive. You're out late." What could her sister-in-law possibly want here at such an hour?

"Mother sent me to inquire as to why the lights were not lit," Olive said stiffly.

Hannah sighed. "Would you care to come in?"

Olive stared at her a moment, then inclined her head. "It's cold. Perhaps it would be best to discuss it indoors."

Hannah opened the door and ushered her inside. The flames in the fireplace illuminated the room. The hip bath still sat by the fire with the clothing and quilt littered beside it. Olive would report back to Mother Thomas on the state of her housekeeping, but she really didn't care. She had ceased trying to be the ideal picture of a daughter-in-law long ago.

"Would you care for tea?"

Olive shivered, then nodded.

Hannah took off her cloak and set to preparing the tea. As she shaved bits of tea from the cube into the caddy, she wondered what Olive's true motive was in coming in.

She could have said her piece at the front door, then hurried back to her warm bed. Did it have anything to do with Birch? Pity for her sister-in-law welled up in her. Criticized by her mother constantly, no wonder the poor girl seemed so desperate.

Hannah carried a tray with tea and scones into the parlor and placed it on the center table. The tea's aroma relaxed her, and she poured two cups, then offered Olive a scone, which she took with a stiff smile of thanks.

"As you can see from the state of the room, this has been an eventful evening. Lydia's skirt caught fire while preparing supper, and she was burned. I was tending her burns and was unable to tend the light until moments ago. Luckily, there seems no harm done."

Olive's mouth dropped open. "Is she disfigured?"

The genuine concern in her voice warmed Hannah. "No, praise God. Only blistered and reddened skin on her legs and hands. She will recover."

"Oh, indeed. God be praised. I shall inform Mother." Olive fiddled with the fringe on her shawl and took a sip of tea. "Ha-have you heard from your former boarder in recent weeks?"

Aha, she was right. She resisted a smile. "No, nothing. But Captain Meredith is a busy man with an important new job. He is unlikely to contact me again."

Olive sniffed. "Your relationship appeared to be more than friendly to the village the day he left. I have heard reports that you kissed him in broad view of the entire population."

So this was the real crux of the matter. Hannah felt the warm tide of color on her cheeks. She had rued the way she had thrown herself at Birch that day. She had expected a visit from the elders of the church, but they had not reproached her so far. But it was coming.

"I must admit emotion stole my sense that day," Hannah said softly. "I had caused his injury and still felt badly about it. But I fail to see why you bring it up now."

"He is a Tory, and the British killed your husband!" Olive wrung her hands.

"And your brother. And you sought to wed him but a few short weeks ago."

Olive's cheeks mottled with color. "But I did not know his sympathies lay with Britain. You did. Mother is very distressed by your behavior."

"I am sorry for that, but she need worry no longer. Captain Meredith is gone, and I doubt I shall ever see him again." Hannah took a sip of tea with hands that shook slightly.

They were from two different worlds. Their paths had crossed for a few short weeks, but he was in New York City where there were many beautiful women who shared his love of Britain. He would not remember a lowly lighthouse keeper from a small village in Massachusetts.

"It would be best for him never to show his face here again. Now that the village knows he is a Tory, he would be tarred and feathered." Olive rose, then hesitated. "Do you know how to get in touch with the captain? Perhaps I should warn him of the danger here."

"I have not heard from him."

Olive sighed. Hannah showed her out and locked the door behind her. She stoked the fire and took the candle to light her way to bed. She didn't want to think or feel anything else today. The emotional toll of the day had left her weary beyond belief. She just hoped she could awaken to tend the light at midnight.

Lydia was much improved by the next morning. Her legs and hands were still sore, but she said most of the worst pain was gone. Hannah wished she might lie abed herself most of the day. She still felt the effects of her late night and lack of sleep. She prepared porridge for breakfast and set the parlor to rights. She carried in a load of wood, then set the kettle over the blaze to boil for tea.

The rattle of a carriage out front brought her to the door. Her heart sank when she recognized two elders from the Congregational church. The minister was not with them, and for that she was grateful. These two would be bad enough.

She inclined her head. "Good day, Mr. Reynolds, Mr. Newsome."

"Widow Thomas." The elder gentleman, Marcus Reynolds, fixed his steely-blue gaze on her. He slipped the gold-tipped cane to one gnarled hand and tipped his cocked hat. "We come on a matter of great importance. Might we come in?"

"Of course." She opened the door and ushered them into the parlor. Lydia looked up wide-eyed at their entrance. She moved to one end of the wooden bench.

The younger man, Roger Newsome, tipped his hat in her direction, and his ferret eyes gleamed with appreciation. "Miss Huddleston."

Lydia inclined her head regally. "Good day, sirs."

Mr. Newsome sat on the sofa. "We were told this morning of your misfortune yesterday, Miss Lydia. We prayed for your safe recovery before we set out."

"Thank you." Lydia sent him a dazzling smile that made him blink.

Lydia's flirting wouldn't help the day. Hannah suppressed a smile. These men would not be swayed by womanly wiles. She seated herself in a chair near the fireplace and folded her hands in her lap. She knew why they had come, and it wasn't to inquire after Lydia's health. She willed herself to be calm and accept their rebuke.

Mr. Reynolds gripped the gold-tipped cane and wheezed as he sank into the chair opposite the bench. "We bear a grievous burden for our community, Mistress Thomas. Our town has certain standards to uphold. When infractions occur, no matter how slight, they must be dealt with before they become rampant sin. It is a charge we do not take lightly."

"I understand, Elder."

He preened slightly at her recognition of his position. He fixed his gaze on Lydia. "A serious matter has come to our attention involving Miss Huddleston."

Lydia almost visibly shrank. Hannah clenched her fists in the folds of her skirt.

"Is it true, miss, that you consorted at the tavern all night with a man, a loyalist, and were delivered home at dawn?" He thundered out the words, and Lydia turned a piteous gaze to Hannah.

"I shall have to ask you to leave, sirs." Hannah rose to her feet. "My sister is not well. We shall answer these accusations at a later time. Perhaps in a week or two when my sister is recovered."

Both men gaped at her, obviously not used to being asked to leave before they were finished. After a moment's silence, Mr. Newsome looked to Mr. Reynolds for guidance.

"It has also come to the attention of the church that you behaved in an unseemly manner in view of the entire village several weeks ago. I fear we must take you to task for that, mistress."

"I know of the incident of which you speak," Hannah said. "I can only say that my actions were innocent affection and not something sinful."

"That may be. You and God alone know the state of your heart," Mr. Reynolds said with another keen glance from those blue eyes. "However, the village witnessed you in the embrace of a loyalist. For that, there must be penance."

162

Hannah struggled to keep her anger in check. "I appreciate your concern, gentlemen, but I assure you my soul is well before the Lord."

He shook his white head. "I fear we cannot take your assurance. We must ask you to appear before the town council to answer questions about your conduct and morals as well as the state of your soul."

"And if I do not?" Hannah wasn't sure where the courage came from to question his edict. She'd already answered the questions as well as she was able.

"I advise you not to test us in this way," he said ominously. "We will expect you tomorrow afternoon at two."

Hannah stood her ground, though inside she was quaking. What would she do if she were banished? Where would she go? She allowed not a hint of her misgivings to show on her face but merely inclined her head. "I shall answer your questions, sirs. But not tomorrow. As I said, my sister is not well. When she is well again, we shall answer your accusations."

Mr. Reynolds' face was thunderous. "The church shall hear of your defiance this day, Mistress Thomas. If you fail to answer to the church in a satisfactory manner, you shall be banished. We do not want to do this, mind you. But we will have no choice. We cannot have such behavior go unpunished."

He glared at her once more, then stomped to the front door, his cane slapping smartly against the floorboards. When the door slammed behind them, Hannah sank into the chair and buried her face in her hands.

A salty breeze lifted the hair on the back of Birch's head and raised his lagging spirits as he took the steps two at a time to his room. He'd found a pleasant rooming house near the quay. He would never be able to stand to live away from the sound of the sea. His landlady, Mrs. Dunwoodie, was a short, stout woman with ruddy cheeks and a wide smile that made Birch feel welcome. His room had one window that looked out on the water. Though small, the room was clean with simple furnishings, and the price included breakfast and supper.

He seldom encountered the two other boarders, a thin, young man with the nervous habit of picking his teeth and an intense man about his own age who often carried a Bible under one arm. Birch vowed to stay away from the Bible-carrying gentleman. He had no interest in listening to him spout off about wrath and damnation. Birch knew all about damnation and wrath. As far as he was concerned, plenty of both abounded in this wretched world.

New York was crawling with British soldiers. It seemed to Birch that the numbers had increased even more in the past few days. He had an uneasy feeling something was about to happen. He needed to find out what was afoot and get word to General Washington. His job as a merchant was a good cover. It was commonly known that he had been transporting goods to the British ships and was merely working until he obtained another ship.

Mrs. Dunwoodie knocked on his door. "Captain? There is a gentleman downstairs who wishes to speak with you. I've put him in the parlor."

Birch frowned and pulled on his coat. He had been looking forward to an evening of reading. But it could be important. He hurried down the steps and into the parlor.

Samuel Rivers rose from his seat on the sofa and thrust his hands in his pocket. "Close the door."

Birch gave him a keen glance, then shut the door. He had never seen his superior look so rattled. Samuel was usually in full command of any situation. Birch's interest sharpened. He was ready for some new excitement.

Samuel waited until Birch came nearer, then put his finger to his lips and tiptoed back to the door. He swung it open quickly, but no one was there. "Just checking," he muttered. He shut it firmly again and motioned Birch to follow him away from the door. "I must be certain no one hears."

"What has happened?"

"The British Army intends to take Philadelphia." Samuel spoke the words softly, still watchful of the door.

A soft exhalation was the only response Birch allowed himself. He itched to take up a musket himself and defend his country's capital. "When?"

"They're on the march now. I sent someone to warn Washington. But I need you to try to learn all you can quickly. Major Montgomery will be at a large party tonight at the home of Molly Vicar. I managed to get you an invitation. Mingle as circumspectly as you can. We need to find out just when the attack will commence and how many men they plan to deploy."

The muscles in Birch's neck tightened, and his respiration kicked up a notch. So, it had come at last. He would meet the man face-to-face who murdered his brother.

Samuel laid a hand on his shoulder. "I

had hoped to keep you away from Montgomery. I cannot stress how dangerous this is. Montgomery seems to have a sixth sense about people, and more than one of those who have tried to get close enough to him to gain information have hanged."

Birch curled his lip, and he could not keep the contempt from his voice. "I have no fear of Montgomery."

"That is exactly why I chose you. He smells fear like a fox smells a chicken. If he sensed you feared him, he would begin to wonder why, and that would be our undoing. If you are found out, we will all go down with you. He will never believe I had a colonial working for me without being one myself."

Birch nodded. The stakes were high, but he wouldn't let Samuel down. Or Charlie. Hugh Montgomery would pay, and tonight would begin the game. He showed Samuel to the door, then hurried to get ready for the evening.

He dressed carefully in his finest clothes — breeches and a crimson-and-gold waistcoat with a black coat over it. He debated about wearing a wig, but he hated them, so he simply pulled his hair back and tied it in a queue. He must look the part of a gentleman of quality.

Candlelight glowed from the windows, and the hum of conversation paused momentarily as a black servant ushered Birch into the drawing room. He looked around for anyone he might know. There were easily thirty to fifty people in the large room.

Standing by a large potted palm tree was Galen Wright. He wore a powdered wig and was flirting with a lovely dark-haired woman in a blue gown. He saw Birch and scowled. The woman turned to see what had disturbed Galen, and her eyes lit with interest when she saw Birch. She turned to say something to Galen, and though his eyes were hostile, he motioned for Birch to join them.

"Well, hello. Do I know you?" The woman laid her hand on his arm.

She was striking, in spite of her age. About forty, her face was arresting with its high cheekbones and dark, expressive eyes. A tide of heat rose up his face at the amusement in those dark eyes. Galen rudely left them without a word to Birch, but he barely noticed with Molly's admiring gaze boring into his.

She smiled again and curtsied. "Molly Vicar, your hostess."

"Birch Meredith." He offered a slight bow and took her hand.

"Ah, Captain Meredith, the brave man who lost his ship bringing food to our troops. I have heard of you, sir. You are most welcome in my home." She tucked her hand into the crook of his arm. "You must have something to drink. Then I shall introduce you to a few people who might be able to help you acquire another ship." She slanted a coquettish look up at him, and a dimple appeared in her cheek. "I can tell you are not totally comfortable on land. You belong at sea."

He warmed at her perception. This party might not be so bad after all. Was there any possibility of getting a ship and continuing his work of smuggling food to the Continental Army? He had thought there would be no hope of another ship until after the war was over. He responded to her gentle tug, and they strolled through the crowd. She found him a drink, then led him to a group of four men and three women who were talking beside the window overlooking the snow-covered garden.

One man with sandy-blond hair and blue eyes smiled when he saw Mistress Vicar. "Lovely party, Molly. Where do you find such delicacies in the middle of a war?"

Her dimples deepened. "Who could resist a request of mine, Major?"

Major? Birch's head swiveled, and he stared at the man. Was this man Montgomery? If so, he didn't look all that formidable. He wore a petulant expression as though he was used to getting his own way.

The man took her hand gallantly. "I certainly could refuse you nothing, my sweet Molly."

She smiled. "Major, this is Captain Birch Meredith. You may have heard of the wreck of his ship several months ago. The disaster took supplies for your troops to the bottom of the ocean. Captain, this is Major Hugh Montgomery. I'm sure you've heard of the marvelous job Hugh is doing against the colonials. When we win this war, we shall have Hugh to thank for it."

His hostess's effusive praise did not seem to cause Montgomery any embarrassment. He smiled and bowed as though she had merely spoken the truth. "Captain. Indeed, I have heard of your tragedy. Many of your crew were lost, were they not?"

Birch returned his bow. "I regret that fact even more than the loss of my ship, Major. Some of those men had served with me for ten years."

The major's shrewd eyes continued to look Birch over. Birch was suddenly glad he'd been warned about Montgomery. He was the kind of man who would enjoy using a man's weaknesses against him.

"I knew a Meredith once. Where are you from, Captain?"

"Virginia." Birch lied without a flicker of an eyelash. It would never do to have Montgomery associate him with Charles.

"Are you related to any North Carolina Merediths?"

"Not to my knowledge."

Montgomery nodded. "A common name."

At least Montgomery had learned the name of the young spy he'd hunted down like a stag. Birch had never been sure.

Molly tapped the major on the arm with her fan. "You are monopolizing the captain and have not even let me introduce him to your companions."

Montgomery grinned and looked even more boyish, but Birch wasn't misled. It would take some time to get closer to the wary major. He would watch for his opportunity, and it would come.

Molly introduced him to the other people in the group. There was a banker and his wife, another officer in the army and Galen Wright, who had so far managed not to speak a word to Birch.

"I have already had the pleasure of making the captain's acquaintance," Wright said with a smoldering glare.

Birch could feel the dislike radiating from Galen. "Lieutenant Wright." He nodded to Galen.

"How fare Hannah and Lydia?"

"It has been several weeks since I left, but they were well at that time." Birch hated to tell him even that much. Anger burned at the thought of this man bothering Hannah.

Molly's eyes narrowed in jealousy. "And who are Hannah and Lydia? I thought I had your heart, Galen." The words were said with a light tone, but there was no mistaking the pique in her eyes.

"Two ladies from my childhood, Molly. No one for you to be jealous of." Galen slid a smile in her direction. "By coincidence, Hannah was the lightkeeper along the coast where the captain's ship was destroyed. He stayed in her home while he recovered."

"Are they traitors to the Crown?" Molly refused to let the subject die.

"Hannah is a colonial, but Lydia is a loyalist," Wright admitted.

"Ha! That would make for some strained sisterly relations," Montgomery said.

Wright shrugged. "They seemed friendly during the brief visit I made. The captain could probably tell better than I, as I was only in the area overnight."

Long enough to destroy Lydia. Birch wished he could fling Wright's treachery in his face in front of witnesses. He kept all indications of his feelings from his face and voice. He must not tip his hand. "Mistress Thomas is much too busy with her duties as lightkeeper to engage in much political discussion."

"Thomas?" Montgomery's lazy expression sharpened. "Was not that the name of one of the traitors who burned New York, Galen? One of those you caught and hanged?"

Wright's eyes snapped wide, and he looked alarmed. "Y-Yes. I think it was."

Birch stared at him. Was that guilt in Galen's eyes? "John Thomas was her husband's name. He was hanged here in New York as a spy."

"One and the same man, I am sure of it!" Montgomery stared at Wright. "Strange connection, Galen. Did you know this man was the husband of this lighthouse keeper? You never mentioned that you knew him."

"Thomas is a common name, sir. I had lost track of Hannah some time ago and did not remember her married name." Wright looked down at the floor and chewed on his thumbnail.

"I see." Montgomery glowered and

straightened his shoulders. "I am sure you must continue your rounds, Molly. I need to speak with Galen for a moment. If you will excuse me." He bowed and motioned for Galen to follow him.

So Galen's hand had been in John's hanging. Birch didn't know what to make of that information. He had known by the way Galen watched Hannah that he had feelings for her. That made what he did to Lydia all the more despicable. He wondered if Hannah and Lydia knew this but decided it was doubtful. Hannah had treated him almost with fear. If she had known he had killed her husband, she would have been enraged. Her soft manner hid a will of iron.

He was tempted to write and tell Hannah what he had discovered. She was a good woman and deserved the best from life, though her God didn't seem to feel the same way. Her life had already been hard for one so young. Widowed at eighteen, tending a lighthouse on a lonely shore, being caretaker of a willful sister — she had many burdens to bear.

"Captain, I believe our supper is ready." Molly smiled up at him and touched his arm again. "Shall we go?"

He took her arm and escorted her to the dining room. He was only too glad to put thoughts of Hannah behind him. It could never be.

CHAPTER 13

Major Montgomery slammed the doors to the parlor closed. The force caused the pictures on the wall to rattle. Galen knew he was in for a scolding and silently cursed Captain Meredith. Why did he have to open his mouth about John Thomas? Galen rubbed the back of his neck and watched his commander. Montgomery always left him feeling a bit unsettled. And why did he have to go on a tirade at a social occasion filled with pretty women? Montgomery liked a pretty woman as well as the next man, didn't he? Especially rich ones.

His lips tight and a muscle in his jaw twitching, the major turned to face Galen. "I do not appreciate being made to look a fool, Lieutenant. It looks to me as though you hanged this John Thomas merely to get to his wife."

How should he play this? Innocent or apologetic? "I have to admit I am as shocked as you are, Major. I had no idea John was Hannah's husband until tonight. Thomas is a very common name and so is John. Truthfully, I did not even remember who Hannah had married."

The major stared at him, then snorted. "Do you really expect me to believe that poppycock? Do you have so little respect for my intelligence that you would try to convince me of such a ludicrous lie?"

Galen wanted to tell him what he really thought of him, but he managed to bide his time. "What can I say to convince you, Major? I know it looks bad, but I had no thought of Hannah when I was merely doing my duty. You had told me to find the men who burned New York, and I did exactly that. A soldier has no time for women during a war like this."

Major Montgomery's tight jaw relaxed. It had been the right thing to remind him that Galen had been merely doing his duty. Galen stifled a sigh of relief, then mentioned something that might soothe him further. "You met Hannah's sister, Major."

Major Montgomery lifted an eyebrow. "Oh? I remember no woman with a last name of Thomas."

"No, sir. It is Huddleston. I delivered a

message from her when I came from Plymouth."

The major's eyes warmed. "Ah, that Lydia. From Gurnet Point. A lovely young woman." He smiled. "She is this Hannah's sister? You know her as well?"

"Since she was a toddler."

The major stared at him speculatively. "I would like to get to know her better. If you could arrange that, I might see my way clear to forgive you this latest stumble. I find myself thinking of her often. Mayhap she would like to see something of New York."

"Her sister would never allow it." Too late Galen saw his error in mentioning Lydia. How was he to get her away from Hannah? Something like this would fan Hannah's distrust, not appease it.

The major laid a hand on Galen's shoulder. "I have every confidence in your powers of persuasion." He dropped his hand and opened the door. "We should rejoin the party. Molly will wonder what has become of us."

Galen followed him across the hallway to the drawing room. He wanted to avoid Birch Meredith if possible. He didn't think he would be able to hold his temper in check if he saw the captain. Had Birch tried to get him in trouble on purpose? It seemed likely.

Birch was leaning against the wall with his arms crossed over his chest. His smile and stance were relaxed and interested, and Molly was basking in his attention. Galen's lip curled. If Hannah could see her precious captain now, she wouldn't look at him with those shining eyes. Perhaps he could find a way to tell her about it. A slow smile emerged. It might be entertaining to have Lydia in New York after all.

When would this party end? It had seemed interminable. Birch's face ached from smiling. This type of spying was not for him. He wasn't good at it.

He supposed it had been a good move of Samuel's to send him, and he had a feeling Molly might know a great deal about British movements. Her home was crawling with English officers.

Hugh Montgomery's appearance had surprised him. He had expected a gruff, older man, not the slim, boyish-looking major. But Birch could imagine him on a horse shooting his brother down like a fox in an English hunt. He tightened his lips. Soon it would be the major who was run to ground.

He looked back at Molly. She intrigued him, and he wasn't the only one. The women deferred to her, and the men flirted. She looked lovely, though the powder accentuated the lines around her mouth and eyes. She wore a blue polonaise gown with the extra material looped back over buttons at the hips and trailing behind her. She smiled into his eyes with a promise that stirred his blood.

He made his way through the throng to her side. "Might I have this dance?"

Molly wrinkled her nose. "I do not feel like dancing right now, Captain. I shall introduce you to someone you should meet." She led him toward a gray-haired man who wore an affable grin. "David, I would like you to meet Captain Birch Meredith. You both have much in common. Birch, this is David Saunders. He is a shipbuilder and merchant."

Mr. Saunders bowed, and Birch returned the greeting.

"I always enjoy talking about shipping and the sea, Captain."

Birch talked with Mr. Saunders while Molly flitted about the room. He watched with amusement as Molly flirted with one man after another. Although older than most of the other women, she turned many heads. There was just something engaging about her.

"Just let me know when you are ready to get back to the sea, Captain. Your prowess on the ocean is well known." Saunders's voice interrupted his thoughts. "I am always in need of experienced captains, especially now that the blockade stands in our way. Most men are afraid of the colonials."

"I hope to get back to a ship when this war is over. I'm not well suited to office work. I would imagine you have been having a lot of trouble with colonials."

Saunders snorted. "The few ragtag ships they have are no match for my vessels, but many men are fearful anyway."

"Would I be allowed to pick my own crew?" Not that he would seriously consider it. Montgomery was here, and Birch intended to stay here until his revenge was complete. But his thoughts raced with the opportunity for the Continental Army. If they could get a man of their own and his crew on that ship, they could fly the British colors and slip close enough to the enemy to cause some real damage.

"Absolutely!" Saunders leaned forward. "I would put the ship totally under your command."

"When would you have another ship ready

to sail?"

"I have one just about to christen now. She's a beauty with a generous captain's cabin. I would even let you name her."

"Let me think about it for a few days. Where can I reach you on Monday?" That would give him enough time to report and see what his superiors wanted to do about the opportunity.

Saunders gave him the address of the shipyard, then clapped him on the back. "You will not be sorry, Captain. I shall make it worth your while."

He would report the matter to Samuel. They needed to seize the opportunity. He'd also found what he had come for. He had to admit Samuel was right. A social place like this yielded much information. Some he could have done without.

It was nearly midnight by the time the guests took their leave. Birch headed toward the door, but Molly stopped him.

"Don't leave," she whispered. "I should like to talk to you when my guests are gone."

He stepped back into the drawing room and sat in a chair by the fireplace. The rest of the guests filed out in haste with bows and curtsies. He watched Molly through the open doorway as she thanked them all for coming. She stepped back into the drawing room and came toward him.

"I cry mercy, I am so glad that party is over." She took the pins from her hair and the dark tresses caressed her silky shoulders. Her eyes invited him to do the same. Molly stepped close and smiled into his eyes. "It's so cold, Birch. You could warm me."

Her voice was deliberately seductive. Her perfume wafted up his nose, and her silk skirts rustled as she moved closer still. He swallowed hard and kept a tight rein on his temptation. He knew what she was offering, and if he wanted to continue to use the contacts she had, he did not dare alienate her with a harsh refusal. But the memory of Hannah's green eyes dampened any response he might have had.

He took a deep breath and patted her hand. "I think there is a robe on the sofa, Molly." He reached over and searched until his fingers found the rough wool of the robe. He stood and draped it around her. "Better?"

"Much, thank you kindly."

The ardor in her voice had cooled, and Birch knew she had taken his gentle refusal graciously. The tension in his shoulders eased, and he bowed. "What did you need to talk to me about? I must be getting home."

She looked startled, then smiled. "I simply wondered what David discussed with you."

"He's offered me a ship, and I have you to thank for that, I think."

She clapped her hands. "Wonderful. I thought you might have much in common with him."

He yawned. "I do not wish to appear churlish, but I should take my leave now. I thank you for your hospitality. Might I call again?"

His request softened the steely gaze in her eyes. "Of course, Birch. I should be delighted to see you anytime." She trailed a finger along his arm. "Make it soon."

He found it difficult to sleep that night. He was eager to tell Samuel what he'd learned at the ball, and he was disturbed by his reaction to Molly. Why had he turned down her obvious invitation? Before he met Hannah, he would not have been so gentlemanly. He shook his head. He didn't want to think of Hannah. He had no time for women now. His duty here in New York was too pressing.

He was certain General Washington would be thrilled at the opportunity to get a ship. They would have to pick the crew with care, and it would be dangerous, but the rewards for the country would be great.

He rose early, washed, and hurried through Lower Manhattan to Samuel's home. He had promised David an answer on Monday. The maid showed him to the parlor. The home was pleasant but not ostentatious, although Birch knew his employer was wealthy. The floor was tongue-and-groove heart pine, the plaster walls were painted a vivid Prussian blue with white woodwork, and the sun streaming through the mullioned windows gave an even cheerier glow to the room. He sat in a high-backed chair and waited for Samuel.

He didn't have long to wait. Samuel, his cravat untied and his hair still loose, rushed in. "My boy, what is it?"

Birch stood and bowed. "I beg your pardon, sir, for disturbing you at such an early hour."

"No, no, of course I want to hear any news of importance you might have. Think nothing of it." Samuel waved a hand.

"First, let me admit you were right. I discovered much of interest."

Samuel grinned. "I love to be right."

Birch grinned, but he felt no levity. His hands still itched to throttle Hugh Montgomery. "Howe did indeed plan to press on to Philadelphia, but his plans have changed. He has offered a pardon to rebel Americans.

If they will appear before a British official within the next sixty days and sign a statement promising to remain in peaceful obedience to His Majesty, they will be exempt from forfeitures and penalties. He thinks that will be enough to defeat us, especially teamed with the other news."

"What news is that?" Samuel's high spirits had vanished.

"General Charles Lee has surrendered in Basking Ridge."

"This cannot be true. Did you hear of this from a reliable person?" Samuel paced in front of the window.

"From a lieutenant who was there. He arrived straight from the battle, and I overheard his conversation last night."

Samuel eased onto a chair. "He was the general the British feared the most. They surely think they've won the war now." He sighed. "Is there more?"

"Do you know of the shipbuilder and merchant David Saunders?"

Samuel stroked his chin. "Of course. A violent loyalist but an excellent shipbuilder."

"He has offered me a ship to outfit and crew as I please. I'm needed here, so of course, I cannot accept myself, but I might be able to persuade him to accept a substitute. With a handpicked crew of good colonials, they could begin to board and take over British ships."

Samuel's eyes brightened. "I see what you mean. Of course, it would be dangerous work with no guarantee of success. But it could not be done undercover. The entire British fleet would begin to hunt for the renegade."

"Not for a while, and not if the captain was crafty. He could be cautious and only take a ship when no other was in the vicinity. The crew could be taken captive and brought to shore so news of which ship was involved did not get back to the British."

Samuel nodded. "A daring plan, Birch, but I expected no less from you. This needs to be taken up with Washington himself. He camps near Trenton. I want you to find him and tell him this news. All of it." He paused, a grave look straightening his features. "Finding a captain and crew will be the most difficult part of this scheme. But Washington will know what to do."

Birch hurried back to his room, dressed warmly, and set out for Washington's camp. He should arrive by midafternoon. Huddling over the horse's neck, he plodded toward the camp. He looked forward to seeing the general again. Sometimes it seemed the life of a soldier was preferable to that of a spy. At least he would be in the middle of action instead of cooling his heels with a bunch of Tories.

He was stopped by a sentry and taken to Washington's tent. When he was bid to enter the tent, he found the general and Captain Hamilton hunched over his desk poring over maps.

"Captain Meredith!" Washington sat up and rubbed his eyes. "I did not expect to see you, but it is fortuitous. I could use you well."

"Are you going into battle?"

Washington smiled. "A surprise attack on Trenton in a few days, Captain."

Birch had expected to find a Washington reeling from the recent defeats. The British army had pushed them all the way back to Pennsylvania, and deserters were fleeing the Continental Army like rats. Yet this man seemed to notice nothing of the adverse circumstances facing them.

Birch shifted. "I hear the Hessians are in Trenton, General."

"I know. But even Germans will make merry today with Christmas upon us. I plan to ferry my men across the Delaware and strike at dawn following the Christmas celebration. They will be sleeping off their beer, and we will rout them." He spoke with confidence and fire in his eyes.

"A bold stroke, sir."

"But what are you doing here, Captain?"

Birch quickly explained his news.

Hamilton waved his hand. "We had heard of Lee's surrender earlier today."

Washington's eyes narrowed. "But it shall not deter me. This news of amnesty is more troubling, but we won't worry about it now. Get some rest, Captain. We shall talk more tomorrow."

Birch saluted and went to find a tent. The next few days he talked with Washington and listened to his plans to take Trenton. It just might work. When Christmas Day came, he was ready to join them.

CHAPTER 14

"Why must we stay here, Hannah?" Lydia's voice was edgy with frustration. "If I stay in this house another day with just the two of us, I shall go mad! Since you made such a spectacle of yourself with the captain, this is the first time we have been invited any-where."

"I think you forget your own part in our shunning."

They would not have been invited to the rare party tonight were it not that she was a Thomas. John's cousin Joseph couldn't have a party and leave her out. She would not go, but there was no reason to deny Lydia a bit of fun.

"Would you have me neglect my duties? The wind will likely snuff out the lamps if I am not here to tend them. But you may go." Hannah suppressed a sigh. Lydia became more fractious as the autumn had turned to winter.

"Thank you, Sister!" Lydia clapped her hands like a child and turned a smile on Hannah.

"I shall write a letter giving my regrets, and you shall take it to Sarah and Joseph. I had hoped to see them too."

"You sound regretful." Lydia seemed surprised.

"Do you think I enjoy never having any fun? I think you have not noticed anyone but yourself, Lydia. If my duty did not demand it, I should very much enjoy wearing a pretty dress and laughing with friends. It happens so rarely." Hannah swallowed the lump in her throat. She didn't want to show Lydia just how disappointed she was. There was no reason to spoil the evening for both of them. But in truth, she doubted if Lydia would spare a thought for her sister left behind on the snowy, windswept hill.

But Lydia surprised her. She laid a hand on Hannah's shoulder. "I shall stay with you. I did not think."

The lump in Hannah's throat grew larger. Mayhap Lydia did love her. "You shall wear my green sacque. The color will suit your hair. I would grieve to know you stayed home on my account. You would be alone in the house while I tended the light, anyway. Put the tongs for your hair in the

191

fire, and we shall make you the belle of the ball."

Lydia squealed with delight and hugged her. "I have often wished to wear that gown. Thank you, Sister." She hurried away to find the curling tongs.

A heavy feeling in her chest, Hannah stared after her. Lydia was like a child. Her pouting could change in a moment to sunshine and smiles. Hannah hoped she would have a good time.

She curled Lydia's hair with the hot tongs until the golden locks were a riot of curls held high on her head with tendrils around her face. She really did look lovely. She would soon meet the right kind of man and forget all about Galen Wright. The more Hannah talked against him, the more adamant Lydia became. It was best to simply let it run its course.

Hannah helped her into the green sacque, and they both waited for the carriage from the Thomas house. Now that Lydia would be seen in public, Hannah knew they would have to face the church. She'd been able to avoid the elders for the past two weeks by keeping Lydia inside. How she dreaded that. Not for herself, but for her sister. If the town elders knew of her tryst with Galen, most of the village probably knew.

The carriage stopped, and the footman helped Lydia climb inside. Her cheeks pink with excitement, she waved at Hannah, and the carriage lurched away. Hannah sighed and went out to the lighthouse. The sting of smoke made her cough, but she went up the iron steps and checked the lights. They were glowing, but the lamps needed cleaning already. The wind caused the whale oil to smoke, and the glass was nearly black with soot.

She coughed again and set to her duties. Her eyes were streaming tears by the time she was finished, and she hurried down the steps into the fresh air. Even the cold wind felt good in her face after the sting of the smoke, though a stab of wind nearly took her breath away.

Once she was back in the parlor, she stirred up the fire and put a pot of stew on to cook. It would be a sorry feast compared to what she might have enjoyed had she been free to attend the ball. She sighed and took out her knitting.

Lydia did not return until nearly eleven that night. Hannah had just refilled the whale oil and cleaned the glass again in the lighthouse. She had thought of going to bed, but she wanted to at least share the party vicariously when Lydia returned.

Smiling tiredly, Lydia entered with the light of enjoyment still shining in her blue eyes and started a bit when she saw Hannah seated by the fireplace. "Hannah, I had such fun! Even Mother Thomas and Olive seemed to be enjoying themselves. Some of the soldiers were home for a few days, so we had some dancing partners too." She sniffed. "Of course they were colonials instead of British officers."

"Did you give Sarah my note?"

Lydia fished through her reticule. "Yes, and she sent you one back. She was quite disappointed you could not come, but she understood." She handed Hannah a folded piece of paper. "I shall go to bed. My thanks for allowing me to go, dear Sister." She dropped a kiss on Hannah's head before going up the stairs. Hannah followed her.

At the top of the steps she turned. "Oh, I almost forgot. Mr. Reynolds was at the ball. He was most solicitous of my health and said he would call tomorrow." She shuddered. "What shall we do?"

Hannah shuddered too. Of all the town elders, he was the one who struck the most fear in her. There was only judgment in his eyes, never mercy or understanding. "The only thing we can do is leave it in God's hands, Lydia."

Lydia nodded and went to her room, and Hannah walked slowly to her own bed-chamber. Before she fell asleep, she prayed fervently for God's dominion in the matter.

She awoke the next morning with a sense of dread. When she remembered what awaited her today, the feeling of impending doom deepened. She dressed in her plainest gown, a gray wool with a black stomacher. It couldn't hurt to appear as unassuming as possible.

She read her Bible and spent some time in prayer as usual. She would not let the threat of what the day might bring cause her so much worry that she neglected her devotions. After about an hour, she put her Bible down and went into the hall.

She peeked in on Lydia, but she still slept, one arm flung above her head and her golden hair in glorious disarray. If he saw her like this, Elder Reynolds would punish her for her looks alone. Hannah sighed and tiptoed out of the room. She went to the lighthouse and extinguished the lights, then went back to the house and cooked porridge for breakfast.

Lydia stirred upstairs and Hannah hurried up to speak with her before she dressed. "Good morrow."

" 'Tis too early," Lydia moaned. "I need

to sleep two more hours."

"I do not know when the elders will be here. Please wear your plainest gown and put your hair under your mobcap."

Lydia nodded. "I had already thought to do that." She stared at Hannah anxiously. "What do you think the town officers will do?"

"I wish I knew. But we shall accept their rebuke with good grace, and perhaps they will be lenient. At least we have been able to avoid it for these past weeks." And though she might be punished for it, she could not regret the memory she carried of Birch's lips against hers, his breath on her face. It would be all she had for the rest of her life.

Lydia compressed her full lips and brushed her hair with angry strokes. "They have no right to sit in judgment on us."

Hannah sighed. "They merely try to keep the public morality. I cannot fault them for their motives. What you did was grievously wrong. Now finish your toilette and join me downstairs. The porridge is ready." Though she agreed with her sister, she didn't want to inflame her further.

Lydia did not answer her but simply began to dress in a brown wool dress devoid of any decoration. Hannah was relieved she didn't argue anymore. If she took that attitude with the elders, she was sure to be severely punished. She could only hope Lydia was as meek and fearful as she had been during the first confrontation.

They had just finished their breakfast when they heard the rattle of a carriage outside. They looked at one another, and Hannah took a deep breath and said a silent prayer. "Hold your tongue, Sister. Allow me to do the talking."

"As you wish."

Even the knock on the door sounded like the clap of doom. Hannah smoothed her skirt and went to open it. The wind brought the scent of snow with it. She curtsied. "Mr. Reynolds, Mr. Newsome, please come in."

"Mistress, we have come to bring you before the town officers. I fear we must insist this time." Mr. Reynolds inclined his head toward the carriage behind him.

"We are ready, sirs. Let me fetch Lydia and our cloaks, and we will join you."

An expression of surprise flickered across his face. He nodded, and Hannah and Lydia hurriedly threw on their cloaks and followed them to the waiting carriage. The ride to Gurnet seemed interminable with both men sitting stiffly and staring out the windows.

Hannah's mouth went dry, and her heart

pounded when the carriage stopped outside the clapboard church. The men got out and helped them down, then led the way inside. The building was frigid and she shivered. The room was almost full of men who turned to watch their progress. They wore identical expressions of gravity, but she searched for a friendly face anyway. Finding none, she and Lydia sat in the two chairs provided for them in the front. She clasped her hands together tightly and prayed for God's hand to guide this ordeal.

As moderator, the Reverend Arthur Goodman cleared his throat. "We have gathered here to judge a most grievous matter, gentlemen." He turned his glowering gaze on Hannah. "First, Mistress Hannah Thomas, you were seen in an indecorous embrace with a man known as a loyalist. This man lived in your home for over a month as well. What say you to this charge?"

Hannah took a deep breath and prayed for her voice to remain steady. "I cry you mercy in this matter, sirs. I meant no harm and thought not how it would look to the town. I grew up in the South where folks are more liberal with embraces. I felt responsible for the captain's injury and knew I would never see him again. Emotion got the better of my sense that day, sirs."

Her apology seemed to take the wind out of his sails, and he cleared his throat. "And what about the fact that you cannot seem to pay attention to the worship in this church, mistress? Do you not know that God expects you to give strict adherence to his Word?"

This was a stickier matter. Her answer would be sure to cause offense. No matter how hard she tried, she couldn't seem to keep her eyes open during the three-hour-long sermons after being up all hours tending the light. If the minister's message was interesting, it might have been easier, but the legalism he espoused had no relevance to the close relationship she had with her Lord. She couldn't say that, though.

One of the other men cleared his throat.

Pastor Goodman turned to him. "You have something to say, Elder Gray?"

Nathan Gray stared at Hannah a moment, then stood. "I am inclined to dismiss these matters pertaining to Mistress Thomas, sirs. I worked at a lighthouse one summer, and I know the arduous task it is to keep the lights burning all night. Mistress Thomas is a woman, and as the weaker vessel, we should give her honor for trying to fulfill her husband's duties. At least she attends the services, though she oft falls asleep."

Murmurs of agreement resounded around the room. Hannah's gaze met that of Mr. Gray's and saw the smile in his eyes. She silently thanked God for his care on her behalf.

"Very well," Pastor Goodman said with ill grace. "Now to Miss Lydia Huddleston. This charge is much more serious to the public morality. She was seen at the tavern in the company of one Galen Wright, a known officer in the British army. It was reported that she went to his bedchamber and was there until dawn when he delivered her home. What say you to these charges, miss?"

Lydia shuddered. "They are true, sirs."

A wave of murmurs passed through the room, and Hannah closed her eyes. At least Lydia had the courage to admit her sin.

"Have you nothing to say in your defense?"

"May I speak, Reverend Goodman?" Hannah dared to interrupt him.

He inclined his head. "As you wish, mistress."

She clutched her hands together in her lap and flicked a glance at Lydia. Her sister's face was white, but she sat composed awaiting her punishment.

"Galen Wright has been a friend of our

family since we were children. In fact, it was assumed I would wed him. When he came for such a brief time, my sister saw nothing wrong with seeking him out and spending some time with him. He was like a brother when she was growing up. She was foolish and willful, I agree, but because of the previous relationship, she didn't see how it would look to others." But would they ask outright if Lydia had committed fornication? If they asked, she must tell the truth.

Reverend Goodman frowned. "You say you knew this man from your childhood? Was he a Tory then?"

"We did not speak of such things then, sir, so I cannot tell what his political views were. But I cry you mercy for Lydia, sirs. She is young and sometimes foolish."

Murmurs reverberated through the room again. "We shall confer for a few moments. Please step into the next room." Reverend Goodman pointed out a door leading to another room, then shut the door behind them.

Lydia burst into tears and flung herself to her knees against Hannah's skirt. She buried her face in the rough wool and sobbed. "They will not dismiss these charges, Hannah. Did you not see the way they looked at me?"

Hannah stroked her head. "Do not lose hope yet, Sister. Perhaps the punishment will not be too onerous. And I only spoke the truth. You are young and did not see the seriousness of your actions. Galen is the one to blame, not you."

Lydia soon calmed, then sat on a chair by the door and folded her hands in a resigned pose. Moments later the Reverend Goodman opened the door and motioned them in. As they entered the room, Hannah's heart sank when she saw their stern expressions.

The minister fixed his gaze on Lydia. "Please step forward, Miss Huddleston, to hear the decision of this body."

Lydia's pleading gaze darted to Hannah, then with shoulders shaking, she complied. Hannah stood beside her. Her face must be as white as Lydia's.

"We are mindful of your youth, miss, but the seriousness of this offense demands punishment. We debated between banishment, the pillory, or a whipping. Have you any sentiments on which punishment you would prefer?" He paused and stared at them. "What say you?"

What a choice. Banishment would not carry any pain beyond emotional. Surely

Lydia would choose that. The stocks lasted all day, and she would have to suffer the taunts of the townspeople and the ignominy of thrown eggs and garbage. Whipping with the cat-o'-nine-tails would be quickest but also the most painful. And depending on the number of lashes, it could even be fatal. Hannah squeezed her sister's hand tightly. She couldn't answer for her. Lydia's foolishness and immaturity had caused this, and now she must suffer the consequences.

Lydia licked her lips. "I wish to stay with my sister, sirs. I have no real home other than with her. I choose —" She broke off and threw a helpless look at Hannah. "I cannot choose any of the three, sirs."

Reverend Goodman nodded. "We are not harsh men, miss. Therefore, we have chosen banishment. You may collect your belongings from your sister's, but we want you gone by the morrow."

Hannah's heart sank, though Lydia's banishment didn't come as a shock. Villages in New England were so suspicious of any newcomers. Where would Lydia go? She had vowed never to return to their parents' drunken home. Hannah frantically tried to think if there was a relative she could send Lydia to, but no one came to mind. Then Lydia let out a soft moan, her grip on

Hannah's fingers loosened, and Hannah caught her just as she fell to the floor in a dead faint.

Chapter 15

The very air reeked with victory in Trenton in spite of the mixture of sleet and snow from the northeast that pelted Birch's cheeks. He pulled his tricorn hat lower and huddled inside his coat.

"None of our boys lost except the two to the cold," Hamilton crowed after the battle. They'd crossed the Delaware at dawn and surprised the Hessians. "Nine hundred thirteen prisoners and one hundred six enemy casualties with at least twenty-three dead. We were twenty-four hundred against their fourteen hundred. We would have captured the rest if they had not run like foxes."

"A stunning victory." Birch turned toward Washington. "Have you thought of the news I brought, General? I promised an answer to Saunders tomorrow. Surely there is a naval captain we can recruit for this duty."

General Washington's face became expressionless for a moment. "The answer is obvious, Captain. You must go."

For a moment a wild exultation seized Birch. The thought of being back on the water again was tempting. "I cannot, General."

"Frightened, Captain? I know it would be dangerous duty."

"Of course not, sir. You know better than that." Birch didn't try to hide his anger at the question.

General Washington nodded. "You are letting your thoughts of revenge come between you and your duty, Captain. There will be time enough to see to Major Montgomery's fate once we are free of Britain's yoke. You must put it behind you, sir. Focus on the necessary duties right now."

It was easy for Washington to say. He didn't have the nightmares Birch did. Nightmares of his brother being hunted down like an animal. Since he had actually seen Montgomery, the torment had intensified. Now in his dreams the figure on the horse had a face. The smirking, self-satisfied face of Hugh Montgomery.

"You have your orders, Captain." Washington spurred his horse and rode ahead of Birch without a backward glance.

"Yes, sir." Only the tightest rein on his

emotions held him silent. In his heart he knew his commander was right. This war was too important to let personal vendettas cloud his mind.

He smiled. Mayhap defeat would be the cruelest blow he could deal Montgomery. Besides, he had no choice. After today's battle, he believed the tide had turned for the country. If he skirted his duty now, this day's victory might be for naught. They must strike at England and worry the enemy the way a dog worries a bone. Montgomery was making plans to rule his small kingdom, but what would he do when it all fell to ashes in his hands?

For a moment Hannah's image hovered in his mind. Mayhap there would be an opportunity to stop and see her once he was back on the sea. He banished the thought. He had to stay focused, as the general said.

Birch was still exhausted by the time he got back to New York, although he had slept a few hours at camp before heading back. His inner turmoil drained him. His dreams of revenge were about to slip through his fingers, but at the same time he longed to feel the sea wind in his face and smell the salty tang of the water. Perhaps with time aboard his new ship, he could lay his plans for Montgomery. This war wouldn't last forever.

Pushing his way through the throng of men at the quay, he found Saunders's shipyard office. A thin, nervous young man behind a desk pushed spectacles up his nose and went to tell his employer he was here.

Birch glanced idly around the room. Posters advertising the speed and comfort of the Saunders ships covered the walls. Just looking at the billowing sails gave him a rush of joy.

"Captain Meredith." David Saunders clapped him on the back. "I was beginning to think you had forgotten me."

"I was out of town a few days and just returned." Birch followed him into the back office.

Ship plans lay rolled up like paper sausages on the chair, and Saunders swept them off with his forearm. "Have a seat. I hope you mean to tell me you will accept my offer."

Birch bowed. "With pleasure, sir. I'd like to christen her the *Mermaid.*"

"Splendid! Let me call for some tea, and we will talk particulars. She comes off the staves next week."

So soon. Birch couldn't help the smile that curved his lips. In just a few days he would stand on the deck and look out on the water, feel the spray in his face, hear the billow and snap of the sails above his head. He sat on the chair and tried not to look too eager. He needed to think about crew too. They would have to be both dependable and colonial.

Over the next week he interviewed every man who wanted a job. Most thought he wanted loyalists and were assertive of their desire to remain part of the British Empire. But he began to find a man here and there who looked him in the eye and told him he would die for America. Men who weren't afraid to declare their loyalty were the ones he sought.

He had several invitations from Molly Vicar but refused all but one. He owed her at least one evening before he went off to sea. The night before the maiden voyage he knocked on her door. He could hear the laughter of the guests inside. Would Montgomery be in attendance this night too? He hoped so. He wanted to impress his image on his mind once more.

The butler showed him to the drawing room. As soon as he entered, Molly hurried toward him with a smile on her lovely face. And she was beautiful tonight. She had likely shocked her guests by appearing with her hair unpowdered once again, but her dark tresses gleamed in the candlelight. Her dress was cut shockingly low, and though her rouge was a bit too dark, it enhanced her dark eyes.

"Birch! I was beginning to think you had found another woman to entertain." She tapped him playfully with her fan.

"Surely you knew better, Molly." He offered her his arm, and she slipped her hand through the crook of his elbow.

Her eyes were warm with affection. She made no effort to hide her attraction to him, and he felt a surge of rebellion. Why shouldn't he take what she had to offer? He swallowed hard at the lovely vision before him. Beautiful or not, she didn't sway him and it angered him. Why did he let the memory of a pair of sparkling green eyes stop him from enjoying what life had to offer?

He smiled down at Molly with a distant smile. "I leave on the morrow."

Her own smile faltered. "I did not know. Where are you going?"

"To sea. Your friend David Saunders has put me in charge of his newest ship."

"Then we must make the most of this night." She smiled seductively and moved closer.

The heady scent of her perfume assailed his senses, and he took a step back. He didn't want this prettily packaged strumpet. And that's what Molly was. He could never see Hannah acting in such a forward way. Hannah's innocence and purity glowed from her eyes, her smile, her caring ways.

Molly didn't miss his slight recoil. "Birch, are you a lover of men instead of women? I know of no man who would turn down what I have offered you. Have you any idea of the men who have sought my favors?" Angry tears sparkled in her eyes, and she gripped his arm with her fingers.

For a moment he was tempted to prove his manhood to her, to crush her in his arms and press his lips against hers. But disgust won out. He was barely able to halt the curl of contempt in his lips. "I am sorry, Molly. Truly, I do not wish to hurt you."

"Hurt me? You?" She gave an incredulous laugh. "You honor yourself too much, Captain." She leaned closer, and her breath touched his face. "If you will not have me as a lover, you shall have me as an enemy. You must choose."

She no longer even looked beautiful. She was spoiled and self-willed, a seeker of pleasure with no thought for the morrow. Duty would not be a word in her vocabulary.

Or true love. Her love would last until the next handsome man came into her orbit.

"Well, Captain?"

"I fear I cannot be your lover, Molly." The very thought made him shudder.

"Then you will be my enemy," she spat out. "And you will find I am merciless." She turned on her heel and flounced away without a backward glance.

Birch took a deep breath. He had handled that badly. It was a good thing he was leaving the next day. He suspected she could be a formidable enemy. Perhaps with him out of town, she would soon forget her threats.

Chapter 16

Lydia felt as though she were in a fog. She huddled inside her heavy woolen cloak as the carriage delivered them home from the church, then she followed Hannah into the house. She just couldn't go back to South Carolina. She just couldn't. She recoiled at the thought of listening to her father's drunken rages and her mother's cries of pain and outrage when he struck her. Her friends would laugh behind her back that she had returned when she'd vowed never to darken their doors again.

Tears pricked the backs of her eyes. Why did this have to happen? Things were going so well with Galen. He had actually written her twice and told her he missed her. In fact, she had been expecting another letter any day from him. There might even be one today. She must write him and tell him she didn't know where she would be, but she would contact him when she was settled.

Tears trickled down her cheeks. It had all gone wrong somehow. All her bright, golden dreams of life with Galen in England seemed impossible now. She would have no choice but to go home. She had to face that fact squarely.

"I have some money put back, Lydia. I want you to take it." Hannah went to the pantry and opened a crock. The coins clinked together as she scooped them up. "It should be enough to buy a ticket home, and maybe you can use the rest while you look for a position." She thrust the coins and notes into Lydia's hands.

Lydia's tears fell faster. Hannah had been faithful. She deserved more from life than she had received. She certainly didn't deserve a sister who spied on her. For the first time Lydia felt shame, and was relieved Hannah had no idea of all she'd done. "My thanks, Sister," she whispered.

Hannah released a gentle smile. Her face was white with shock and fatigue, and her green eyes were shadowed with pain. "If I could go with you, I would, Lydia."

Lydia grimaced. "The lighthouse, always the lighthouse. It is a harsh taskmaster, Hannah. Why do you not leave it and come away with me? We could seek our fortune together in New York or Boston. Your in-laws bear you no love. Why do you stay?"

The pain in Hannah's eyes deepened. "I promised John. And it is an important task. Important to the revolution and to all the ships that ply these waters. Faith, but where would I go? Here I have a roof over my head, important duties, and a tie to my husband."

"A husband you never loved." Lydia didn't understand her sister. She placed too much importance on duty. Did she never long to do what she wanted for a change? Her life was slipping by, and soon she would be too old for adventure.

"Maybe not in the way you mean. But I revered and honored him. He was good to me. But more than that, I need to be needed."

Lydia had never heard her admit something like that before. "I need you too. Come with me and we can help each other."

"I cannot."

Lydia heard the finality in her sister's words and nodded. "So be it. I shall let you know where I am. Now I had better pack my things."

The next morning Lydia's heart was heavy as Hannah took her into town in the trap. She dropped her at the stage stop. "You get your ticket and I shall duck into the general store a moment. I will meet you back here."

Lydia nodded and hurried into the stage-coach office. The man behind the desk smiled knowingly as she approached. He obviously recognized her by the way his gaze raked her figure. "Where to, miss?"

She opened her mouth to say Charles Town, then hesitated. She would have to go through New York anyway, so why not simply buy a ticket there first and see if Galen had any suggestions to offer? "New York," she said with an airy smile.

She was still smiling when Hannah joined her a few minutes later on the bench by the fire.

"You have your ticket?"

"I took the last seat."

Hannah nodded. "Make sure you write the minute you get home."

"I will."

"And don't talk to strangers."

"I shall work on my knitting and ignore all other passengers." Hannah smiled at her light tone, and Lydia smiled too. "I shall be fine, Sister."

Hannah nodded and dabbed her eyes with a hanky. "But I am not so sure about myself. I have grown accustomed to your presence, and I will miss you dreadfully."

Lydia's own eyes filled with tears at her

admission. She had wondered if she had been a burden to Hannah. "I will write when I get there." The stage pulled in, and she stood. "I must go. Say good-bye to Olive and Mrs. Thomas for me."

"I shall." Hannah hugged her fiercely, then gave her a small shove. "Go then. And remember my prayers go with you."

Lydia nodded and rushed to the door before she could embarrass herself further by breaking into sobs. She had been happy here. Anger burned in her belly, and she set her jaw and marched to the stage. She would show these hypocrites that they couldn't tell her how to live her life. Someday she would come back through this place with her head held high. She would be dressed in fine clothes with a handsome husband beside her, fine children, and enough money to buy whatever she wanted.

And even Hannah, though she was different from the hypocrites at the Congregational church, viewed life through the narrow strictures of the Bible. Lydia would have to show her that duty wasn't so terribly important. Someday she would show her. Shaking her head at the footman's offer of help, she climbed into the stagecoach by herself and settled into the middle of the cushion where she would be warmer.

She ignored her companions' attempts at friendliness and planned what she would say to Galen when she found him. She had enough money to pay for a cheap room for a few weeks. Mayhap Galen could help her find work in New York. She did not dare even hope he would suggest they wed immediately. Just to be near him would be enough.

A cold, sleety rain was falling when the stage stopped in New York. After days on the stage, Lydia was tired, dirty, and sore. She made her way to the same boardinghouse she and Martha had found on the way out. It was close to headquarters, and she would begin the search for Galen on the morrow. There was a vacant room, so she took it for two days. That would be long enough to find Galen.

She fell into bed with a sigh of thankfulness and did not awaken until the sun shone in her eyes the next morning. She dressed in a hurry with a sense of anticipation. It seemed years since Galen had held her in his arms, had kissed her and told her he loved her. But she might actually see him today. She just hoped he wasn't gone from New York right now.

A different soldier was manning the desk

at headquarters when she arrived. "I need to see Lieutenant Galen Wright."

"I'm sorry, miss, Lieutenant Wright has gone to New Brunswick. He is expected to be there for several weeks at least."

Lydia's heart fell, and she stumbled back to the street. All her plans crumbled around her. She couldn't wait here that long. But she couldn't go back to South Carolina. She just couldn't. The pellets of freezing rain struck her cheeks, but she hardly felt them. What was she to do? A great lump grew in her throat. Everything and everyone was against her. Just when she thought she had things figured out, the rules changed and she was left on the outside again.

She walked blindly back to her room. She had to make a decision. Her money wouldn't last until Galen returned. She sat on the edge of the bed and burst into tears. The past few days had drained her. Ripped from a safe, though dull, existence in Massachusetts, she was alone in a big city with no one to count on but herself. She'd never been in such a predicament.

She could go to New Brunswick.

The tears stopped at the thought. Of course, she could go find Galen there. Why hadn't she thought of it before? She threw her cloak around her shoulders, grabbed her valise, and raced down the steps and out the door to the stage station. Most people wouldn't harm a woman. She had to take the chance.

Snow had begun to fall overnight, but Lydia didn't care as she boarded the stagecoach for New Brunswick. Tonight she would be warm in Galen's arms. Would he be as thrilled to see her as she was to see him? She smiled at the thought of his surprise. She knew he would be delighted. Hadn't he told her he wished they could be together always? Other men had their wives with them in camp. She would be no different.

When she arrived at New Brunswick several days later, she found the streets teeming with soldiers. She heard snatches of conversation about a great rebel victory in Trenton. The soldiers seemed to be readying for battle — cannons rumbled along the streets, and lines of men marched alongside them. She scanned the crowd for Galen but saw no familiar faces.

An old man dressed in rough tweed brushed by her, and she stopped him to ask for directions to a boardinghouse.

He stared at her as though she were mad. "Are ye daft, miss? Every available bed is taken with the British soldiers. You'll not find a place to stay here. I suggest you travel on down the road a piece." He didn't wait for her response but walked away with a muttered oath.

No place to stay? Nothing? That didn't seem possible. She approached an older woman with a baby on her hip and asked her, but the response was the same. No places available. Panic rose in her throat, but she tamped it down. She would just have to find Galen, that's all. He would know what to do.

She wove her way through the throng until she found the British headquarters. As soon as she opened the door, she heard a familiar voice. Galen stood talking to another officer in the doorway. Lydia just stood and drank in the sight of him. How splendid he looked in his scarlet uniform! She must have made a sound, for he turned.

His eyes dilated at the sight of her, and his jaw dropped. "Lydia?" He strode toward her and took her hands.

"Hello, Galen." She searched his gaze. He was glad to see her, wasn't he?

He drew her to the side, away from the men stomping the snow from their boots and shouting orders to the men behind them. "What are you doing here?"

"I came to find you. I was banished from

Gurnet."

"Banished." He frowned. "What did you do?"

"Knowledge of our tryst that night became known."

He gave a bark of laughter. "Count yourself fortunate those hypocrites did not put you in the pillory or whip you."

"They considered it." Why didn't he sweep her into his arms and tell her how happy he was to see her? Disappointment, sharp as a dagger, stabbed her heart.

He put an arm around her and hugged her as a brother would. "Where are you staying?"

"I know not. I have been told there is no housing left."

His face darkened. "You came all this way with no plans, no provisions for yourself?"

"You are angry with me." She could see it in his face, in the muscle that twitched in his jaw.

"It was very foolish, Lydia. What if I had been moved and you did not find me? What would you have done?"

"I would simply get back on the stage and go to New York," she said stiffly. He must not see how much he had hurt her.

He shook his head. "Wait here. I will see what I can do." He walked over to a soldier at a table and spoke for a few moments. When he came back, his face was still flushed with temper. "There is nothing available. You shall have to share my room for the time being."

Joy bubbled inside her. Stay with him? That was what she wanted to do. Wasn't he happy about that at least? She touched his arm. "I do not mind, Galen."

"Well, I mind. People will think you are a strumpet."

The joy increased. He was concerned for her reputation. That was all. He was glad to see her, he just wanted to protect her. "I don't care for my reputation. I would give up any good name I have for your sake." But why couldn't he see how that little problem would be corrected with marriage?

Instead of the smile she expected, his frown deepened. "Come with me," he said abruptly. He took her valise and offered her his arm.

She slipped her hand through the crook of his arm. He would soon lose that surly countenance. She would charm it out of him and shower him with love and kisses. How could he resist her?

She practically ran to keep up with his long stride. They pushed through the crowd, and Galen led her to an imposing brick home at the end of the street. He opened the door and looked around, then motioned her to follow him up the steps. She felt a warm rush of love for his thoughtfulness at making sure no one saw her go into his room. If they had been so circumspect in Gurnet, she wouldn't be here now.

He opened the door, hurried her inside, then shut the door. Lydia looked around at the clothes tossed haphazardly over the chair and the rumpled bed. He needed a woman to look after him.

"Now we must get something straight, Lydia." Galen scowled. "If this is a ploy to force me to wed you, it will not work."

He thought she would try to trick him? Tears pooled in her eyes. "How could you think I would do such a thing? I had nowhere else to go, and I thought perhaps I could find work near you so we could be together." She struggled to keep back the tears. Hadn't he said he would marry her if he could? Why was he saying these hurtful words now? Surely he didn't mean them.

His sharp gaze softened at her tears. "Very well, then. I shall see what I can do." He sat on the edge of the bed and smiled at her. "Now come kiss me and tell me how much you missed me."

CHAPTER 17

The saltbox house on the top of the cliff echoed with loneliness. Even the friendly glow from the lighthouse did nothing to cheer Hannah's mood. Aggravating as she could be with her rosy view of Galen, Lydia was bubbly and energetic. She had brought life to Hannah's lonely world. The only inhabitants in the empty rooms now were memories. Memories of John, of Lydia, and most of all, of Birch.

How had he wrapped himself around her heart so completely and in such a short time? She just didn't understand it. Tending the light in the wee hours of the night, she looked out over the dark water and wondered where he was. Did he ever think about her? In spite of his silence, she allowed herself to hope and to dream.

The knocker on the front door fell, and she dried her hands on her apron and hurried to answer it. Olive stood on the doorstep, her hands thrust into a fur muff and her cheeks red with cold.

"Olive, what a surprise. Come in, and I'll fix some tea." Hannah opened the door wider and smiled. She was glad to see someone, anyone. The last time another voice had spoken on this property had been the day Lydia left.

Olive shook her head. "I cannot stay. I am on my way to town. Mother would like you to come to dinner tonight." Her gaze darted past Hannah into the room behind her.

Hannah suppressed a sigh. Olive still thought Birch would come back some day. Every time she came to the house she looked for him. Hannah wished she could be so certain herself. "I would be delighted, Olive. What time?"

"Come about four. That way we can visit first and you can come home before dark. Shall Mother send the carriage for you?"

Hannah shook her head. "I shall enjoy the walk." It was just down the hill.

"Very well. Four o'clock." Olive scurried back to the waiting carriage.

Hannah shut the door behind her sister-in-law and went back to her laundry. What had prompted this invitation? Whatever it was, she was glad of it. She was tired of sitting in this house alone. Besides, she really wanted to try to mend her relationship with John's family. He would be grieved to know such strain existed between them.

Today was Wednesday. Lydia had been gone nearly a month. Perhaps there would be a letter today in town. She finished her laundry, then pulled on her heavy coat and rowed across the choppy seas to town. She could have hitched the horse to the cart and taken the long way around, but the weather was warmer than usual today, and the thought of being in the sunshine, even though it was cold, enticed her. She tied the coble to the dock and hurried to the general store.

Ephraim offered a polite nod when he saw her, but his wife pointedly ignored her. It had happened too often for Hannah to feel the slight anymore. Ever since Lydia was expelled from the community, some people had shunned her. She supposed word of her own behavior with Birch had traveled around the small community as well.

"Got a couple of letters here for you, mistress." Ephraim riffled through a pile of papers under the counter and handed her two letters.

Her heart jumped, and she flashed him a wide smile. He blinked, then glanced nervously at his wife. Hannah felt a mixture of joy and relief at the sight of Lydia's hand-writing. Until this moment she hadn't realized how much she had been worrying about her sister. She had been traveling without a chaperone, and Hannah had tried to push away the fear as she'd waited for news. She handed Ephraim a list of items she needed and went to a chair by the stove to warm up. Curious at the second letter, she was surprised to see it was from John's brother, Harlis.

She broke the seal on the first letter and opened it.

Dearest Hannah, I hope this letter finds you well. I know this will come as a great surprise to you, but I decided not to go to Charles Town. I am in New Brunswick with Galen, and we shall soon be going back to New York. I know this will distress you, but pray do not worry about me. I am very happy, and Galen promises we shall be wed soon. He has introduced me to many of his friends, and I have found them more than willing to accept me into their circle. Please, dearest sister, please try to be happy for me. I know this is not what you would have chosen for me, but you must let me make my own choices. I

chose Galen long ago, and I am so
happy he loves me.

Your loving sister,
Lydia

Hannah stared at the words until her vision blurred. Shock and disbelief choked
her. How could Lydia do such a thing? How
could she throw off the way she had been
taught so completely? She knew fornication
was wrong — she had just been punished
for it. Had she no moral fiber, no knowledge
of right and wrong? Tears sprang to her
eyes, and she took a deep breath. There was
nothing she could do about it. She bit her
lip.

If only Lydia had been allowed to stay
with her, this might not have happened. The
church officials should have had more pity
on a naive girl. They professed to be Chris-
tians, but they had shown nothing of
Christ's pity for her sister. Of course, Lydia
had done wrong and deserved punishment,
but some kind of punishment that led her
gently back to Christ would have accom-
plished more.

She opened Harlis's letter and read the
short missive in disbelief. He wanted her to
wait for him. He felt his brother would
expect him to care for his widow and of-

fered to wed her. Hannah shook her head. She would never marry Harlis, but it was sweet of him to offer. She would write him tonight.

She took her gunnysack of supplies from Ephraim woodenly and hurried back outside. The shock of the cold air cleared her head, but even thinking clearly she knew there was nothing to be done to salvage the situation now. Lydia had willfully started down a path to destruction. Only God himself could save her now.

She tossed her supplies to the back of the coble and climbed in. Rowing back to Gurnet Point, her thoughts tossed her emotions to and fro like the waves tossed her boat. She prayed for wisdom. Was there something she could say that would make Lydia stop and think about right and wrong, about eternity?

Galen would never marry her. Hannah knew this in her heart. He was using sweet, unsuspecting Lydia for some nefarious purpose of his own. If he had been here in front of her, Hannah would have flown at him. She knew she should not hate, but, God have mercy on her, she hated Galen Wright. Perhaps now was the time to reveal the whole truth to Lydia. Would it make a difference?

She pulled the coble to shore above the tide line and walked up the steep path to the house. She put her foodstuffs away and went to the fireplace. After rereading the letter, she was struck by the contentment in the tone of it. Lydia truly seemed not to understand the magnitude of what she'd done.

Hannah buried her face in her hands and wept. She had lost her sister.

She felt lethargic and drained when she prepared for the evening at Mother Thomas's. The thought of making small talk all evening filled her with dismay. What could she say if her mother-in-law asked about Lydia? She couldn't lie, but she couldn't bear to see the expression of frigid distaste Mother Thomas was sure to wear.

Hannah rubbed her eyes and put her hair up. She couldn't change anything, so she simply must bear it. She sighed and slipped her mobcap over her dark curls, then went down the steps. Before she departed, she sat down and wrote a kind letter to Harlis refusing his offer. She'd best not tarry on that task.

Twilight came early in the winter, and the sun was far down in the west. She lit the lamps in the lighthouse, then trudged through the snow down the path to the stately Thomas residence. The news from Lydia had sapped all enjoyment she might have felt from the invigorating walk.

Mother Thomas smiled when Hannah was shown into the parlor. "There you are, dear Hannah. Come in and have some tea before supper." She patted a spot on the sofa beside her.

Hannah curtsied and sat beside her where she'd indicated. What had happened to make her so agreeable? And was that genuine pleasure in her smile? She glanced at her mother-in-law uncertainly. Could this be the start of a new relationship for them? She allowed herself to hope.

Bridget, the serving maid, brought tea, and they chatted about the latest news from the war, then Olive joined them. Even her smile seemed genuine. Hannah had always hoped to have Olive as a real friend. Her hope intensified, but she was confused over what could have caused the change.

They had a lovely supper of battalia pie with hot crusty bread and sweet butter followed by plum pudding. Hannah relaxed in the friendly atmosphere of good food and conversation. After supper they retired to the parlor.

"Hannah, dear, have you given any thought to your situation?" Mother Thomas laid a gnarled hand on Hannah's forearm.

"My situation? What do you mean?" A sense of unease gripped her throat.

"A woman all alone doing a man's job is prey for any handsome face that happens along. Have you thought of remarrying? John has been gone nigh on five months. I would see you safely wed to a good man who would take the burden of keeping the lights from you."

Hannah gaped at her. Was this truly concern for her or something else? The thought of being responsible only for her house was appealing, but she did not want another marriage of convenience. She suppressed a smile. What would Mother Thomas think if she knew of Harlis's offer?

The image of Birch's dark hair and eyes flashed through her mind, but she quashed it. "I have not given it any thought."

"Well, you should. In fact, I have a suitor for your hand." Her mother-in-law smiled at her slyly. "A finer man is not to be found, Hannah. What say you to Mr. Nathan Gray as a suitor?"

Nathan Gray. Her thoughts flashed back to the way he had defended her when she and Lydia were brought before the town board. She respected him, but he was old, even older than John had been. He had to be at least fifty. She didn't know what to say. Her gaze darted from Mother Thomas to Olive. Olive appeared happier than she'd ever seen her, and Hannah realized her sister-in-law wanted her safely wed if Birch ever came back.

"Well?" Olive said eagerly. "What say you?"

"I know not what to say," Hannah said slowly. "Faith, but I have not considered remarriage. Mr. Gray is a fine man, but I do not know him."

"Shall I tell him he may call on you here every Saturday?"

Mother Thomas was inexorable, and Hannah didn't have the courage to tell her no. "Very well. But I make no promises. I am willing to become friends with Mr. Gray, but that is all I can say at this time."

"I shall tell him it is to be friendship only for the time being." Her mother-in-law's voice was filled with self-satisfaction.

Hannah took her leave moments later. Her head was spinning, and she wanted to get home before it was too dark to see. The moon had risen, and it cast a silver glow over the snow as she trudged along the path. Surely this was about Harlis. Mother Thomas would not want to see Hannah wed another of her sons.

Why had she not told them no? This was likely to tangle things even more. But she couldn't stop the tiny thrill at the thought of having something to do every Saturday, of having a friend she could talk to. She had never imagined loneliness such as this. Every day she awoke to an empty house, worked all day with only her own voice for company, and went to bed in a silent house with the wind howling in the eaves. She didn't know how much longer she could bear it. If she just had a friend to talk to.

Perhaps Olive would be open to a friendly relationship now. If that was true, Hannah would not need to find one in Nathan Gray. Olive lived in her mother's shadow; surely she would be glad of someone younger as a confidant. Hannah resolved to try harder with her sister-in-law.

She stopped at the lighthouse and climbed the steps to the first tower. She coughed at the heavy smoke and trimmed the wicks a bit until it abated. The wind blew through the top of the tower, and Hannah folded her arms and looked out to sea. She saw the lights of a ship and stared at it. It seemed rather close. Perhaps it was even anchored offshore.

With a last glance she turned to go. She thought she heard a sound at the bottom of the steps and paused. Her hand flew to her throat, and she listened, her pulse thumping against her fingers. Nothing came back to her ears except the sigh of the wind. She turned her gaze a final time to the sea. The lights were still there. The ship bobbed beyond the rocks. Mayhap it was a merchant ship waiting until dawn to seek safe harbor.

Suddenly she heard firm footsteps on the stairs. "Hello," she called uncertainly. Who would be calling at this hour?

The steps didn't falter but made a fast ascent. A man's steps, from the sound of the heavy tread.

"Who's there?" Was it an enemy soldier? Alarm kept her immobile a moment. She looked around for a weapon. She spied a heavy iron pipe in the corner and seized it, then spun to face the doorway with it over her head.

A man's head, topped with a tricorn hat, came into view. Her eyes skimmed the scarlet British uniform, then settled on the man's face — dark, pirate eyes above that rakish grin. Her eyes widened, and she dropped the pipe with a startled gasp.

Birch's dark eyes held laughter. "And here I thought you'd be glad to see me."

CHAPTER 18

Birch stared at Hannah from the doorway to the light tower. Faith, but he had forgotten how beautiful she was. Why had he come? It would have been better to have buried her memory in work and activity. Seeing her again would make this strange longing worse. He had no time for a woman in his life. The surf crashed against the rocks behind him, and staring into those mermaid eyes, green as summer, he felt like a pebble tossed by those waves.

He still couldn't believe he had stopped here. The nearer the ship had come to Plymouth, the more he told himself he would not stop. But when Gurnet Light had twinkled into view, he had impulsively given the order to drop anchor. He knew the men had wondered at his sanity when he had them drop the ship's boat over the side and he had rowed ashore.

He took a step nearer, and she raised a

hand to her throat. She blinked as though she wasn't sure he was real. Was that really joy in her eyes or his own wishful thinking? She opened her eyes again, and his gaze was caught in hers. He wanted to rush forward and gather her into his arms, but he wasn't sure how she would react. She had kissed him good-bye in a way that still haunted his waking hours, but mayhap it would be best to step back and start anew.

"I imagined you in New York. How long can you stay?"

"Not long. A few hours. I should not have tarried here now, but I found I could not pass by without stopping." He took a step nearer. "Have you been well? Methinks you seem thinner and more tired."

She touched his face with her small hand and smiled. "Faith, but I have just been lonely. How is your leg? I did not notice a limp."

"No limp. It does not even pain me."

"Come to the house, and I shall fix you some tea. Have you supped?"

Regret flashed in her eyes before she stepped away to go down the spiral steps. Until he saw her again, he hadn't realized just how important she had become to him. He followed her down the steps to the house.

He glanced around as they entered the house. The memories of talking with Hannah about everything from politics to trading on the high seas swept over him. The house seemed empty. "Lydia is gone? Did she go home to Charles Town?" He really didn't want to talk about Lydia, but Hannah was not completely at ease yet. The separation had been too long for them to just assume the easy camaraderie they had enjoyed in the fall.

Hannah took her time pouring the hot water into the teapot as though to avoid the question. She put the lid on the pot and set it aside to steep a few minutes. "No, I fear she did not, Birch." When she turned around, he saw the tears sparkling in her eyes.

He took a step closer and put a comforting hand on her shoulder. The loneliness in her eyes touched him.

She took a deep breath, and a scarlet tide surged up her face. "She is in New York with Galen." She raised miserable eyes to meet his. "She is living with him, though not married."

Birch had seen that and more since the war began. Women who flung themselves at any uniform just to have enough to eat. But Lydia had no such excuse. If she had been here, he would have wrung her neck for distressing her sister. No wonder Hannah had been lonely. He didn't like the idea of her alone in the lighthouse. The enemy would like nothing better than to find her defenseless.

He thumbed a tear from her cheek. "You can do nothing about it, Hannah. Let it go. She must make her own choices."

She shook her head. "She has no shame, Birch. There was no apology for her actions in the letter she sent. No real remorse for the heartache she causes me." Hannah shuddered. "I have not been able to write our parents and tell them. If Father knew, he would kill her." She turned away and poured the tea into cups and handed one to him.

He wrapped his cold hands around the hot cup and blew into the steaming liquid. The aroma warmed him as much as the heat. He didn't quite know what to say to Hannah, how to comfort her. He pulled his pocket watch out surreptitiously. He could only stay an hour, and they must go with the tide. He had no time to waste with talk of Lydia.

He followed Hannah to the sofa by the fire. The crackling blaze drove shadows from the room, and he could see her pensive expression.

"I saw Galen in New York. He seemed to have plenty of female companionship there."

Hannah sighed. "It is as I feared. When he tires of Lydia, he will cast her off. I do not know what will become of her. It is in God's hands, I know, but it is hard for me to leave it there."

He frowned. He could do without her talk of God. God had done nothing for him that he could see. Or for Hannah either, for that matter. Widowed at eighteen, stranded on a lonely outcropping of land with only the seagulls for company, dealing with difficult in-laws. No, God had done her no favors.

"You still scowl whenever I say anything about God." A tiny frown marred the smooth perfection of her forehead. "I had hoped you would have put your anger at him behind you."

"I shall never be satisfied until my brother's murderer pays for his deed. I will not wait for God to bring justice." Birch had served God faithfully for years, and then he had taken the one person Birch loved most in the world. The betrayal had rocked the faith he had thought unshakable.

There was another matter he felt she needed to know. It was the excuse he'd used to convince himself to stop. "Did you know

Galen was the one who arrested and hanged your husband?"

He was sorry he had been so abrupt when he saw her blanch and draw back.

The teacup fell from her numb fingers and shattered on the floor. "Galen? He-he killed John? Surely you are mistaken."

Birch shook his head, then knelt and picked up the broken shards of pottery from the floor. "No mistake, Hannah."

She took the pieces of teacup he handed her and stared at him with ashen cheeks. "Are you sure of this?"

He hated to cause her more distress, but Hannah needed to be on her guard against Galen. The man had an agenda, and Birch wished he knew what it was. "Galen asked how you and Lydia were. When his superior officer heard the name Thomas, he mentioned it. Galen tried to pretend he had no idea John was your husband. I admit the name is common, but there was something in Galen's manner that made me think he was lying. Watch him with care, Hannah."

She wrung her hands and rose to her feet. "Lydia . . . She has no idea with whom she has taken up. What can I do? How can I possibly save her? I knew what Galen was capable of years ago, but I had hoped, I prayed he was older, wiser, gentler." Tears shimmered in her eyes.

What did she mean? What had Wright done to her in the past? A wave of protectiveness swept over him, and he clenched his teeth. He would make sure the man never hurt her again. "If you like, I could investigate further when I go back to New York."

"You would do that for me?"

Did she not realize he would do just about anything for her? Where she was concerned, he was weak and helpless. "Of course. I will make inquiries as soon as I return."

"I must get word to Lydia once I know the truth." She made an effort to smile. "But let us talk of something else. I see you have another ship. I thought you were going to work in New York." A shadow crossed her face as though she suddenly remembered they were on different sides of the war.

He longed to tell her the truth but looked into the fire instead. "I met a man who offered me the chance to captain a new ship. I missed the sea, the sound of it, the smell of it." He turned and smiled. "I would have been mad to refuse such an opportunity."

Her dimpled smile flickered. "I should love to go to sea someday." She leaned her chin against her fist. "My mother taught us to read, and I found escape in books. When my father would be in a drunken rage, I often ran to the water and prayed to be on a passing ship." She sighed. "Where will you go? To China or Africa? I would love to see China."

He felt a stab of regret that he couldn't smuggle her aboard and take her to sea with him. "Wherever the navy sends me for supplies. Most of my trips will probably be back and forth to England, transporting ammunition and food for the soldiers."

Her frown came again. "I cry you mercy, but I keep forgetting we are enemies." She gave a light laugh, but the troubled expression in her eyes didn't fade.

He could never be enemies with this woman. What had he been thinking of to come here, knowing he had to keep the truth from her? He glanced at his pocket watch again. He had to go soon. Did he dare a kiss? And would her embrace still move him like the first one?

"Does not the Good Book say we are to love our enemies?" He leaned closer to her and slipped an arm around her shoulders.

Her green eyes looked startled, and she drew back slightly.

"Methinks we should begin." He bent his head and his lips found hers. A vast ocean of longing swept over him, and he pulled her close. Her lips were soft and pliant beneath his. Was this love? He had not yet given a name to the way he felt about Hannah, but he had never felt like this about anyone else. His breathing quickened, and he drew her closer still.

She tore her lips away, and he felt bereft. "I cannot," she gasped. She stood and turned her back to him. Her shoulders shook with the intensity of her emotions.

He rose and placed his hands on her shoulders. "What is it, Hannah? Do you not care for me as I care for you?" Fool that he was, he had hoped she felt something for him.

A sob shook her small frame, and she shook her head frantically. "It isn't that, Birch." She clamped her lips shut as though she feared what she might reveal.

"We are on different sides of this war, but the battle will not last forever, and there is much I would tell you. Trust me, Hannah. Things are not always as they seem." If he had to tell her the truth, he would.

Fresh tears trickled down her cheeks. "I must not love you, Birch. God says I must not. You must put aside this bitterness you hold first."

God again. He squeezed his eyes shut at

the pain in his heart. Must God take every-thing he loved in this world? Did he mean to treat Birch as he did Job?

Birch opened his eyes and took a deep breath. "I would not talk you into something you have no wish for." He knew a feeble excuse when he heard it. So be it. If she loved God more than him, it was best he found out now.

He dropped his hands from her shoulders. "I must go. The crew will wonder what keeps me."

She dabbed at her tears with a handker-chief she had pulled from her pocket and nodded slowly. "I shall walk you to your boat."

"There is no need for you to come out in the cold." He just wanted to get away. If he ran far enough away from this cold cliff, maybe he could forget this mermaid girl someday.

"I want to." She handed him his coat, then slipped her cloak about her shoulders. "Where do you journey now?"

"To England." The flicker of pain on her face shamed him, but he shrugged it away. She had made the choice, not him. He would never let her know how much her words had wounded him.

She nodded and followed him out the

door. The wind struck her, and she staggered. He took her arm to steady her, and they trudged down the path to the beach, stopping at the bow of the boat. The incoming surf lapped at the stern of the boat, and the moon glinted on the snow like quicksilver.

The silence between them stretched out like the ocean. For a moment Birch was tempted to take her in his arms again, to kiss her obstinacy away. Something in her eyes told him he might succeed, but he would not play that kind of game. She either loved him or she didn't.

"Will I see you again?" Hannah asked timidly.

He wanted to tell her she had destroyed any chance for them, but the words caught in his throat. The thought of never seeing her again tugged at his heart. "Maybe, if I come this way again." He would make no promises. He would try to purge this love from his life.

She nodded and turned her face up to the moonlight. "I shall pray for you, Birch. I shall pray that God heals the hurt in your heart and brings you back to him."

A shaft of pain pierced his heart. Didn't she realize that her love could heal him? Why did he need God for that? "Take care

247

of yourself," he said gruffly.

He wanted to kiss her again but couldn't bear the thought of another rebuff. He simply squeezed her hand and shoved the boat into the icy waves. Setting his back to the oars, the last glimpse he had of her was atop the bluff with her hand raised in farewell. She reminded him again of an elusive mermaid, almost a twin of the figurehead on the bow of his ship. But she had felt all woman in his arms, and he wasn't sure he could ever get the feel of her out of his mind.

CHAPTER 19

"You wanted to see me, sir?" Galen stood at attention in front of the battered desk in the British Army's makeshift office. The room had originally been the elegant parlor in this commandeered home. Galen wondered idly what had become of the owners. They would likely be distressed at the scarred floors and soiled furniture.

"At ease, Lieutenant." Major Montgomery smiled genially. "Sit a moment." He indicated the chair to Galen's right.

Galen sat on the edge of the chair and stared at his superior. He didn't trust him when he was too friendly. Of course, he really didn't trust him much in any circumstances. The man was a lightweight and a fool. It chafed at Galen to have to kowtow to Montgomery, but he bided his time, hoping his stellar qualities would be noticed and he eventually would be the one in charge.

"Tea?" The major poured a cup of tea and offered it to Galen.

Galen shook his head. "Thank you, but no. I just had some at the shop down the street."

Nonplussed, the major stared at the cup, then set it down in front of himself. He made an obvious effort to cover his irritation by leaning back in his chair to stare at Galen over his steepled fingers. "If you recall, Lieutenant, I asked you for a particular favor several months ago."

Favor? Galen thought back and could remember no such request. "Sir?"

Montgomery frowned and sat forward with a thump of his chair. "At Molly's party," he snapped. "You agreed to bring Lydia Huddleston to New York. She's here, all right, but as your doxy." He stared at Galen accusingly.

Galen had forgotten. A smile tugged at his mouth, but he bit his lip. Lydia might prove useful to him after all. He had grown weary of her tiresome entreaties for marriage. This might be a way to get rid of her and bring about Montgomery's downfall, all in one fell swoop.

He shrugged. "The woman came of her own will, Major. I think she tired of me as soon as she saw you at a few parties." The lie slid off his tongue with ease.

"She did?" The major leaned forward like an eager young boy. "There is a ball on Friday. I should like her to accompany me."

"I think that could be arranged. Maybe you should look for suitable housing for her, Major. A small house of her own where she could enjoy your visits privately as well as act as your hostess."

Montgomery's pale-blue eyes gleamed at the thought. "You are certain she would be agreeable to this arrangement?"

"Of course. As I said, she has pestered me with questions about you. Methinks you made quite an impression on her when you met in Gurnet."

Montgomery smiled. "See to it then, Lieutenant. I shall commandeer a house for her."

Galen stood and saluted. "Yes, sir." He hurried from the room and turned toward his quarters. He would have a hard time convincing Lydia, but he was confident he could accomplish his mission. The little fool would do anything to help him. All he had to do was make her believe his very life hung in the balance. Which shouldn't be too hard. She still believed he would marry her.

■ ■ ■ ■

Lydia plunged Galen's clothes into the tub and scrubbed them against the washboard. Humming, she rubbed at a spot on the neck of the wet shirt. It was wonderful to have her own man to care for and look after. The lye stung her eyes, and she wiped the tears with the back of her arm. Galen should be home soon. Mayhap they would go out tonight. She was tired of these four walls, but she knew he was simply trying to protect her. The whistles and catcalls from the other men distressed him when he took her out, although she tried to assure him it didn't matter.

The laundry finished, she laid it over a couple of chairs by the fire to dry. Peering in a mirror, she removed the hairpins and let her golden locks fall down her back as she changed her gown for a clean one. Galen liked her hair loose on her shoulders. The small house was in readiness for his arrival. It was important that his home be a haven for him from the stress of his day. Since their arrival in New York, it had seemed almost as if they were married.

The front doorknob rattled. He was home. She smiled and hurried to greet him. He was scowling when he shut the door, and her heart sank.

"Let me take your coat," she said with a coaxing smile. She helped him off with his coat and hung it on the hook by the door.

"Fix me some tea and biscuits. My stomach is rumbling."

"Rough day?" She stroked his arm.

"We shall discuss it over tea," he said ominously.

Her heart fell. It must be terrible news. She'd never seen him in such a state. She took the teakettle from the fire and poured the water into the waiting teapot. While the tea steeped, she put some biscuits on a plate with some butter and jam, then carried it all over to the sofa.

Galen sighed and stuck out a foot. "Pull."

She set the tray on the table and tugged off his boots. Sitting beside him, she poured two cups of tea and handed him one, then prepared a biscuit and gave it to him as well.

He popped the biscuit into his mouth and took a gulp of tea. Leaning back against the sofa, he stared at her.

Were those tears in his eyes? Fear gripped her, and she put a hand to her throat. "What is it? What is wrong?"

"Everything. I am being transferred to another detachment, one on the front lines.

I shall likely not survive another month. The colonials target the officers."

The impact of his words took a few moments to sink in. Horror filled her. "No, Galen, that cannot be! You are valuable here. They would not dare do this." The image of his blood-splattered body on a battlefield made her shudder.

"Tell that to Major Montgomery." His shoulders drooped. "There is only one thing that would save me, but I refused his offer."

For a moment she felt as though she couldn't breathe. There was a way out, and she had to persuade him to take it. She laid a hand on his arm. "No matter what it is or how distasteful, you must do it." He set his hand over hers. The unexpected gesture of tenderness almost broke the tenuous hold she had on her grief.

"It is out of the question. I would not ask a woman I love to do such a thing."

"Me? Can I do something to save you?" Confusion filled her. She had thought he would have to bend his pride or apologize for harsh words. What could she possibly do to alter the situation?

He heaved a sigh. "You met Major Montgomery in Gurnet, did you not?"

"You know I did. The major is the one who has made this decision? I shall speak with him myself about it. He seems a most reasonable man." For the first time, she felt hopeful. She liked Major Montgomery and had seen the admiring glances he had sent her way.

"He was quite taken with you, Lydia." Galen leaned forward and lifted her hand to his lips. "And with good cause. You are the most beautiful woman in New York."

Her heart swelled with love and joy at his words. Sometimes she had wondered if he regretted her arrival, but such high praise soothed her fears. Finally, he had put his feelings for Hannah away. He was hers now, and Hannah would never move him again. "I am surprised he would notice me. Does he want me to go back to Gurnet? I could ask to be allowed to stay with Hannah again and take the pillory as punishment." She hated the thought of spying on her sister again, but she would do it for Galen's sake.

He smiled tenderly. "Nothing so arduous." He turned her hand over and kissed her palm.

The touch of his lips on her palm made her shiver. How she loved him. No task would be too great if it saved him from death. The thought that she wielded such power over his fate gave her a sense of purpose. "What does he want me to do?"

She could make a good spy.

He sighed again. "He wishes —" He broke off and shook his head. "It is impossible."

"Tell me!"

He directed a pleading gaze at her. "He wishes you to accompany him to a ball on Friday. And he would like to give you a nice house where he might visit with you and get to know you better. Do you realize what that might mean, Lydia? What he probably expects?"

Her heart sank, and a knot squeezed in the pit of her stomach. She knew what Galen meant. She wasn't the innocent fool she'd been a year ago. She rose and clasped icy hands together. She couldn't do such a thing. To go to a man she didn't know, much less love? To leave Galen, the love of her life? She shook her head. She couldn't do it.

Galen stood and turned his back to her. "I told him it was impossible, of course. Would you help me pack my belongings? I shall pay for you to stay in the house for the next three months. That's all the money I have. When I'm dead and the time is up, maybe you can go back to your parents."

When he was dead? The seriousness of the situation struck her. What good was her love if he was dead? She shuddered as she began to seriously entertain the idea he proposed. "Would I still be able to see you?"

"I suppose, but you cannot do this, Lydia. I cannot allow it."

As long as she could still see Galen, still be held in his arms and feel his lips on hers, she could bear anything. Anything, if it meant Galen wasn't dead and buried in the cold ground. She shuddered again. "I must do it, Galen. If this is the only thing that will save your life, how can I do otherwise?"

For a moment she wondered if she should take back those words and trust Galen's fate to God, but she didn't have the faith Hannah did. She often wished she did, but turning to God would require giving up Galen. She couldn't do that.

He turned around to face her, and tears glimmered in his eyes. "You would do this for me?"

"I told you I would do anything for you, Galen. Anything." She stepped into his arms and cuddled her head against his chest. His uniform smelled of wet wool and tobacco, a comfortable, familiar scent. She must treasure every moment they spent together. The steady cadence of his heart thudded beneath her ear, and she tightened her arms around him. "Will the major give me time to get to — to get to know him?"

"I am certain he will." He kissed the top of her head. "I know not how to thank you for saving my life, Lydia. Say nothing of this to the major. He must think you came to him of your own free will, not under duress."

A slight shudder ran through her, and Galen's embrace tightened. Bile rose in her throat, but she choked it back. No sacrifice was too great. Her good name was gone anyway.

She knew her sister would entreat her to trust God and let him work it out. That was always Hannah's advice. But these were desperate times, and she had seen too much death. Many of the laughing young officers she'd met at balls over the past three months were now dead and buried. As long as she drew breath, that wouldn't happen to Galen.

How could she tell Hannah?

She wouldn't. She would let her think she was still with Galen. Sweet, pure Hannah must never know the depths to which her sister had fallen. Lydia didn't think she could bear to see the pain and disappointment in Hannah's eyes.

"You will enjoy the parties and soirees the major enjoys. He will certainly find a nicer house than this. You will merely entertain him a few nights a week and act as his hostess for soirees and balls."

Soirees and balls? That sounded promising. She could endure the other for the fun of parties. Would the major buy her new gowns? That prospect thrilled her. And she did like him. He was attractive and clean with good teeth.

"I can find out his schedule and see you on nights when he is otherwise occupied." Galen caressed her hair. "Then when the war is over, we can be wed."

Lydia sighed. It would be all right. This was but a wrinkle in their plans. As long as Galen loved her, everything would turn out for the best.

CHAPTER 20

May 5, 1777

"Hannah, what are you doing up there?"

She looked down from her perch on the side of the leeward tower of the lighthouse. Olive appeared farther away than she sounded. Since she'd first crawled out the window with the rope around her waist to apply a fresh coat of whitewash to the lighthouse, she hadn't dared look down. Now that she had, a wave of dizziness swept over her, and she tightened her grip on the railing.

"Come down this instant! What if someone saw you in those breeches? 'Tis disgraceful." Olive's voice rose in pitch to a near screech.

Hannah dragged her gaze from her sister-in-law far below her and began to inch her way back to the open window. The railing was narrow and treacherous, and even with the rope securing her, she felt uneasy. The wind blew incessantly, and the pounding of the surf below the bluff filled her head and made it hard to concentrate. She marshaled her thoughts and focused on sliding her hands along the rail until she reached the safety of the window and crawled inside the tower. She let out the breath she'd been holding and shuddered. She would be glad when this job was done. After putting down her bucket of whitewash, she descended the spiral stairs, the metal clanging in her haste.

Olive's face was pale when Hannah exited the tower. "You must hire that job done, Hannah. What if something happened to you?"

Hannah put a hand on Olive's shoulder. "Come inside for tea. You must not worry. God is in control." She would have had to stop anyway. Fog was beginning to roll in from the ocean.

Olive sighed. "Methinks you should preach instead of Pastor Goodman. At least you tell me of God's love and care." She followed her sister-in-law to the house.

Piercing the shell Olive had wrapped around herself hadn't been easy, but she had been right to think the young woman needed a friend. The past few months had yielded the fruit of friendship between them.

"What were you doing up there?" Olive

shaved slivers of tea into the caddy and handed it to Hannah. "I was affrighted just watching you."

"The lighthouse is in a disgraceful condition." Hannah poured the tea, and the women took their cups to the chairs and table by the window. The fog had grown so thick, she couldn't see the surf. Which meant any ships out there would be unable to see the light. "If the inspector were to come, I would be fired. I must reapply the whitewash and clean the windows. Now that spring is here, I can put it off no longer." Neither were duties she relished, but they had to be done. It was her responsibility.

Olive shuddered. "Hire a man from the village to do it. Spending the money would be better than falling to your death."

"There is no man able to do it. The young ones are gone to war. Can you imagine someone like Ephraim Baxter on that railing?" Hannah smiled at the thought.

"Nathan would do it," Olive said with a knowing wink.

Hannah laughed. "He would probably try. But he is too old to be up there." She would rather avoid mention of Nathan. Daily he pressed his offer of marriage more earnestly.

"He is not that old." Olive waved her hand. "Faith, but I do not understand why you hesitate to accept him, Hannah. He would make you a good husband."

"Are you so eager to share me with a husband?" Hannah teased. "Then I should not have time to listen to your woes. What brings you by today? You seem a trifle distracted." She'd noticed the way Olive pleated the folds of her skirt, a sure sign of distress in her sister-in-law.

"You know me too well." Olive sighed and took a sip of tea. "Mama is determined to marry me off."

" 'Tis nothing new, Olive." Indeed it wasn't. Finding a man to wed her daughter had become Mother Thomas's mission in life.

"But now she has got it into her head to send me to Aunt Maddie in Boston. She thinks I shall find a suitable husband among the wealthy there." Olive shook her head. "Why can she not see that no man would pick a wife with a face like mine? I overheard the last man tell his friend that he expected me to whinny any minute!" Tears of mortification sparkled in her eyes.

Hannah bit her lip. She had once thought the same of her sister-in-law's long, horsey face and shrill voice, but the cruel words were painful to hear now that she loved her as a sister. She'd seen a change in Olive since they had become friends too. It was almost as if Olive was imitating Hannah's manners and voice. She'd moderated her tone and dressed in more feminine ways. Surely some man would see her qualities if she was patient.

"Such a man does not deserve you." Hannah patted Olive's hand. "But why seek a husband at all? Are you not happy and content as you are?" She was. She had no wish to come under the protection of another husband. Thoughts of Birch hovered near the surface, but she resolutely buried them deep inside again.

"Mama is determined I must wed." Olive sighed. "You know how relentless Mama can be when she's resolute. I think I would rather stay unwed than take a man for whom I have no real feelings."

Indeed, Hannah knew. Mother Thomas had pushed Nathan Gray at her for the past three months, but Hannah was determined not to be rushed. She felt nothing for Nathan but friendship and slight fondness. He insisted that was enough for him, but she wasn't so sure.

"I suppose I shall have no choice but to go to Boston for the season." Olive lowered her chin to her chest.

Hannah opened her mouth to console her

sister-in-law when she heard the fearsome sound of a ship tearing itself to pieces on the rocks. "Ring the bell for the village, Olive!" She sprang to her feet and ran out the door and down the path to the beach. Was it a British ship or one of their own?

Heavy fog blanketed the beach and the sea beyond. It had rolled in swiftly and made it impossible to see the lighthouse warning. She shoved the coble into the waves and jumped inside. The wind carried the screams of the crewmen and the squeal of timber against rock to her ears, and she pulled hard on the oars in her haste to reach the sinking ship.

She didn't wait for Olive who had feared and hated the water since she'd nearly drowned as a child. The large swells hampered her boat. Pieces of shattered hull, kegs of supplies, and other flotsam were already floating toward her. The shapes looked strange and twisted in the fog.

She paused from her rowing and stood. Scanning the waves for bobbing heads, she saw three men clinging to a piece of wood off to her left. She paddled to them with all possible speed and pulled them, one by one, into the boat. They lay gasping while she searched for more survivors. This looked to be a merchant ship.

Behind her, the bell pealed out above the roaring wind. The villagers would be here soon. She spied another man clinging to wreckage and managed to haul him aboard too, in spite of his girth. His weight put her boat dangerously low in the water. She would have to take these men to shore and come back out. She looked over the wreckage in regret and rowed to shore.

When she helped them out onto the sand, one man refused to get out. "Mistress, I will help you rescue my men."

He must be the captain. She didn't have time to argue, so she merely nodded and shoved the boat back into the water. She guessed the man to be about thirty-two. He was not handsome with his thinning hair and round face, but there was a strength about him that was attractive. His clothing seemed to be of fine quality, and she had to wonder who he was.

They found five other survivors, and by that time, the men from the village had arrived. Hannah glanced behind her. Olive in a dinghy by herself, rowing valiantly against the waves.

She gasped and the captain gazed at her with a question in his sober gray eyes. "My sister-in-law. She should not be out here. She cannot swim and does not know how to row a boat."

He stared over the waves at Olive. Her face was screwed up in concentration, and then she saw Hannah. She stopped rowing and stood in the boat and waved.

"Sit down!" Hannah almost stood herself in her agitation. Olive would tip the boat. Then as if the very thought had caused the action, a swell struck the small boat and pitched Olive over the side.

Hannah screamed, and the man dove headlong into the waves. Olive flailed about in the water, then her head went under the waves. *Please God, let him get to her in time.* Her lips moved silently as she prayed.

She couldn't see Olive. Then the swell died and her head popped up above the waves. She thrashed about again, just as the man reached her. He caught her up in his arm and towed her to the dinghy. Guiding her hand to the side of the boat, he waited until she had steadied herself, then heaved her over the side. He slipped to the other end of the boat and climbed in himself.

Hannah had to admire him. Not many men would have jumped back into the water after being rescued. She picked up the oars and rowed to shore, reaching it just as the man was lifting Olive out of the boat.

"Where can I take her?"

"To the house." Hannah pointed out the path, then looked around to make sure the shipwrecked survivors were being cared for by the townspeople. Seeing no need to stay, she hurried up the path after Olive and the man.

She caught them at the top of the bluff. Her stomach churned as she stared at Olive's pale face. She was only half-conscious and clung to the man as though to a lifeline. Hannah hurried ahead and opened the door as he carried Olive inside and deposited her on the sofa. The spring air was still cool, so Hannah stirred up the fire and got it blazing. She was shivering in her damp clothes, and Olive must be freezing after being in the frigid water.

Hannah fetched a blanket from the chest and draped it over her sister-in-law. She should change Olive's clothes, but she couldn't do it with the man standing there. She turned to face him. "My thanks, sir."

"No, I should be thanking you." He bowed a bit stiffly. "Stephen Brewster at your service. I owned yonder pile of kindling." He shook his head. "Now my goods lie at the bottom of the sea or in the hands of your good village folk. Still, I have my life, and for that, I thank you."

Hannah curtsied, and as she did, she realized she still wore the breeches and hunting shirt. Heat rushed up her face. What must everyone think to see her dressed so immodestly? She could probably expect another call from the town elders. Suppressing a sigh, she forced a smile. "Hannah Thomas, sir, keeper of Gurnet Light. This is my sister-in-law, Olive Thomas, whom you saved from the sea this day."

"A woman lighthouse keeper?" He raised an eyebrow. "Although I must admit you performed your lifesaving duties admirably." He glanced down at Olive again. "Methinks she will be all right, but I would suggest you change her clothing and yours as well. I would hate for either of you to catch a chill."

She was grateful he made no mention of her unusual attire. Mayhap he thought it the usual clothing for a female keeper, but it did make the job of rowing easier.

She nodded. "I shall, sir."

"Have you an idea where I might find accommodation, Mistress Thomas?"

She glanced at Olive. Mother Thomas would want to thank the man who had saved her daughter's life. She nodded. "Follow the path behind the house. It will take you to Olive's home. Tell her mother what has happened and ask her to send the carriage for her. I know Mother Thomas will insist you stay with her."

Olive moaned, and they both turned. Hannah knelt beside her and placed a calming hand on her forehead. "Shh, 'tis all right, Olive."

Her eyes flew open, and she struggled to a sitting position. "I was drowning," she cried. Her gaze traveled to the man behind Hannah, and her eyes widened when she took in his round, pleasant face. "You saved me. How can I thank you?"

A flush bloomed on his face. "Think nothing of it, Miss Olive. I was just glad I was there."

Before Olive could speak, someone pounded on the front door. It swung open and Nathan Gray rushed in. "I cry you mercy for barging in, Hannah. I had to see that you were all right. I heard a woman was pulled from the water." His gaze took in Hannah's unusual garb, and he frowned. Then he saw Olive, wet and shivering on the sofa, and his face cleared. "I just thank Providence you are both well."

Olive's teeth chattered, and Hannah turned to look at her. Her lips were blue, and she was as pale as salt. "I must ask you, gentlemen, to leave us now so we might get into dry clothing."

Nathan eyed Stephen with suspicion, but

they both nodded and turned toward the door.

"One moment." Hannah rushed up the stairs and into her bedroom. She took some clothing of John's from the drawer as well as his good shoes and coat. She hurried back to the parlor and thrust them into Stephen's hands. "Here are dry clothes for you, sir. Nathan, would you show Mr. Brewster to my mother-in-law's? She will want to thank him properly."

Nathan nodded. "This way, sir."

As soon as the door was closed behind them, Hannah latched it and stripped Olive's wet clothes from her and helped her dress in a clean shift, petticoat, and day gown. It was a snug fit, as Hannah was smaller than Olive, but at least she was dry. Then she changed her own clothes.

"What a strong man." Olive sighed as Hannah combed and plaited her hair in front of the crackling fire. "I felt so safe in his arms."

It was likely the closest Olive had ever been to a man. Hannah suppressed a smile. Wouldn't it be lovely if something developed between the two of them? Mr. Brewster seemed a very kind man.

They heard the rattle and jingle of the carriage outside, and Hannah went to the door.

Nathan climbed out and hurried to her. She felt a flash of irritation that he would be back so soon. All she wanted to do was crawl into bed and rest.

"Is Olive ready?"

Perhaps he wouldn't stay but would escort Olive to her home. Hannah nodded. "She is eager to get home."

Nathan touched her shoulder as he passed, and she stepped back. Why must he always find a way to put his hands on her?

He helped Olive to her feet. "The carriage is outside, and your mother is eager to assure herself that you are all right. Let me help you."

"I am fine," Olive said with dignity. She paused in the doorway and hugged Hannah. "Thank you, my dear sister," she whispered.

Nathan helped Olive into the carriage, then stepped back down and shut the door. He wasn't leaving. Hannah suppressed a sigh. She just didn't feel up to dealing with him after all she'd been through today. Why couldn't he see how exhausted she was? Birch would have known with one look. He would have insisted on fixing her some tea and then tucked the blanket around her and made her rest.

Birch, Birch, always thoughts of Birch.

Why couldn't she forget him as easily as he had forgotten her? This shipwreck brought it all crashing back. It had been three months since that dark night he had surprised her in the light tower. Three months of silence, three months of heartache as she tried to banish him from her thoughts. Most of the time she was so busy she was able to keep the pain at bay. But not tonight.

She wanted to sit by the fire and weep, to remember. Dealing with Nathan was not on her agenda. She had to make him see she just wasn't up to company tonight. She stood squarely in the doorway to the house. He would have to push her aside to gain entrance, and she hoped he was too much of a gentleman to do that.

When the carriage pulled away, he turned back to face her. "Might we go inside and talk a bit, Hannah?"

She shook her head firmly. "Not tonight, Nathan. Faith, but I am so tired I would not be good company. I want to seek my bed and rest."

He nodded, but he didn't seem keen about it. "I would discuss something with you, though, Hannah. Might I call tomorrow?"

She had no choice but to agree. He took his leave, and she went back inside. She needed to tell him she could never marry him. The memories brought back by the shipwreck had convinced her of that. She would marry no one but Birch, so she would likely never marry. Until Birch found his peace with God and came back to her, she would wait. If that never happened, then so be it. She would accept God's will.

She knew Nathan was tiring of the way she kept him at a distance. She would tell him firmly that he must not wait for her any longer. He would just have to accept her decision.

CHAPTER 21

Birch squinted through the spyglass at the white dot on the horizon. A ship, its white canvas billowing, sailed toward them. It was likely a British ship, and he smiled in anticipation. They had boarded five ships in the past three months. After taking the crew captive, they had taken the booty for the Continental Army, then blasted a hole through the hull and watched the ships go to the bottom of the ocean. So far they had been lucky — and crafty. They only took ships alone in the empty sea, like the ship coming toward them now. The British didn't know it was their own *Mermaid* who held the hidden pirate in their midst.

The people had called 1777 the year of the hangman because all the sevens looked like gallows. They had predicted that Benjamin Franklin, John Adams, Thomas Jefferson, and George Washington would all be swinging from gibbets before the end of the year. Birch intended to do his part to prove that prediction wrong. And he and his crew were getting rich in the meantime. They sailed to ports in the South and sold the luxuries aboard to eager consumers. The food and ammunition were sent to the Continental Army.

It would be at least an hour before the ship was near enough to fire on with his cannon. Birch leaned against the railing and gazed out over the gray sea. It was choppy today, with small whitecaps kicked up by the wind. What was Hannah doing right now? He sighed. Did she ever think of him? His lips tightened, and he shook his head at his own foolishness. She had made her feelings perfectly clear. So why couldn't he forget her?

Her clear-green eyes haunted him. His mermaid, his love. He knew he would never feel about another woman the way he did Hannah. She brought out the best in him. In spite of his resolve to put God out of his life, he found himself listening to that still, small voice in his heart.

He gave a bark of laughter at his own fanciful thoughts. God was done with him too. What madness made him think God still spoke to his heart? Hannah had said she would pray for him. Did she still pray?

He gazed out at the horizon again. The ship was close enough to see men moving about her deck. They would likely see the British flag he flew and think they were safe. He pressed his lips together in a grim smile. They would soon find out differently.

"Ready the cannon," he ordered his first mate, Riley.

Riley had been invaluable. An Irishman of about forty, he knew what the orders would be sometimes before Birch did. Birch had found him in the sea clinging to a bit of splintered wood and surrounded by sharks. He had jumped from a British floating prison hulk. He would rather be eaten by sharks than go back to that rat-infested, diseased hole, he'd told Birch.

Readying for battle, his men scurried around the deck. The deck was painted red so the men wouldn't be shocked to see blood staining it, and he'd ordered sand spread to keep it from being slippery in the heat of the battle. He was not anticipating much battle today, though. He intended to try a new tactic Riley had suggested.

The *Mermaid*'s sails were down, and he put on his British uniform coat. All was in readiness. The ship sailed nearer. He could make out her name printed on the side. A British-owned merchant ship with several cannons mounted on her deck. *Prosperity.* A fortuitous name.

He nodded to a crewman to wave the flag of distress. He climbed to the prow of the ship and lifted his hand in greeting. "Ahoy, *Prosperity*!"

A crewman aboard the British ship answered his summons. "Ahoy, *Mermaid.* How do you fare?"

"We have a torn sail," he called. "Can you tow us to shore?" They were only about thirty miles out, so it was a reasonable request.

There was silence as the crewman consulted with the captain. "Aye, *Mermaid,* throw us your line."

Birch bit back a smile of triumph. Riley was a genius. He leaned over the railing again and called to the ship. "I would like to invite your captain to sup with me this night. The men have caught a shark, and I would share it with him."

The man conferred with the captain again. The captain shook his head, and Birch knew the plan would work.

The seaman shouted across the water again. "The captain says to bring the fish and come here. Our cook is the best in the fleet."

"I shall be there." Birch waved at the

captain who acknowledged his gesture with an upraised hand of his own. He wanted to dance in victory. He left the bosun to throw the line to the other ship while he hurried from the deck and told Riley to prepare the men. Then he stopped by the galley and had the cook cut a huge slab of shark meat for him and wrap it in burlap. The captain of *Prosperity* would have his supper, and something he might not like as well.

The ship moved beneath his feet as the *Prosperity* towed the *Mermaid* toward the shore. He slicked his hair back and caught it in a ribbon at the nape of his neck. After donning his hat, Birch took the steps to the top deck two at a time. He climbed down the ladder to the ship's boat bobbing beside the ship, and two sailors rowed him to the *Prosperity.*

The captain met him at the top of the ladder with an outstretched hand. After he was safely aboard, the man bowed. "Captain Robert Gristol."

After a swift glance at the unkempt ship, Birch returned his bow. "Captain Birch Meredith." This man deserved to have his ship taken. He was unshaven and dressed in breeches black with grime, and the same lack of care was in evidence in the ship itself. Decks were unwashed, the crew was lackadaisical with mismatched uniforms, and the yards were badly mended.

"Welcome aboard, Captain Meredith. Ah, I see you brought the fish. I must admit your invitation was welcome after over a month of hardtack and water."

"We have one of the best fishermen in the colonies aboard." Birch handed the shark to a waiting sailor.

"Come along, and let me show you my ship," Gristol said. They strolled along the deck, and he pointed out their cannon and big guns. He spoke of the battles he'd been in and the rich cargo he carried belowdecks.

Making suitable sounds of appreciation, Birch followed him around but grew more appalled at the condition of the ship. When a sailor announced their dinner was ready, he trailed Gristol to his cabin.

Captain Gristol took a deep sniff of the air and sighed. "There's nothing like fresh fish."

Their dinner was spread out on the table. Birch had brought potatoes and tea as well, and he knew it looked like a feast to the other captain. He would let him enjoy his last meal of freedom.

"I shall soon have enough money to retire to the West Indies." Gristol leaned back in his chair as they lingered over their meal. "I have made much in the slave trade." He belched.

"You have slaves aboard?" A slaver. He had supped with a slaver. He felt nauseated.

Gristol shook his head. "Not this trip." He belched again. "That was a fine meal, Captain Meredith. It was a fortunate wind that blew us together."

"I fear you will no longer think that in a few moments, Captain." He drew his flintlock pistol from the hidden inner pocket of his coat and pointed it at the other man.

Gristol set his chair forward with a thump. "What is this, Meredith?" He started to stand, but Birch stopped him.

"Please remain seated, Captain. You are my prisoner, you and your ship." He knew Gristol would need a few minutes to fully believe what had happened to him. Birch was in no hurry. The plan had worked so well he wanted to savor the success.

Gristol laughed. "My men will cut you to ribbons." He idly picked a sliver of meat from between his teeth.

"You will order them to throw down their weapons."

"You are mad, Meredith. Why would I do that?" He shook his head. "Captain, you are outgunned."

"Look out the porthole." Birch grinned.

Gristol sighed but did as he was told. Birch came up behind him and signaled to Riley. Moments later hidden doors dropped on the *Mermaid* and revealed the hidden cannon.

"Now we are going to go top deck, and you will order your men to lay down their arms." Birch dug the gun into Gristol's back.

"I think not, Meredith. Let us ask the men, shall we?"

"What we shall do is go up to the top deck, and if you do not do as I ask, I fear you will not like the consequences." He drew his knife out of his other pocket. "Have you noticed the sharks following us?"

"Of course." Gristol stared at the knife, and beads of sweat broke out on his upper lip.

"If you do not do as I say, exactly, I shall cut your leg and let the sharks have you." He held his breath at the bluff. If Gristol didn't believe him, he would have no choice but to try to fight his way out of the situation. He nodded at the porthole again. "Methinks I saw at least five shark fins yonder. Make your decision, Captain, or I shall do as I said."

Gristol's shoulders sagged. "Very well, Captain. You have outfoxed me." He attempted a feeble smile. "Would you accept a bribe? Look in yonder chest. All that is yours if you take your pistol and get back in your boat."

Birch shook his head. "Sorry, Captain. You may keep your gold. Now shall we go topside?"

Gristol shrugged. "I had to try, Meredith." He picked up his hat and walked up the steps with Birch close behind him.

"I have my finger on the trigger, Gristol. Remember that."

The captain hesitated at the top of the stairs, and Birch poked him with the pistol again. "Throw down your weapons, men," he shouted with a surly glare at Birch. "We have been boarded."

The sailors stared at Birch, consternation painting their faces. They started toward the two captains, but a sharp word from Captain Gristol stopped them. "I gave you a direct order. Throw down your weapons!" His face grew redder with each moment that passed.

Swords, pistols, knives, and muskets clattered onto the deck. "Very good," Birch said. "Now step away from them, all of you. I want you down in the hold."

The men looked at one another, then slowly filed to the steps and down into the hold. Birch pulled the door shut behind them and pulled a padlock out of his pocket. He slipped it over the latch and locked it.

Captain Gristol watched him balefully. "What do you intend to do with us?"

"We will sail to Boston and deliver you to the authorities there. You will spend the rest of the war in prison." He bound Gristol's hands and signaled his men to come aboard.

Within minutes his men swarmed over the railing and searched the ship for what cargo it carried. Riley strutted up to Birch with a grin.

Birch smiled and clapped him on the back. "Good thinking, Riley. We took the ship without firing a single shot."

Riley preened. "I hoped not to have to fish you from the sea this day, Captain."

"Captain, over here!"

Birch spun around at the call. His bosun, Richards, waved urgently from the stair to the hull where the enemy was confined. He waited to see if Birch was coming, then disappeared down the steps. Birch strode across the deck, then followed him. His men had herded the enemy into the tack room and confined them so the rest of the hold could be searched. It took a moment for his eyes to adjust to the dim light, then he hurried to the room where Richards stood waiting.

"What is it?" Richards wouldn't have called him down here unless it was important. He glanced around as he moved to meet the bosun. The slaves had been kept here. The outer hold bristled with iron cuffs and leg irons. Nausea gripped his stomach at the stench of human misery.

"See for yourself, Cap'n." Richards stepped aside so he could enter the cramped room.

On a cot lay a young woman, obviously part African, although her skin was fair enough to have passed for white. She was also obviously dead, though her body was still warm. Birch's gaze traveled from her face to the bundle in her arms. A baby. The child moved restlessly and sucked on its fist. A pretty infant with dark, curly hair and fair skin. There was no obvious trace of African in the child, though Birch knew she must be the woman's child. The father must have been white and diluted the African blood even further.

"Do you know anything of the mother?" For a moment the baby reminded him of his own brother. He had been the first one to hold Charles.

Richards shook his head. "Nor of the

father. Perhaps it was one of the crew."

Birch knelt and put his hand out. The baby opened its eyes and grasped his finger. The alert expression in the infant's dark eyes and the firm grip on his finger told him this little one wanted to live. It was like a miracle to find this small scrap of life in the midst of war. He pressed his lips together. He must save this child somehow, though it would be hard to keep the child alive with the mother dead.

Birch pulled the dirty blanket back and looked the child over. A girl, obviously dirty and wet, but otherwise fine. He snatched a cleaner blanket from the other cot and wrapped the baby in it. Cradling her against his chest, he took her up on deck. He hadn't held a baby since he was eight when he used to cart Charles around and was surprised he remembered how.

Gristol clenched his fists when he saw the burden Birch carried. "What are you doing with her? Where is Letitia?"

"If you are referring to her mother, she is dead."

Gristol stared at him as if to see if he was telling the truth, then shrugged. "Just as well. I had tired of her anyway and would have sold her on my next trip south."

Birch stared at the man with loathing. He

was the father, obviously. "What about your daughter?"

Gristol shrugged again. "What about her? She would have gone with her mother. Do with her what you will."

"You would have let her go into slavery?" Birch was sorry now he hadn't had the hard heart necessary to pitch Gristol to the sharks.

"Of course. Letitia would have insisted on keeping her. The woman was wild about that baby. It made her quite tiresome."

Birch turned away before he did something he would regret. He had never loathed a man as much as he did Gristol in that moment. The man had no conscience. Birch tightened his arms around the baby girl. Now Gristol had no claim on her. He didn't deserve a fine daughter like this. Birch sent one of the crew to find cloth to cut up into nappies and another back to the cabin to see if there was clothing for the baby.

The men hoisted the yards and, with a stiff wind to their backs, set sail for Boston. Time was of the essence. They would make Boston by daybreak, and he would see if he could find a wet nurse. He managed to fasten a makeshift nappy on her and dressed her in the dirty gown the sailor found. She was fretful and hungry, but he dipped a cloth in sugar water and let her suck on it. It only pacified her momentarily, and she began to wail and suck on her fist.

He paced the deck with her over his shoulder and watched anxiously for the Boston harbor. The child's wailing would make the trip even longer.

"Ye look like nursing a baby is a common occurrence for ye, Cap'n," Riley said with a sly grin. "Have ye a wee one at home?"

Birch's cheeks warmed and he shook his head. "I walked the floor with my brother Charles many times." A lump grew in his throat at the memory of toting Charlie around the house. Mama had been ill after Charlie's birth, and Birch had taken his brother under his wing. He flinched from the memory.

"Land ahoy!"

Birch's head swiveled at the call from the lookout. Boston, at last. He didn't know how much more of this crying he could bear. He handed the baby to Riley, who took her gingerly as if he wasn't quite sure what to do with her, then went to the bow and watched the land grow nearer. The ship rolled with the swells, and he braced his feet against the deck.

An hour later they dropped anchor and made their way down the gangway into the teeming city. Birch found a man who directed him to a woman he knew who just had a baby. He paid her well, and she disappeared into a back room with the infant. He would pick up the child later when the ship was ready to sail. He'd already decided what he would do with the little one. He would take her to Hannah.

CHAPTER 22

The newly whitewashed lighthouse gleamed in the May sunshine. Hannah was proud of her work. She'd been terrified the entire time she'd hung over the catwalk painting it, but now that it was finished, she could relax and enjoy it. She had managed to avoid Nathan for the past week, but he was coming late this afternoon, and she could delay the confrontation no longer. The thought of hurting him brought her no pleasure, but neither did continuing to refuse him. The time had come to end it.

"Hallo, at the lighthouse!"

She turned to see Stephen Brewster and Olive coming up the path from the big house. She smiled and waved. She hadn't seen them for three days and relished the thought of their company. Stephen walked slowly and helped Olive over the stones and rough areas of the path.

Hannah suppressed a smile. Mayhap a

romance was blooming there. She hoped so for Olive's sake. Mother Thomas's choice would not offer Olive much more than a proper station. The man obviously seemed to care for Olive by the way he held her arm and hovered over her so attentively.

Olive's cheeks were pink, and she was out of breath when they reached the lighthouse. "You finished the painting without me." A frown wrinkled her brow.

"I wanted to be done before the weather changed again. Besides, you are still recovering from your dunking." Hannah directed a smile to Stephen. "You both seem to be well. Would you care for some tea?"

Stephen shook his head. "We stopped to see if we could persuade you to come to supper."

"I would, but I am expecting Mr. Gray. Another time before you go."

Olive's face fell. "I so wanted you to be there, Hannah! We wanted you to be the first to know."

"Know what?" But looking at their shining faces, she knew what they wanted to tell her. While she was happy for Olive, her heart sank at the thought of being alone and friendless again. Olive would go with Stephen.

"Olive has consented to become my wife,"

Stephen said with a broad smile.

Hannah clapped her hands together and hugged Olive. "Methinks I knew before you said the words. Olive's face was like the lighthouse beacon."

The pink in Olive's cheeks deepened. Happiness had made her almost pretty, and Hannah had to hug her again just from the sheer joy in her sister-in-law's face. "When shall you be wed?"

"Next week. Stephen must get back to Boston and his business concerns there."

"And try to untangle the details of this shipwreck," Stephen added.

Next week. She would be alone again in a week. Hannah swallowed the lump in her throat and forced back tears. She would not let them see her sorrow. Nothing should mar their happiness this day. "We have much to do in seven days."

"You must be my attendant," Olive said. "You are the best friend I have ever had."

"I would be honored if that is your wish. But methinks you should consult your mother. I have yet to be chastised for my public appearance in breeches. It may not be prudent for me to appear beside you."

Olive waved a hand. " 'Tis what Mother said as well, but we care nothing for their opinion. We shall be gone from here." She smiled. "Stephen says we shall travel the world, Hannah. It is a dream come true for me."

Hannah pushed away the stab of envy. It would be a dream come true for her too. Could that be one reason she could not accept Nathan? She knew he had no desire to travel beyond the confines of Gurnet.

"Come, Olive. We must get back. Your mother will be expecting us." He bowed to Hannah, and she curtsied.

Olive hugged her. "If your plans change, join us tonight."

"I will." Hannah waved as they went back down the path.

Her life was about to change again, and not for the better. Her only confidant was leaving. Tears filled her eyes, and she let them fall this time. There was no one around to see. Loneliness would be her only companion.

She was being silly. She loved Olive and was happy she had found a suitable husband, but some days Hannah felt she would go mad if she didn't get out of this place. She wanted to stand on a ship and smell the salty tang of the sea in her face, to hear the strange languages and see the different customs of a country not her own. But she needed to put such childish longings behind her.

She had some tea and biscuits for luncheon, then went back outside. It was too lovely a day to spend inside, though she had cleaning she could do. She took her spade and began to dig in her tiny garden plot behind the house. She could plant peas and beans here and let them grow up the trellis. When she looked out the kitchen window, she would be able to see them.

She worked steadily for a few minutes, then threw down the spade. Her heart just wasn't in it. She didn't know why she was so restless. Mayhap she should row to town and pick up supplies. That might calm her unsettled spirit.

She rounded the corner to fetch her shawl and ran into a tall figure. She tilted her head back and looked up into a sunburned face. Her mouth dropped. "Birch?"

"Why is your mouth open every time I see you?" he asked with a grin. "Have you not been watching for me?"

She wanted to fling herself into his arms, but she remembered their parting too well. She would not suffer that pain again. There was no future for them until Birch could put his bitterness behind him. "I was not sure I would ever see you again." He carried a bundle, but Hannah could not see what it was.

"I was angry. But I find I cannot stay away, my Hannah."

Joy flooded her heart at his admission. Mayhap God would reach him yet. "I missed you."

"Did you pray for me?" His dark eyes probed her face.

"Daily."

The bundle in his arms squeaked, and he looked down with a grin. "I have brought you a gift, Hannah." He pulled back the blanket to reveal an exquisite child. Dark curls framed a round face with a little pointed chin. With rosebud lips and pink cheeks, the child looked as though it belonged in a fine knit wrap not a rough wool blanket.

"Oh," she breathed. "How beautiful. Is it a boy or girl?" What did he mean, a gift? Did he intend to leave the child with her?

"A girl. Her mother died on board ship. If she has a name, I do not know it. You may call her whatever you like."

She stared into his face. "You want *me* to keep her?" She longed to take the child and cuddle her close. Her childlessness had been a source of great heartache, but she couldn't quite believe she would gain a daughter in such a way.

"She will need a wet nurse or you will have to hand-feed her. I will be at sea with no means to care for her. I knew you would not have me leave her for the buzzards." His dark eyes never left her face.

Joy welled in her soul. Hannah held out her arms, and Birch placed the baby in them. She inhaled the sweetness of her. She took a small hand, and the baby's fingers closed around hers. A fierce protectiveness and love welled up in her heart. This would be her daughter, her child. She kissed the petal-soft skin and cuddled her close.

Birch was watching her with an expression almost of pain. What was he thinking? Did he yearn for a home and family the way she did? His gaze caught and held hers. The love and hunger in his eyes took her breath away. She had to be strong. God wasn't finished with him yet. She looked back down at the baby.

"Before you agree, there is one thing you must know." Birch's voice was sober.

Was the child his? The thought caused a stab of pain so sharp, she almost gasped with the fierceness of it.

"She is part African. I know she doesn't look it, but 'tis something you should know now. Does that make a difference?"

Relief flooded her. The child was not his. She was shamed the thought had crossed her mind. "That matters not to me. I shall love her." She gazed tenderly into the child's face. "What shall I name her?" The words were more a question to herself than to Birch, but he answered it.

"I thought of calling her Charlotte after my brother Charles." His tone was diffident, but there was no mistaking the longing in his voice.

"She looks like a Charlotte. 'Tis what we shall call her." She stared up into his eyes again. "I'll have to get supplies for her. It would be too difficult to find a wet nurse willing to come here for feedings. One of the farmers in town has a milk goat for sale."

He nodded. "If you like, I will go with you now. I would like to buy the things she will need." She started to protest, but he held up his hand. "She is mine too, Hannah. I want you to understand that. I shall return to see her." He paused a moment. "And you."

The last two words were so soft, she wasn't entirely certain she heard them. But the burning glance he sent her warmed her heart. She nodded. "As you wish."

They walked along the rocky path to the beach. Hannah couldn't take her eyes from her new daughter, and Birch steadied her several times as she stumbled. He helped her into the round-bottomed coble and rowed them across the inlet.

Hannah was relieved Ephraim's wife was not in evidence at the general store. Ephraim exclaimed over Charlotte's beauty and helped them pick out needed supplies. They purchased a small bed, blankets, bottles, nappies, clothing, and myriad other small items. Hannah was shocked at the total, but Birch just peeled off pound notes and thrust them in the shopkeeper's hand. Then they stopped at a farm on the edge of town and bought a goat.

Charlotte was beginning to fret when they finally got back home. Hannah was thrilled to see she had dark eyes. She would think of Birch every time she looked into those eyes. She changed the baby's nappy while Birch took a stab at milking the goat. He was just outside the open kitchen window, and she had to suppress a giggle when she heard him berate the goat for trying to chew his coat.

He came in looking a bit worse for the wear. His coat was frayed where the goat had chewed it, and his dark hair was loose on his shoulders. "The goat ate my ribbon," he said with a scowl when he saw the question in her eyes. The frown turned to a grin when she giggled. "You shall see, mistress," he said teasingly. "She will eat anything. So beware!"

She giggled again, and he just shook his head. He took a step closer and touched her chin. "You will make a fine mother, Hannah. I shall remember you here with Charlotte."

Her heart sank at his heavy tone. He was leaving. "You are going?"

He nodded. "I must. We weigh anchor in an hour. My men will be wondering where I am."

"Do you know when you will be back?" She wanted to hold him here with her a few more moments. Impressing his image in her mind, she stared at him through a sparkling sheen of tears. Her pirate. Biting her lip, she forced the tears away. She would not send him off with tears.

"Mayhap in the fall." He stared into her eyes, then stroked her cheek.

Hannah trembled at his touch. He bent his head and brushed her lips with a soft kiss. "Take care, my Hannah. You hold my heart."

"You hold my heart." The poetic words pierced her soul. She clung to him, and the

tears spilled over. "I, too, hold you in my heart."

Before he could respond, a knock sounded at the door. She pulled away and went to answer it. Nathan. His smile faded when he saw the babe in her arms and Birch standing just beyond her.

"Have I come at a bad time, Hannah?"

She wanted to tell him to leave, but she just shook her head. "Of course not, Nathan. Come in."

She introduced the men. "Captain Meredith has brought me a new daughter," she said proudly. She held Charlotte up for Nathan's inspection.

He frowned. "Methinks you do not need to take in some captain's by-blow." He shot a glare at Birch. "We shall have children of our own one day soon. I would not have you concerned with wiping the snotty nose of a guttersnipe."

Hannah gasped, hurt and rage narrowing her vision. She wanted to glance at Birch to see if he believed she was marrying this man. "How dare you! I have never promised to wed you. You have no right to dictate anything to me." How could he say such things of this innocent babe? "I would like you to leave, Mr. Gray."

"Who is this man," he demanded. "Is he

the reason you refuse my suit week after week? Do not bother to deny it. I can see the truth in your face. This is the same captain with whom you made a spectacle of yourself last fall, is that not right?"

"The lady asked you to leave her home."

The rage in Birch's face frightened Hannah. Birch must not do anything to jeopardize himself. He was an outsider here and a Tory.

"Just go, Birch," she said quietly. "I shall handle this." She turned to Nathan. He had deceived her. She would never have imagined he could be so angry and jealous. That part of his personality had been well hidden from her. "Please leave, sir."

"Oh, I shall leave. But I will be back with the town elders. You will not escape their judgment so easily this time. I will not defend you again, Hannah." He stomped toward the door and slammed it behind him.

Birch came up behind her and put his arms on her shoulders. "I have done you no favors this trip. You will have more trouble now."

She gave a long, low sigh. "In truth, he will agitate the elders against me. But they were already angry when they saw me in breeches. I was painting the lighthouse

301

when a ship needed rescuing. The towns-people all saw me dressed immodestly."

"I should like to have seen that sight," he said with a twinkle in his dark eyes. "Come away with me, Hannah. We will take the goat and the babe and sail the seas together."

A wild longing gripped her, and she trembled with the temptation of it. She swallowed hard. "I cannot, Birch. I am needed here, and there is still the matter of your relationship with God. He has not yet given me leave to follow my heart. He may never."

His face darkened. "God, always God. Is he so important to you, Hannah? What of me?"

A sob tore from her throat. "He is everything to me, Birch. I would not disobey him and hinder him from his work in your life."

"He has no place in my life," he spat out. "He has taken everything from me and still withholds the thing I covet most." He spun on his heel and stormed out the door.

Hannah flinched at the slam of the door. Tears trickled from her eyes and dripped onto the folds of Charlotte's nappy. Why must their times together always end in pain and discord? She shook her head wearily and went upstairs. She spent the rest of the hours until bedtime arranging the baby's room and trying not to think of Birch. It was difficult with this tiny reminder.

The next morning she fed the child and dressed in her most somber gown and stomacher. She was ready when the men came for her.

CHAPTER 23

Lydia laughed gaily and smiled at her guests as she moved through the party and mingled in the crowd like the skilled hostess she had become, but she felt anything but happy. How was she to tell Galen? Her stomach roiled at the thought.

Hugh had been patient with her for two months, but his patience was gone. The house he had provided was lovely, with high ceilings and imported rugs, pretty things and tasty delicacies for her, but Hugh expected something in return. Something she was unable to give. Why had she not expected something like this to happen? She had been foolish. Willful and foolish. Tears pricked the back of her eyes, but she suppressed them. She must not disgrace herself further.

"Having a good time?"

Lydia jumped. Hugh Montgomery had come up behind her in utter silence. He often did that, moving so quietly through the house like a cat, and she would turn and find him there. It was quite unnerving. She forced a brittle smile. "Lovely."

"You look a little pale. Are you feeling well?" His pale-blue eyes bored into hers. "I wouldn't want anything to spoil our evening. Especially . . . later." He leaned forward and kissed her cheek. "Our guests will be leaving soon."

Bile rose in her throat. She couldn't go through with it. She just couldn't. Galen would understand when she told him the reason. But how could she tell him when he avoided her? She stared at him with longing. He stood near the window laughing with two ladies who were obviously besotted with his blond good looks. Jealousy tugged at her heart. He didn't look at her that way anymore. Now he stole in by cover of night and was gone before daybreak.

She smiled until she thought her face would crack. Hovering as near Galen as she dared, she waited for an opportunity to talk to him. He glanced at her several times, and she tried to signal him with her eyes, but he always turned away. Near tears, she wandered away and slipped across the hall to the library. After shutting the door behind her, she sat in a chair in the darkness and buried her face in her hands.

Sobs shook her body, and she hugged herself to keep them quiet. It would never do for the guests to see her terror and despair. After a few moments she took a deep breath and stood. She would have to smile again and go back before Hugh missed her. With her hand on the doorknob, she felt it turn and stepped back into the shadows. A dark figure entered the room, but she stayed silent until she heard a whisper.

"Lydia, are you in here?"

Galen. He had seen the plea in her eyes and come to her. She rushed forward with a soft moan. "Here I am, my love."

He shut the door behind him. "What is wrong with you? There was no missing the way you were mooning over me, and I had no choice but to follow you. You must stop it. If Montgomery were to find us, I would be sent to the front of the fighting. Is that what you want?"

"No, no, Galen. But I had to speak with you." She wrung her hands. "Hugh presses me. He says he is staying with me this night. I cannot do this when I love you."

"You should have thought of that before you agreed to this plan, Lydia. Now wipe your eyes like a good girl, and pull yourself together. We must go back to the party. By this time tomorrow, you will wonder what all the fuss was about." Galen spoke to her as though to a recalcitrant child and took her arm.

She wrenched her arm from his grasp. "No, Galen, you do not understand! I-I am with child." There. She had said the words, though she wished she might have broken the news to him more gently.

"With child? You are *with child*?" Galen was no longer whispering but nearly shouting. "You little fool! How could you let this happen?" He took her by the shoulders and shook her. "You listen to me, Lydia! You are going to wipe your face and go back to that party with a smile. You will coo and woo Montgomery this night. When he discovers you are breeding, he will think the child is his. Do you understand me?"

She stared at him in disbelief. The moonlight through the window illuminated his face, eyes bulging and mouth twisted with anger. She swallowed hard and nodded.

The door swung open, and a figure stepped through and shut the door again. "I, too, understand, Galen. Now I finally see why Lydia turns from my kisses and caresses."

Hugh Montgomery looked like a vengeful

fiend in the moonlight. His lips were drawn back to reveal his teeth, and she could see the glare of his eyes. Lydia's vision doubled and the room swam. She clung desperately to consciousness. She must not faint. Curling her fingers around the back of a chair in front of her, she took a deep breath.

Galen took a step back. "Major, I know not just what you heard, but —"

"Do not bother with trying to deceive me further, Lieutenant. You were trying to pass your by-blow off on me. Obviously, you have been enjoying Miss Huddleston's favors while I have been paying the piper." Montgomery spat out the words.

"I had no idea of this until tonight, Major," Galen said.

Montgomery glared at Lydia. "So, miss, tell me the truth. I will be able to tell if you are lying, and you will not like the consequences. Have you entertained this man since you moved here?"

Lydia had no strength for lies. His merciless stare left her legs weak. "Yes, Major."

"How many times?" The implacable voice demanded an answer. Even though Galen threw her a pleading glance, she could not refuse to answer. "At least three times a week," she whispered.

Montgomery shook his head. "I am a fool,

a bloody fool." He drew a deep breath. "You will pack your belongings and be gone this night, both of you. I do not want to ever look on either of you. Lieutenant, I will transfer you to General Howe's unit, effective immediately. I care not what you do with your strumpet." He turned and stalked from the room.

Lydia crumpled to the floor. She had failed Galen. He would go into the heat of the battle after all, and her baby would be fatherless. She burst into noisy sobs.

"Fie, you cry now. Why could you not have shed those tears sooner and saved us this disgrace?" Galen said through tight lips. "If you had begged him, he might have relented."

She couldn't answer him; she had no strength for words. "We can go away from here, Galen. I can come with you as other women do. When we are wed and the babe is born, we will forget this rocky start."

He stared down at her incredulously. "Are you mad? Do you think I would wed you when you have lost me everything?" He turned away from her. "I cannot speak to you now, or I would throttle you." He strode from the room and slammed the door behind him.

She stared at the shut door and stumbled

to her feet. He couldn't leave her. He loved her, and she loved him. They belonged together. She pulled the door open, and a group of curious onlookers stared at her ravaged face. She stumbled past them and hurried up the steps. She would gather her things and go back to their home. Galen would have calmed down by then.

In a near frenzy she stuffed her clothes into her valise, snatched up her cape, and ran back downstairs. The guests had departed and she saw Montgomery, his head bowed, sitting in front of the window. She hesitated at the sight of his dejection. He raised his head and saw her standing there.

"I really cared about you, Lydia," he said with a twisted smile. "I had even thought to wed you." He gave a short bark of laughter. "I, the son of an English earl, was ready to wed another man's doxy."

Her face flamed at the term. She was no doxy. Hadn't she proved that by keeping herself only for Galen? She stood mutely, unsure of what to say.

He scowled. "Take your pity and leave me." When she hesitated, he stood and pointed a finger toward the door. "Go, I tell you. Go to your lover and leave me in peace. If I see you again, I shall offer you to the men in camp."

She gulped, knowing it was no idle threat. "I-I did like you, Hugh," she said in hushed tones. "If I had met you before Galen, mayhap —" She broke off at his glare of rage. "Farewell."

She took her valise and let herself out into the heavy spring air. The black night closed in on her, and she hugged her valise to her chest. She had never been out at night in New York unaccompanied. If she had money, she would have hailed a carriage. The rocks and stones bit through her thin slippers and hurt her feet before she'd gone two blocks, but she hurried on. She had to get to Galen.

A candle glowed in the parlor of the small house she had thought of as home. Galen was here. A wild tide of joy gripped her heart. Until that moment she hadn't realized how fearful she was that he would just leave her behind. The door was unlocked, so she let herself in. She set her valise down by the front door, then tiptoed into the parlor.

Galen looked up. "I thought you would come." He shook his head. "What are we to do, Lydia?"

She hurried toward him and knelt at his feet. "We will be all right, my love. We have each other. And Hannah. She would help us, she and her captain."

His head jerked toward her. "Her captain? Meredith has come back?"

She nodded. "I think they will wed."

"Never." His blue eyes narrowed. "I shall have a word with Molly, and we shall see what we can do about ridding ourselves of the good captain."

Lydia frowned. "Why do you care, Galen? Hannah's nothing to you."

He shook his head again. "You weary me, Lydia. You are like water dripping on stone. I must get away from you before you wear me down to nothing."

He wasn't making any sense. She took his hand and kissed the palm. "Come to bed, love. Things will not seem so grim come the morrow."

"You go to bed, Lydia. I shall be gone when you awaken." He rose and picked up a bag by the door. "I do not intend to fight. Mayhap Washington's troops can use me."

Lydia gasped. "You would betray England?" She stood and followed him to the door.

He chuckled, a dry rattle with no real mirth. "It would be a way to keep my head on my shoulders. But no, I would not do that. I will offer my services to Howe as a spy. Methinks he can use me there."

"You cannot leave me, Galen." She clutched at him with desperate hands. "Take me with you."

He seized her wrist and tore her hand from his arm. "I should never have taken you in, Lydia. You have become like a viper in my bosom. I do not want to ever see you again." He stomped from the room without a backward glance.

She cried out and ran after him, but he shook her off and slammed the outer door in her face. She wrenched it open, but he disappeared in the fog. Eyes burning and throat sore from sobbing, she fell to the floor in a paroxysm of weeping. She had thought she had no more tears left, but she was wrong.

After several long moments, she pulled herself wearily to her feet and shut the door. She felt lifeless, drained. What was she to do? She had no money, no friends. The so-called "friends" she had made while with Hugh wouldn't help her. If she went home to Hannah, her sister wouldn't turn her away, not even with a babe in her belly. Of course, she'd have to take whatever punishment the town elders ordered, but anything would be better than being alone. But Gurnet was too far to walk, and she had no money for a stagecoach.

She shivered and went up the stairs. She would think of something tomorrow. She crawled into bed and wept again at Galen's scent on the sheets.

Vendors hawking their wares on the streets below awakened Lydia. The sun was high overhead when she pushed back the bedclothes and stumbled out of bed. She threw open the shutters and looked down onto the street. The newsboy shouted about the latest battle, carriages rattled across the cobblestone streets, and soldiers practiced their movements on the field behind the house. Everything seemed so normal, so familiar. But the reality of her situation seemed all the more dire against the normalcy of the day.

She was penniless, friendless, and pregnant. Her situation couldn't get much worse. She pulled her gown and petticoat over her shift and rummaged for her stomacher. Her stockings had a hole, but she didn't care. She combed her hair and put it back up, then went downstairs to find something to eat.

There was not much food in the kitchen. A crust of bread and some tea was all she could find. What had Galen eaten? After she'd finished, she took a deep breath and sallied forth to see what could be done about her situation. By two o'clock she was disheartened. Hugh refused to see her, as did the few women she would have called her friends. They had all been at the party last night and knew of her fall from grace. Her last hope was Major Grayson, who had spoken kindly with her on several occasions. She assumed he would refuse to see her as well, but she had to try.

His office was empty when she stepped inside the door. The soldier who usually manned the desk must have been on a break. She hurried to the major's inner office and knocked on the door.

"Come."

Lydia pushed open the door at the peremptory command and stepped inside. His gray head bowed at what appeared like maps, Major Grayson looked up at the sound of the door. His blue eyes widened at the sight of her. "Miss Lydia!" He stood and came around the desk. "What are you doing here? And unescorted?"

At his kind voice Lydia burst into tears. "I had no one else to come to, Major. Please do not turn me away." Hopeful for the first time, she clung to his hand.

He patted her shoulder and guided her to a chair. "Sit down, miss. I was just about to enjoy a cup of tea. Surely you would join me." He picked up the teapot and poured the steaming liquid into a cup. After handing it to her, he poured one for himself and sat in the chair next to her. "Now tell me what troubles you, my dear."

In a frantic burst of energy, Lydia spilled the story. His face grew graver and more disapproving as she told of her abandonment and condition.

"You have been foolish, my dear. What can I do? I do not know of a midwife in the city, though I am sure there are some. Mayhap you could find one and rid yourself of the babe."

Lydia placed a protective hand on her stomach. "Major, I would not kill Galen's child. I know he will want us both when he has time to think." She was certain of that fact. He loved her, she knew he did. He was just upset at the destruction of his plans.

Major Grayson shrugged. "Then what do you wish of me?"

"A-a job, mayhap?" She stuttered at the shuttered expression on his face. He wouldn't help her. She placed her cup on the desk with trembling fingers. "I can see I should not have come. I will go, Major. I cry you mercy for disturbing you." She stood on wobbly legs.

He held out a hand. "A job, you say? Mayhap I would have something. Sit, Miss Lydia, and we will discuss it."

A wave of relief left her giddy. She eased back into the chair. "What kind of job, Major?"

"Would you like to serve England?"

"Oh yes," she breathed. "More than anything."

He nodded with satisfaction. "I have need of a spy in Washington's camp, and I think you might suit for the position."

"A spy?" Lydia's heart pounded. "I reported events in Gurnet to Major Montgomery's men when I lived there with my sister, so I have some experience."

He laughed. "All the better. What I have in mind is a bit more dangerous than that, I fear. But I will pay you handsomely, and when the time comes, I will make inquiries and obtain a competent midwife for you." He rose and patted her shoulder. "You need not fear, Lydia. I will take good care of you."

Lydia stared into his smiling eyes and felt a niggling sense of unease, but she squelched it. This was her only hope, her only chance to salvage her life. If she could help England win the war, she and Galen could go there and have the perfect life she dreamed of. She didn't care what she had to do.

Chapter 24

The men were seated at a table in the front of the church while Hannah stood facing them with Charlotte in her arms. The censure in their faces made her mouth go dry.

"Well, Mistress Hannah, I see we have you before this body once again." Town elder Marcus Reynolds glared at her over his heavy eyebrows. "I had hoped you had learned from your sister's example."

Hannah bit her lip and reminded herself that the Good Book said to have respect for those in authority over you. It was difficult, though, when she felt the men were being so unfair. She curtsied. "I cry you mercy, Elder Reynolds, but may I know what the charges are against me?" She had a pretty good idea, but she wanted to hear the men say exactly what they held against her. She looked around the room at the men seated there. Nathan refused to meet her gaze, and she felt a stab of hurt.

Mr. Reynolds looked through the spectacles perched on his nose at the book in front of him. "Appearing in public with immodest dress, consorting with a known Tory and entertaining him without a chaperone, and bastardy."

Bastardy. Hannah gasped. She had expected the other, but could they honestly believe the child was hers? She glanced down at Charlotte, sleeping peacefully in her arms. She would be interested to hear how they planned to accuse her of that crime.

"What say you, mistress?" His stringent voice broke through her musings.

"I am not guilty of any of these things, sirs."

"That remains to be seen." He turned to Roger Newsome. "You may present your accusations, Mr. Newsome."

Newsome, a balding fisherman with ferret eyes, stood and cleared his throat. He didn't look at Hannah. "Gentlemen, I was shocked to see Mistress Hannah Thomas clad in men's breeches the day the *New England* went down. She exposed herself in this immodest fashion to men from the village as well as sailors from the ship. Even after the danger was over, she continued to parade

320

herself in men's clothing."

The murmur of disapproval echoed in the room, and Hannah flinched. She doubted they would even listen to her explanations.

"Mr. Gray, present your testimony."

Hannah blanched. Though she knew he would not defend her, she didn't expect him to speak against her. She stared at him, but he still refused to meet her gaze.

Nathan stood and shuffled his feet. "I regret to tell you all that I found Mistress Hannah entertaining Captain Meredith just yesterday. There was no chaperone present. We reprimanded her for consorting with this known Tory just last fall. Obviously, she did not listen to our advice."

He finally met her gaze, but no pity dwelled there. A tear escaped, but his face still didn't soften. "Finally, there is the matter of the babe. I wonder if this is her own child that has been hidden away. She introduced her as her own daughter."

Caught by her own words. Her arms tightened around Charlotte. Charlotte's dark curls were very like her own, which would be damaging. But she would have a chance to defend herself. *God help me. Give me the right words to reach them.*

Mr. Reynolds gestured to her. "You may defend yourself, mistress. What say you to these charges?"

Hannah took a deep breath. "As to the charge of wearing men's breeches, it is true, sirs." A mutter of anger spanned the room. "But I was painting the lighthouse when the wreck occurred. It was not safe or modest to do so in a dress, and since I was alone at my home, I thought it would be permitted to do what was necessary in privacy. If I was to save the shipwrecked men, there was no time to change clothes."

The censure slackened on the faces of some of the men, and two of them nodded. Encouraged, she went on. "As to consorting with Captain Meredith, I was not expecting him. He found this babe with her dead mother and brought her to me. He knew of my childlessness and thought I would welcome a daughter of my own. From the moment he placed Charlotte in my arms, I was her mother. But she is not the child of my own body, sirs. Surely you cannot believe such a horrendous lie."

"He is a Tory. You should not have allowed him access to your home." Mr. Reynolds glowered.

"He was a friend, sir. I would not turn a friend away, no matter what his political persuasion." Hannah didn't know what else she could say. She spoke the truth. Surely they could see the accusations were lies. "And the child would have died without his intervention. Surely, that should account for some sympathy from you."

"We will retire and discuss this matter," Elder Reynolds said.

The men filed out of the room. One or two cast a sympathetic glance her way, and she took heart at their concern. Charlotte slept the entire time they were gone.

After nearly half an hour, the men came back in. She couldn't tell from Mr. Reynolds's expression which way the vote had gone. What would they do to her if they found her guilty? She found it difficult to breathe as she waited for them to be seated.

Mr. Reynolds steepled his fingers together and stared at her over the tops of his hands. "Mistress Hannah Thomas, we find you guilty of these charges."

She gasped and put out a hand to steady herself. A tide of heat swept up her neck and face. Guilty! How could this be? Did these men not listen to God at all? Were they so caught up in appearances and censure they had no compassion? What had she expected, though? They had dealt harshly with Lydia as well.

"After much discussion of your punishment, we have decided on a whipping of the prescribed ten lashes for bastardy. I know this may be less of a punishment than you expected with three charges against you, but in light of your gender and your occupation, we have decided to be lenient."

A whipping. She felt faint.

"However, there is one recourse for you to avoid this punishment. Mr. Nathan Gray has generously agreed to take responsibility for your future actions if you consent to become his wife. I think you will agree this would be an acceptable ending to this matter." Mr. Reynolds appeared pleased, as though he had personally thought of this solution.

Hannah clung desperately to her composure. She must not act like a fishwife, though she longed to throw accusations in Nathan's face. His pleased smile infuriated her. He thought he had her, did he? He would find out differently.

"When is the punishment to be carried out?" she asked quietly.

Nathan's smile faltered, and Elder Reynolds frowned. "Did you not hear me, mistress? There will be no punishment. Mr. Gray has agreed to wed you."

She lost the tenuous grip on her temper. "But I have not agreed to wed him. You would have me wed a man who manipulated me and lied about my good name? A man who does not know the meaning of the word *truth* and who mocks this court's justice? Nay, sirs, I would rather suffer any punishment than that. You are guilty of straining out a gnat and swallowing a camel."

Red suffused Nathan's face. He jumped to his feet and pointed his finger at Hannah. "Must we listen to more of this woman's slander?" he shouted. "She chooses the lash rather than comfort as my wife, so let her feel its sting today. Have we need to wait?"

The angry murmur swelled in the room, and the men rushed forward to take her. Charlotte was ripped from her arms, and her frightened wail pierced Hannah's heart. Rough hands bore her outside. She was thrust against the whipping post and her hands tied to it. It happened so quickly, she barely had time to be frightened. Someone, she could not see his face, ripped her dress from her back and laid it bare to the whip.

She cried out at the first bite of the lash and writhed to get away from the second. The knotted cat-o'-nine-tails sliced through her skin with each stroke. The fury in the lash made her wonder if Nathan held the whip. Her body spasmed with each stripe, her breath whistling through her teeth in agony. Finally, it was over. The men untied her, and she crumpled to the ground.

Her back screamed when she tried to move. She gathered the tattered pieces of her bodice to try to cover as much of her body as she could. She cried out in pain and forced herself to her feet. Looking around, she found that all of her accusers had gone, though several onlookers still gaped and called out rude jeers. She staggered back to the church. As she neared the front door, she could hear Charlotte's frantic wail.

Barely hanging on to consciousness, she pushed open the door and stumbled inside, away from the curious spectators and the shame of her ordeal. Charlotte had been left on the hard floor alone and wept piteously at her abandonment.

"There now, sweet one. Mama's here." Groaning from the exertion, she lifted the baby into her arms and sank into a pew. How was she to get home? She did not have the strength to walk home with Charlotte in her arms. No one in town cared enough about her to help her. *God, help me. I have no strength left.* Tears fell onto the babe's face, and Hannah wiped them away with a trembling finger.

After a few moments, she struggled to her

feet again and moved toward the door. She had to try. She couldn't stay in this place all night. Charlotte was hungry, and Hannah knew her wounds would need treatment.

Olive could help her. She lurched outside and found the streets nearly deserted. Thankful to escape more prying, derisive eyes, she shuffled painfully down the street toward home.

The city limits were still in sight when she was overtaken by a mule and wagon. The man who drove it was a stranger with kind brown eyes and a steady smile. "Have you need of a ride, mistress?"

"You are an answer to prayer, sir." She climbed into the back of the wagon. The sweet smell of hay was comforting, and favoring her back, she lowered herself into its welcome softness with a muffled groan. "Thank you most kindly."

He smiled and flicked the whip over the mule's head. "I intended to pass you by, but God bid me to help you. Thank him, not me."

Hannah let out a weary smile. "I did the moment you stopped, sir." In spite of her pain, she felt a deep joy to know that God had seen her in this hour of great need. Just that encouragement strengthened her.

The lurch of the wagon lulled her to sleep,

and when she awoke the wagon had stopped outside her house. Groggy, she sat up. Charlotte had fallen asleep as well. Hannah gathered the babe into her arms and tried to scoot to the edge of the wagon. Tears sprang to her eyes at the pain in her torn flesh.

"Let me help you." The farmer jumped from the seat and hurried around to the back of the wagon. He gently helped her to her feet and lifted her and Charlotte down. "Is there anything else I can do?"

She shook her head. "Thank you, but no. God bless you, sir."

He tipped his hat. "And you, mistress." He sprang back into the seat and the wagon rattled away.

Hannah stood watching him a moment, then went inside the house. Charlotte was fretting for food, so she placed the baby in the bed and, moving stiffly, took a bottle of milk from the springhouse. She poured some into a cup and went to feed the baby. It was hard getting Charlotte to drink from a cup. She still wanted to suckle, but the goose quill Hannah tried had proved to be a failure. It took nearly an hour, but the baby finally managed to fill her stomach. She fell asleep with her head on Hannah's bosom, and Hannah laid her in the crib.

She needed to try to cleanse her wounds, but the thought of managing the stairs was too painful to contemplate. She curled on the sofa with her back exposed to the air and slept again.

The shadows were long when a knock on the door woke her. She was in no shape for company. She glanced out the window and breathed a sigh when she recognized the Thomas family carriage. Slowly and painfully, she made her way across the room to the front door.

Olive's smile faded when she saw Hannah. Her mouth formed an O, and she put a hand out to her sister-in-law. "We heard what happened."

Hannah leaned against the doorpost for support. She opened her mouth to explain, but for some reason the room wouldn't stop spinning. Stephen stepped forward to catch her as she slid to the ground.

The lights. She must see to the lights. Hannah opened her eyes and tried to sit up. The cool cloth on her forehead fell to the floor. She couldn't see. The lights weren't lit. She forced herself to move though her back felt as if it were on fire. Struggling against the entangling bedclothes, she swung her feet to the floor. She could feel the bandages on her back. Olive must be here somewhere. And what of Charlotte? What would Olive do with her?

Her head spun, but Hannah felt much better than she had earlier. Her back still screamed, but the pain was manageable now. She struggled into a gown and shoes, then opened the bedroom door. Moving slowly down the hall, she could see Olive rocking Charlotte in the chair by the window. Holding on to the banister for support, Hannah descended the stairs. She must see to the lights, but she didn't quite know how she was going to climb those steep spiral steps.

Olive looked up at the slight sound Hannah made in the hall. "You are awake." She put the baby on a pallet on the floor and hurried toward her. "Faith, but you frightened me." She examined her from head to toe. "You look better. Would you like some stew?"

"The lights. I must light them," Hannah said. Her voice was hoarse.

"Stephen just went out to light them." Olive took her arm and led her to the sofa. "I heard what happened today. Why did you not call for me to come to your support? I would have reminded them whose money paid for most of the town." Her eyes sparked with retribution.

Hannah sagged into the cushions. "I regret I did not. By the time I realized how serious the situation was, they had seized me and tied me to the whipping post." She let out the breath she'd been holding. "I feel sorry for them, trapped in their rules and failing to see the true nature of God."

Olive shook her head. "Is it true they offered to stay your punishment if you would wed Nathan?"

Hannah nodded. "Why does he wish to marry me, Olive? He obviously bears no love for me if he would allow me to be publicly whipped."

Olive flushed. "I do not know the full story, but I overheard Mama offer to settle a sum on you if you would marry. She does not want you to carry the Thomas name. Harlis told her of his intention to wed you once the war was over. Nothing Mama said would dissuade him."

So that was it. Hannah understood now. Nathan had merely wanted the money Mother Thomas had offered. Why hadn't her mother-in-law asked her whether she intended to accept Harlis before trying to manage her life? Now the family was further disgraced by her whipping. She shuddered at the thought of facing the townspeople again.

Hannah sighed. "I see you and Charlotte have become acquainted. Did the local gossips tell you who she is?"

Olive's flush deepened. "It was said she is your and Captain Meredith's by-blow, but I told the silly wags it was not true. There was not even time for her to belong to the captain. You only met him eight months ago."

Hannah squeezed her hand, grateful for her defense. "We must put it behind us now. I care not what wicked tongues say. All that matters now is my daughter and my lighthouse."

"And the captain?"

Tears burned Hannah's throat. "I leave him in God's hands."

Galen sipped tea from the fragile teacup and smiled at Molly who perched on the sofa across from him. Her beautiful face was alert with interest since he'd stated his business of searching out spies in the city.

"You say you have information to give me?"

"Mayhap it is nothing, but I have heard whispers that Samuel Rivers might be a spy for the colonials."

"I have heard nothing of such rumors, but mayhap it would be intriguing if I found such information true. I dislike Samuel's associate Birch Meredith most heartily. Could the good captain be a spy as well?"

Galen kept his expression calm and shrugged. "I know not, mistress, but it would seem a possibility. Mayhap you can uncover more than I."

Her smile held triumph. "Believe you me, if such a matter exists, I shall discover. I thank you much for bringing me this information, Major."

"Of course. I am always at the service of the Crown and you, milady."

The thought of seeing Meredith eliminated from Hannah's presence brought him great joy.

Chapter 25

Birch held the spyglass to his eye and scanned the placid sea. Nothing. He longed for the sight of a white sail on the horizon, not that it would do him any good in this becalmed ocean. The British had grown canny, and he seldom saw an unescorted ship. They usually sailed in groups of three or more, and he had to watch them helplessly as they sailed past.

He sighed and put the spyglass down. He looked with longing toward the west. How was Hannah getting along with Charlotte? Several times over the past four months he'd almost set sail for Gurnet Point but had managed to restrain himself. What good would it do? Hannah had made her decision perfectly clear. Her God was more important to her than he was.

"Cap'n."

He turned at the sound of Riley's voice.

His first mate wore a worried frown. "What is it?"

"The mast has a crack in it, sir. We're only ten miles from New York. Shall we put in there and have it checked out?"

Birch frowned and stared at the mast above his head. "How serious?"

"Bad enough I would hate to test it in a gale."

Birch nodded. "Very well, put in at New York." He hated to waste the time, but he would regret it if an early nor'easter blew in and toppled his sail. Besides, it wouldn't hurt to check in with Rivers.

The September breeze teased strands of his hair from the ribbon at the nape of his neck, and he retied it. He leaned against the railing and stared in the direction of the city. Was Montgomery still there? He scowled. Someday he would pay for Charles's death. Someday soon. Birch had only agreed to stay justice for the sake of his country. Once they had shaken off Britain's shackles, he would make Montgomery pay.

Two hours later the ship glided into the harbor and dropped anchor. When they went ashore, Riley went to have the ship looked over while Birch pressed through the teeming throng and headed to Rivers's office. He'd forgotten how much he hated this city. The people, the noise, and dirt. It all made him long for the clean, salty wind in his face. A festival was in full swing, and revelers crowded the streets.

The office was deserted when he arrived, though it was only four in the afternoon. Dust and sand littered the floor, and the room had a musty, closed-up odor. The desks were still in place, and he pushed the door to Samuel's office open. He stopped and gaped a moment. Papers littered the floor, filing cabinets lay strewn about like blocks, and the desk had been upended.

Alarmed, Birch left the office and headed for Samuel's home. He had a sinking feeling that Samuel's true identity had been discovered. When he arrived at the house, he was relieved to see it looked inhabited. He knocked on the door. Hopefully, Samuel was home at this time of day.

The door swung open, and he stared into Molly Vicar's face. He took an involuntary step back. What was she doing in Samuel's house?

Her eyes widened when she saw him, then a smile lifted the corners of her mouth. A touch of malice glittered in her gaze. "Captain Meredith, we meet again. Please, come in." She stepped aside and motioned him in.

"Where is Samuel Rivers?" He didn't trust the gleam in her eyes, but he had to find out about Samuel.

"Let us not argue on the steps for the neighbors' enjoyment. Come to the parlor, and I shall explain what has become of Samuel Rivers."

Her dark eyes mocked him, and his sense of unease deepened. He wanted to turn around and escape from her presence. His throat tight with apprehension, he inclined his head in agreement and followed her to the parlor. She paused outside the parlor door a moment. "Go on in. I need to give my butler some instructions."

The parlor looked very different from when Samuel had lived here, more feminine and fashionable with silk wallpaper and floral rugs. Molly soon joined him.

Dressed in a green silk gown, she looked as though she were about to depart for a party, but she sat on the sofa and arranged the folds of her dress about her. "I did not think to have the pleasure of seeing you again, Captain," she drawled. She rang a small silver bell on the table for the maid. "We shall have some tea and get re-acquainted."

He bit back the sharp words on the tip of his tongue. He would get further by being pleasant.

She leaned back against the sofa and smiled at him seductively. "How good is your memory, Captain?"

"Very good." She was enjoying herself entirely too much. Birch leaned against the fireplace mantel and tried to act unconcerned.

"Then doubtless you remember what I told you the last time we met."

The maid brought a tray of tea and cookies and set it on the table. Molly leaned forward and poured two cups of tea. "Sugar?"

"No, thank you." He took the cup. He well remembered the last thing she told him. What did that have to do with Samuel?

She took a delicate sip of tea. "I told you I'd make a formidable enemy, did I not?"

"So you said."

She chuckled. "You sound as though you did not believe me. You will find I never exaggerate, Captain." She picked up a cookie and took a bite.

Hurried footsteps sounded in the hall, and the parlor door shuddered with the pounding of a fist on the other side. Molly's smile deepened as the door flew open and four British soldiers burst into the room.

Birch resisted the impulse to bolt from

the room. He must not act guilty.

"Is this the traitor Galen Wright told us about, Mistress Vicar?" A young lieutenant with sandy-blond hair and hazel eyes toyed with his saber as though he would like nothing more than to run Birch through with it.

Molly stood. "This is the man, Lieutenant." She turned to Birch. "You see, Captain, knowing of your relationship with Samuel, I had Galen investigate and found him to be a rebel spy. I know that does not mean you are also a spy, but Galen thought it likely. With a bit of persuasion, Samuel confessed your role in the recent loss of five of our British ships, and we hanged him. Your body will soon join his. Take him, Lieutenant."

Birch jumped forward and overturned the table. The first two soldiers stumbled into it, and he grappled with the third for several moments before tossing him into the path of the fourth soldier who had hurried forward to assist.

"Take him!" Molly screamed. "I shall have you hanged if you let him get away!"

Birch ran out the door with the soldiers hastily recovering their balance and following closely on his heels. One snatched at his jacket just as he reached the street, but he jerked loose and melted into the throng.

For once he was glad of the crowds.

He rounded a corner and paused in a dark alley to catch his breath. He heard their shouts and darted his gaze around for a place to hide. A discarded crate had been tossed beside the doorway of a brick building. He knelt behind it and drew his sword. He heard the men run past, and then their voices faded in the distance.

He rose with caution and peered around the corner. No sign of the soldiers. What should he do now? He didn't dare go back to the ship. Soldiers had likely been dispatched there as soon as Molly had summoned them. He hoped his men got wind of the news and didn't try to return to the ship either. New York was firmly in the grasp of the British. With Samuel gone, he had no choice but to find Washington's camp and tell him what had happened.

He waited in the alley until dark, then slipped into the crowds and made his way to a livery. No horses were available, so he gathered supplies and information until nearly midnight, then stole a horse outside the British headquarters. He had a long way to ride. Washington was at Philadelphia defending the capital from the British.

He pushed his horse as hard as he dared. Even so, it was three days of hard riding before he came to the outskirts of the Continental Army's camp along Brandywine Creek, twenty-six miles from Philadelphia. He was stopped by a sentry, then taken to General Washington.

"Captain Meredith!" Weariness lined Washington's face, but he stood and shook Birch's hand. "I hope you bring good news."

Birch slumped in the canvas chair the general indicated. "I fear not, General. Samuel Rivers is dead, hung as a spy, and my cover is blown as well." He still found it hard to believe. If only his mast had not cracked, he would still be at sea.

Washington was silent a moment. "He was a good man. What of his family?"

Birch shook his head. "Gone. I assume they found refuge somewhere."

Washington expelled a heavy sigh. "Get some rest, Captain. We will discuss your next assignment on the morrow."

Birch nodded and trudged through the camp. He passed a peddler woman who looked at him strangely. Did he look as bad as he felt? He unsaddled his horse and pitched his tent under a towering evergreen tree. After crawling inside, he was asleep within moments.

"Birch."

The hushed whisper penetrated his mind.

Was he dreaming? Moonlight streamed through the open flap of the tent and illuminated the figure huddled near his head. He sat upright and fumbled for his saber. He opened his mouth to shout for help.

"Birch, 'tis me, Lydia."

Lydia? His groping stilled, and he stared at her in the moonlight. This old hag? He narrowed his eyes. What trick was this?

Seeing the disbelief in his eyes, she pulled the wig off her head and revealed her golden hair. The color of her smooth skin had been altered somehow; it seemed dark and coarse. She moved closer. "Truly, Captain, 'tis Lydia."

"What are you doing here?"

"I might ask the same of you," she said with a toss of her hair.

That was the old Lydia. She never did like being questioned. She had to be a spy. That was the only explanation. "Where is Galen?"

Her eyes filled with tears. "I know not," she whispered. "I tried to find him, but he left orders no one was to tell me where he had gone." She took his hand. "Mayhap you could find out for me."

"Forget him, Lydia. He is a bounder."

Her shoulders shook as tears coursed down her cheeks. "I wish I could. I try, Birch, but I cannot stop any more than I can no longer breathe." She coughed, a fierce, convulsive spasm that left her gasping for breath.

"You are sick, Lydia. Let me fetch the doctor." He rose, but she put her hand on his arm.

"He would see beyond my disguise." She coughed again, then took his hand. "I want Hannah. My child and I need her."

His fingers tightened on hers. "You have a child?"

She smiled. "Not yet, but soon." She took his hand and guided it to her stomach. "Galen's son."

He felt a movement and jerked his hand away.

"Can you help me get home to Hannah?" She hesitated and dropped her eyes. "You owe her that much for the pain of the lashing she endured on your behalf."

He stared at her. "Lashing?"

"Ten lashes for bastardy with you. Her back was laid open."

He squeezed his eyes shut at the awful image her words summoned. He clenched his fists. Someday the men who had done this to Hannah would pay. "Is she all right?"

"She will be once she has me safely home. You know she would want you to help me. I know I wasn't always kind to you, Captain, and you have no reason to help me. But for Hannah's sake, I ask it anyway."

She was sick and pregnant. He should turn her in to Washington, but she was Hannah's sister. If he whisked her out of here, she could do no more harm. He told himself it was only for that reason that he would go back to Gurnet Point, but he couldn't still the sudden leap of his heart at the thought of seeing Hannah again. "Are you able to travel? It is a long trip."

"I will do what I must. Then when I am with Hannah again, you will find Galen and tell him he has a son."

The bounder. Did he know she was pregnant? Was that the reason he had cast her off?

Lydia saw the question in his gaze and dropped her eyes. "He will want me and the babe when he knows the child is a boy. No man would refuse to claim his son."

The desperate hope in her voice broke through Birch's resistance. She was deceiving herself. "You've been spying for Galen, have you not?"

She stared back at him. "Not for Galen, but yes, I've been reporting Washington's troop movements to the British as any good citizen would. Thanks to my work, several spies have been hung."

344

Even now she failed to see her own corruption. His lips twisted and he stepped back. "I'll take you."

Lydia clasped her hands together. "Thank you, Captain. I shall be ready to leave on the morrow." She pressed his hand again, then slipped back into the night.

Birch lay back down when she was gone, but it was a long time before he slept. His sleep was fitful, plagued by dreams he couldn't remember when he woke. He sighed at the bugle call and dragged himself up from his pallet. He felt as though he'd just lain down. He should tell Washington about Lydia, but he couldn't do it. He couldn't hurt Hannah any more. He'd get Lydia away.

He obtained permission from the general to take a few weeks' leave for personal business. The general was hesitant to let him go, but since Birch had never enlisted in the army, he had every right to do so. He assured Washington he would return as soon as he was able. Birch rounded up some supplies and waited for Lydia by the creek.

She came rattling down the track on a cart pulled by a sway-backed mule. Even though he knew it was she, this dirty, unkempt peddler bore no trace of her true identity. She smiled at him, and he swung onto his horse and led the way north.

They talked little as they traveled. The mule was so wayward, it took all her concentration to keep him from stopping and investigating the tasty tufts of grass on the side of the road. Birch was too tired to make conversation, though he was determined to find out how she came to be spying in the enemy camp. Duty demanded he turn her in, but love for Hannah stilled his tongue. At least he would stop her spying by removing her from camp.

They stopped for the night in a glen beside a clear stream. He tethered the horse and helped her down from the cart. Her face was drawn with fatigue, and she rubbed her back. "Sit and rest. I shall care for the animals."

She nodded and knelt beside the water. "Do you suppose I could have a bath?" she asked wistfully. "The fleas nearly drive me mad. I have a tin tub in the cart."

"I'll build a fire for hot water." He could do with a bath himself. Then he wanted to have a talk with her. He had to see if she had discovered any information that would be damaging to the revolution. If so, he had to keep her from giving it to the British.

While he set up camp, she heated several kettles of water and filled the washtub. She paused several times and rubbed her lower back. This trip would be hard on her. He set up a tent around the tub, and she smiled at him.

"You go first," she said. "I would hate for you to get any of these fleas."

"You bathe. I'll use the stream."

She looked more like herself after the bath. Her wig was gone, and her golden hair was clean and shining. Some of the darkness had disappeared from her skin as well.

He handed her a tin plate of beans and hard bread. "I need some answers, Lydia."

Her eyes darkened. "I have told you everything."

"What were you doing in the camp?"

"The same as you, obviously. We're two of a kind." She smirked. "Gathering information."

"How did you come to be there? I would have thought you would have stayed in New York with your friends." She looked away, but not before he saw the sparkle of tears in her eyes.

"I had no friends," she said softly. "An acquaintance arranged for me to become a peddler, and I thought I might as well do something useful for England. Besides, I hoped Galen would hear of my heroism and forgive me."

"And do you have any new information he would be proud of?" Birch desperately hoped not.

"Only the latest troop movements." Her eyes gleamed. "The information is vital. We shall surely pass a British unit on our way, and I can tell them. Washington plans a surprise attack on Howe's troops near Philadelphia on October fourth. He thinks he can retake the capital. If they heed my warning, we may yet see him hang in this year of the hangman."

Birch's heart sank. He must keep her from being suspicious or she would surely find a way to deliver the information herself. "I will find a loyal courier to pass the news to. Wait here." He strode off in the direction of camp. He would stay gone long enough to allay her fears. There was no way he would allow that information to get in the hands of the British.

CHAPTER 26

Hannah blew a stray strand of hair from her eyes and pummeled the bread dough in front of her. The day was unseasonably warm for October, and the exertion left her hot and sticky. Charlotte, happily banging a tin plate and cup, sat at her feet. She was beginning to toddle and had become quite a handful, but she had filled Hannah's days with purpose and delight. Hannah plopped the lump of dough into a bowl to rise and covered it with a damp cloth.

After stirring the stew that bubbled over the fire, she washed her hands and knelt beside Charlotte. "Well, darling, shall we go to the beach for a while and look for seashells?" She touched her daughter's dark curls lovingly.

The baby lifted chubby arms. "Shells," she said, excited, though it sounded more like "yells."

Hannah scooped her up and blew bubbles

on her sweet-smelling neck. Charlotte giggled and squirmed, and Hannah kissed her plump cheek. "Mama loves her little angel."

"Mama." Charlotte planted her small hands on Hannah's cheeks and lifted her face for another kiss.

A lump formed in Hannah's throat, and she silently thanked God for this baby. How had she survived the loneliness before Charlotte's arrival? Birch may have thought he saved the baby on his own, but Hannah knew God had caused him to pity the motherless mite. The Lord God had planned to give her a child of her own, and Birch was merely his instrument.

The thought of Birch made her heart ache. Where was he now? Was he even still alive? Surely she would feel his death in her soul. She closed her eyes a moment and prayed for his safety and for God to speak to him. She sighed and took Charlotte to the beach.

The sun beat down without mercy, and she squinted against the brilliant light shining off the water. She took off her mobcap, shoes, and socks, then removed Charlotte's shoes and stockings as well. Taking the baby's hands, she helped her walk in the soft sand.

Her daughter squealed with delight at the wet sand on her feet. "Yells." The baby jerked her hands from Hannah's and knelt in the sand. Her chubby fingers dug in the sand and held up a small shell for her mother's inspection. "Yell."

"Yes, angel, a shell." While the baby played in the sand, Hannah threw a quilt out and sat on it, burrowing her feet in the sand. The gritty sand felt good. Gazing across the blue sea, she strained her eyes for the sight of a white sail. No ships out there right now. She imagined standing on the rocking deck of a ship with the wind in her hair while she watched an exotic port like Singapore grow nearer. She sighed and shook her head. Such a thing would never be.

The afternoon shadows began to lengthen. Her dough would be ready to bake. Hannah shook the sand out of her quilt and rolled it up with her shoes and mobcap inside. She would retrieve them later. She carried it in one hand and scooped her daughter up in the other. Charlotte, sticky with wet sand, protested being removed from her favorite pastime. Hannah jiggled her and promised her a treat when they reached the house.

As she came up the sloping path from the beach, she saw a cart carrying a man and a woman lurching along the track from the village. Shading her eyes, she tried to make out the faces, but the sun blinded her. Who would visit her? She hadn't had any callers since Olive moved to Boston. Her mother-in-law had ignored her since she had refused Nathan and suffered a public whipping.

They would reach the house before she did. She groaned. She would have no time to become more presentable. With no cap, her hair down, and her feet bare, they would think she looked like a fishwife. Trying to brush the worst of the sand from her skirt, she hurried to meet the visitors.

The man's back was to her as he helped the woman, heavy with child, from the wagon. The woman looked vaguely familiar. Then Hannah gasped. "Lydia!" She ran forward. Pregnant. Lydia was pregnant. But at least she lived.

Lydia looked up, and she released a joyous smile. "Sister!"

The man set her on the ground and turned. Birch. Hannah's heart lurched and her steps slowed. Birch had found Lydia. He had not forgotten his promise to her. Tears burned her eyes, but she forced them back and quickened her pace again. Lydia opened her arms and stepped forward to greet her.

The unfamiliar bulge under Lydia's skirts felt strange as Hannah hugged her sister with one arm, the other occupied with Charlotte. Though her sister was plump around the middle, the rest of her was gaunt. It appeared that everything she'd eaten had gone for the baby.

Hannah frowned. "I shall have to feed you, Lydia. You are much too thin."

She could sense Birch's dark eyes on her, and she turned to greet him, then curtsied. "Captain."

"My daughter seems well."

My daughter. The words gave her a strange sensation, half pain, half joy. They would never share a child between them as long as he still carried that bitterness. And he carried it still. She could see it in the cynical twist of his lips. She swallowed the lump in her throat. "She is well and happy. As am I."

His eyes narrowed. "Your back?"

"Lydia told you?" She shook her head. "No matter. The skin is healed." Though she would carry the scars for her lifetime.

His hands clenched and unclenched. "I would avenge this travesty for you. Tell me who did this."

She shook her head. "I've already forgotten."

The grimness around his mouth softened, and he shook his head. "I know not what to make of you, Hannah."

His eyes told her more than his words. Love for her still glowed in his pirate eyes. She wanted to rush into his arms, to feel his lips against hers again, but Hannah kept a tight rein on her emotions. She would continue to pray for him, though. God could reach him when she could not.

She turned back to Lydia. The babe must be Galen's. She would ask no questions yet. Lydia would tell all when they were alone. " 'Tis almost supper time. Come bide at the table while I prepare your food."

Birch took Lydia's arm and helped her to the house. Hannah was touched by his obvious concern for her sister. He was a good man, a kind man. Why couldn't he give up his hatred? It ate at his soul and was the cause of the lonely expression hidden deep in his eyes. She could see his eagerness to hold Charlotte, to talk to the babe. She smiled secretly. He would soon find what a bright and lovable child she was. Mayhap her sweetness could reach him where Hannah had failed.

Birch seated Lydia in a chair. She held up her arms for the baby. "Let me keep her while you prepare supper."

. Hannah handed Charlotte to her and kissed the baby's head. "She will get sand on you."

"I care not." Lydia seemed delighted with the baby and sang to her. Hannah had forgotten what a sweet voice her sister had. Charlotte stared at her with wide eyes and reached up to touch a lock of golden hair.

Hannah smiled and turned to find Birch's eyes on her, not the pretty picture Lydia and Charlotte made. Her smile faltered. "The tide is coming in." The intensity of his gaze took her breath away. The loneliness in his eyes touched her as nothing else could, but she could change nothing so long as he clung to his hatred.

The parlor faced the water, and the sea blew its salty tang through the window. Birch took a deep breath of the briny air. "Ah, the smell of the sea. I shall stroll along the beach after supper. I have been away from it too long."

"You can see we just came from there. I must look a sight."

His gaze traveled from Hannah's bare head to her toes just peeking under the soiled hem of her skirt. His lips twitched, then he gave up the fight to keep the smile from his face. "You look lovely. Like a mermaid."

"You *have* been away from the sea too long. It has addled your brain." Still, his words gave her a warm glow. The softness in his eyes when he called her a mermaid told her how special that compliment truly was. "I would call you home, if I could." She gazed into his eyes.

"I have been away from you too long."

She stared into his sober eyes. The long moment hung between them like an actual touch. She tore her gaze away. "I must prepare supper. You are both probably starved."

"Can I help?" he asked.

Part of her longed to get away from his probing gaze while another part wanted him in sight at all times. She gave up the struggle. "You could cut the bread while I ladle up the stew." He followed her into the kitchen. "Smells good, especially after eating my own poor attempts for the past few weeks. Lydia was in no shape to do any cooking after traveling hard every day."

Hannah washed her hands and began to ladle the stew. She put the bowls on the table and turned to face Birch. "How did you come to find her? Where is Galen? The babe is Galen's, is it not?"

He nodded. "The scoundrel tossed her out when he found out she was breeding. I found her in Washington's camp masquerading as a peddler."

Hannah put a hand to her throat. "She-she was spying?" She felt as though she couldn't breathe. How could Lydia do such a thing? The dangers to which she had subjected herself and the unborn babe were too horrifying to contemplate.

Birch looked away. "Aye. At least she wasn't selling herself. There were others there who were."

That much was a comfort, but still Hannah clenched her fists. She wanted to march to the parlor and demand an explanation from Lydia for her behavior, but it would do no good. Lydia had never seen her actions as traitorous to her country. She would not begin now just because her sister chastised her.

Hannah stared at Birch. "What were you doing in Washington's camp? Were you spying as well?" She narrowed her eyes.

She saw his hesitation, the way he looked away from her probing gaze, and her heart sank. She didn't wait for him to admit it. "You were spying." She gripped the back of the chair and sat down. Somehow this seemed worse than the fact he was a Tory, a loyalist.

"And if I was? Would that change your

feelings for me?"

Did it? She examined her heart and discovered it changed nothing. She was helpless to stamp out this love she carried for him. She swallowed hard. "No." If she could, she would tear this love from her heart, but it was as though he were part of her.

His dark eyes glowed, and he moved toward her. "There is something I must tell you. I am not what I seem."

She stared at him in puzzlement. "You are not a ship's captain?"

He grinned. "Yes, that I am, but not for the British. I serve General Washington as he sees fit to use me. I had wanted to tell you so many times, but I had to hold my tongue to protect my cover."

"Y-you're not a Tory?" Her spirits lifted at this wondrous news.

He stroked her cheek. "Can you forgive me for deceiving you?"

"There's nothing to forgive. You were simply doing your duty." She laid her own hand over his and pressed her cheek against his palm. "Have you always been a rebel?"

"Always. It was British soldiers who killed Charlie." His black eyes grew even blacker, if possible. "The British must pay for that."

Mouth gaping, Lydia appeared in the

doorway of the kitchen with Charlotte in her arms. "You are not a Tory?" she shrieked. "You've lied to us all this time?"

Hannah snatched the baby from her sister. "This does not concern you, Lydia. I realize it is distressing to you, but I rejoice in this news."

"You would!" Lydia spat out. "I gave him important information to deliver to the British. You didn't deliver it, did you?"

Birch shook his head. "No, Lydia."

She bit her lip and looked as though she would say more, but her shoulders sagged. "Then all my work was for naught," she whispered.

Hannah rose to her feet. "Sit at the table. 'Tis almost ready." She ladled three more bowls of stew and placed them on the table. Putting Charlotte in her chair, Hannah took a cloth and washed the baby's grubby fingers, then sat beside her.

"I should like to say grace," she said. Lydia still seemed stunned from the news that Birch was not her ally, but she and Birch bowed their heads. Hannah closed her eyes. "Oh, Lord God, thank you so much for bringing Lydia and Birch safely here this day. We praise you for your protection and care. Bless now this food and bring us all into your kingdom. Amen."

" 'Men," Charlotte echoed.

Birch laughed at the baby's imitation. "Methinks she has heard her mama pray before." Hannah flushed. "We pray in the morning when we get up, at meals, and at bedtime. I am determined that my daughter know the true ways of God, that he is loving and merciful and sees to our needs if we but ask."

Lydia folded her arms over her chest, anger brewing on her face. "If that is true, why am I here without Galen? I need him as a husband and father to this babe."

Hannah's heart broke at the willfulness in Lydia's voice. Her sister still did not see that her own actions had brought about her downfall. "He sees to our needs, Lydia, not always our wants. We need to seek his will. Did you seek his will before you pursued Galen? I think not."

Lydia glared at her. "I should have known you would still persist in your hatred of Galen." She got up from the table and took her bowl of stew. "I shall eat in my room. Away from the likes of you!" She stalked from the kitchen.

Hannah sighed. "I did not mean to appear judgmental. Lydia has never seen anything as her own fault."

Birch's dark eyes probed her face. "And

what of those like my brother who are hurt through no fault of their own? Where is God in that?"

What could she say? How could she reach him? "I cannot claim to know the unsearchable ways of God, Birch. We see through a glass darkly, but God sees the entire picture. He works in ways we cannot see or comprehend. I want to show you something." She went to the parlor and carried her needlework back to the table.

Holding it upside down with all the colors and strings of thread crisscrossing the backside of the material, she held it out to him. "Can you tell me what this portrays?"

He took it and stared at it, then shook his head. "No, 'tis too jumbled together."

"Turn it over now."

He flipped it over to reveal a garden scene she had almost completed. "Lovely."

"Sometimes our lives look like the backside of that tapestry, all mixed up with no sense or pattern. But 'tis only the part we see, Birch. God sees the other side and is molding us to fit the picture he has in mind."

He was silent a moment. "I see no reason for Charlie's death. Are you saying God had a reason, a purpose?"

Hannah sighed. "He always has a purpose

for us. The Bible also says, 'Precious in the sight of the Lord is the death of his saints.' Charlie was a believer, you told me. Have you stopped to think about the fact that he is with the Lord now?"

Birch frowned. "But the pain and terror he went through first was a terrible thing. Why can you not understand that? I saw his body!"

Hannah pressed his hand between hers. He stood and pulled away from her, then stared out the window. Hannah stepped behind him and touched his back. "What happened to Charlie was horrific. But it would be even worse if you let it mold you into the wrong kind of man, a man filled with bitterness and hatred. Charlie would not want that."

She had to make him understand. "Your error is that you think this world is the reality. In truth, eternity is the reality and this life is but a shadow, a place to develop our character and grow more like Jesus."

He spun around, his dark eyes full of suffering. "You say this world is but a dream, a chimera? Then it should not matter if we marry or not, if we love or not." He took her in his arms, and his black eyes probed hers. "Can you say that this doesn't matter?"

He bent his head, and his lips claimed hers. Wild elation billowed through Hannah, and she clung to him as her only stability in a storm-tossed sea. He pulled her close, and she was lost in a tide of love and longing as vast as the ocean she dimly heard crashing on the shore. When he raised his head, she felt bereft.

She opened her eyes and took a deep breath. "I cannot deny the love I bear for you, Birch. But some things are more important than love. Your soul is more important."

"You can save me, Hannah. Tell me you will marry me, and I will not seek Montgomery's death." He gripped her shoulders. "Tell me!"

Shuddering, she pulled away from his grip. He still didn't understand. "I cannot save you, my love. You must look to Jesus for that."

CHAPTER 27

The surf pounding on the shore soothed Birch's battered feelings. Why did she torment him? He clamped his hands to the sides of his head. He couldn't get her words out of his thoughts. *"I cannot save you, my love. You must look to Jesus for that."* He wanted nothing more to do with Jesus. He had seen his brother follow God with his whole heart, but God had betrayed his love and trust.

He shouted into the wind and surf, "Leave me alone, God!" Then he stormed back to the house. He would just get his things and go. Maybe away from her gentle eyes, he could forget the storm in his soul.

The house was dark when he let himself back in. He picked up his haversack and walked out into the hall. Charlotte's door was open, so he stepped into the room. She lay on her stomach, one chubby leg out of the covers, her thumb corked in her mouth.

He leaned over the crib railing and covered her up. Touching her soft curls, he smiled at the thought that he had done at least one good thing in his life.

He slipped down the hall and stopped outside Hannah's room. Torn between saying good-bye or simply leaving, he stood with his hand on the doorknob. He closed his eyes and took a deep breath. He didn't trust himself in her bedroom. When she found him gone, she would understand.

The steps creaked under his weight as he slipped downstairs to the parlor. A shadow moved by the window, and he startled.

"Birch?" Lydia's voice was fretful. "What are you doing?"

He walked toward her. "Why are you awake? You went to bed hours ago."

She sighed. "You only thought I did. I sat on the steps and listened to Hannah lecture you first. Now I cannot get her words out of my head. Why does she blame me? I heard her say I never see anything as my fault. I only did what Galen wanted. How could it be my fault that he left me with a babe on the way?"

"I think that was the point, Lydia," Birch said dryly. "It was your fault you listened to Galen's lies. Anyone could see the type of man he is. You were foolish to believe him."

He pushed away a wave of irritation. Even now she was angry with her sister instead of Galen.

Lydia gripped his arm, her fingers digging into his flesh. "Galen loves me, Birch. I know he does. But he was bewitched by Hannah long ago. If he had never met her, things would be so different." Her voice was filled with malice. "I hate her!"

He took her by the arms and shook her. "Stop it, Lydia! Stop blaming Hannah for your own actions. Galen loves no one but himself. You are willfully blind."

She jerked herself away and almost fell. He put out a hand to steady her, but she stepped back again. "You are just as bad as Galen," she hissed. "You are bewitched by her as well. She looks at a man with those big green eyes, and he has no sense left." She sat in the chair and began to weep with helpless sobs. "I hate her. I hate her. I wish she would die."

She couldn't mean what she said. Birch knelt beside her. "You must get some rest, Lydia. You love Hannah — you know you do. You are not yourself tonight." He felt a stab of unease at her wild babbling. She sounded almost mad. He wasn't sure it was entirely safe to leave. Would she try to harm Hannah or Charlotte? It was too horrible to contemplate.

Her shoulders drooped. After a long moment she raised her head and stared at him in the moonlight. "Faith, but you are right. What on earth was I saying?" She sounded bewildered. "Of course I love Hannah. She would never do anything to harm me."

He released his pent-up breath and rolled his shoulders to alleviate the tension. She was calm now. It must have been a momentary fit of hysteria. "Let me help you to bed. You shall feel better in the morning."

She clutched his arm. "You will look for Galen, will you not? He is likely to be in one of the rebel camps. He thought to act as a spy for General Howe."

"Oh, I shall look for him all right," he said grimly. He would look for him and see him hang as a traitor.

She stared at him uncertainly. His harsh voice must have frightened her. He put a hand on her arm. "You must get some rest. Come along now." He gently propelled her toward the stairs.

She stopped at the foot of the steps, her eyes wide. A pool of water at her feet glimmered in the moonlight. "My-my baby. It is coming!"

Birch didn't have much experience with childbirth, but he remembered the same thing happening before Charles was born. He scooped her into his arms and hurried up the stairs. Stopping outside Hannah's door, he hammered on it. "Hannah, the baby is coming!"

He rushed down the hall and put Lydia into bed. He would buy Hannah a new mattress. Before he could turn to see if she'd heard him, he heard the creak of Hannah's door, then her footsteps down the hall. He lit a candle and held it aloft as she came through the door.

He felt a surge of love for her when he saw her standing there in her nightgown with her dark curls hanging to her waist. Squeezing his eyes shut, he turned his back to her. He couldn't look at her, or he would take her in his arms and kiss her resistance away. He focused on Lydia.

"Her waters have broken." His uniform was soaked from carrying her up the stairs. "Shall I go for a midwife?"

Hannah stepped to the bed and placed a soothing hand on Lydia's head. "It will likely be many hours yet. Our mother often acted as midwife. I helped her many times, so I shall care for Lydia."

Lydia clutched her hand. "I want no one but you, Hannah. Am I going to die?" Her young voice was frantic.

"Of course not," Hannah said soothingly. "This little one wants to see his mama, and we shall oblige him."

Lydia lifted her lips in a weak smile. " 'Tis a boy. I know it, Hannah." She sighed, then her eyes widened. "Oh!" Grimacing, she put her hands on her stomach.

"The pains have begun?" Hannah asked.

Lydia nodded. "I am frightened, Sister." She sat up in bed and reached for Hannah's hand again. "Promise me you will care for my child if I die."

Hannah laughed. "You know that I would. Do not fret so. You will be fine. You are young and healthy. Now try to rest between pains. It will be a long night." She pushed Lydia back against the pillow. "Let me get you a dry gown."

She seemed almost startled to see Birch, as though she had forgotten he was there. "You may go to bed, Birch. I will see to Lydia."

He wanted to tell her he was leaving, but he couldn't leave until the baby was born. "Is there anything I can do for you?"

She shook her head. "Later you can fetch me some water, but it will be many hours yet." She touched his arm and smiled. "Sleep while you can. Soon there will be two children here with their demands." She seemed pleased at the prospect.

Birch grinned. "Methinks you would be happy with a dozen." What a wonderful thing it would be to have such a large, happy family. He could not still the thrust of hope the image gave him. But he would never have that family as long as Hannah was so stubborn.

She blushed. "Go now. I need to change Lydia." She gave a slight shove toward the door.

It took all Birch's strength to move toward the door. She looked so delectable with her hair around her shoulders like that. He wanted to bury his face in that mass of curls and inhale the sweet scent. He thrust his hands into his pockets before he did something he would regret. "Call me if you need me."

She nodded and turned back to her sister. "If you hear Charlotte, you might see to her."

"I will check on her." He pulled the door shut behind him and went down the hall. Peering into the baby's room, he saw the noise had not disturbed her at all. He pulled her door closed and went to his own room. Sitting on the edge of the bed, he pulled his boots off and removed his damp coat. He started to undress and put on a nightshirt, but he might be called out in the night. Shaking his head at his own vanity, he lay down on top of the bed fully clothed.

He was certain he would not be able to sleep, but to his surprise, the sun streaming through the window awakened him. He bolted upright in the bed. Had the babe arrived? No sound in the night had awakened him. Padding down the hall to Lydia's bedroom, he listened at the door. Nothing. He raised his hand to knock but heard sounds downstairs and let his hand drop.

Hannah looked up when he entered the kitchen. Her eyes were shadowed with fatigue, but she smiled when she saw him.

"How is Lydia?" he asked. She had dressed sometime in the night, and he wasn't sure whether to be glad for the reduced temptation or sad to see her prim and proper again. She wore a brown cotton-print gown with a tan stomacher, and her mobcap covered that glorious dark hair again.

"Holding up well. The babe likely will not make an appearance before this afternoon. The pains are not bad yet. She finally fell asleep, so I left to let her rest." She turned away and continued to shave tea into the caddy. "Would you care for some breakfast?"

"You rest, and I shall prepare it." He took the cube of tea and the knife from her hands and propelled her to a chair. "I'll watch Lydia while you sleep this morning."

She chuckled. "And what would you do if the babe began to come on your watch?"

He shrugged and grinned. "Bellow for you, of course. You would just be down the hall."

"I am tired. Mayhap I shall take you up on your offer."

"I shall insist on it." He dropped the tea caddy into the teapot and poured hot water over it, then set the lid on for it to steep. "I only know how to prepare porridge. Will that suit for breakfast?"

"I had thought to just have some bread and jam with tea."

"I can do that too." He cut slices of still warm bread — she had evidently baked it earlier this morning — and slathered them with butter and jam. "I see the goat has kept you in dairy."

"Quite nicely. Charlotte has thrived on the goat milk, and I have become quite adept at making cheese and butter." Hannah yawned and propped her head on her hand. "How did you happen to hear Lydia last night?"

His hands stilled, then he put the plate of

bread in front of her and poured two cups of tea. "I was leaving."

A shudder shook her shoulders, and she closed her eyes. "I feared that was what happened. You would leave without a farewell?"

"I did not trust myself in your bedroom." He didn't trust himself anywhere near her. She was as necessary to him as breathing, and it hurt to know she didn't love him the same way. It was easier when he didn't have to look in her face or hear the low melody of her voice. He finally dared a glance at her and saw two large tears slip down her cheeks.

"If you wish to leave me, I shall not stop you," she whispered. "I had hoped you would listen to my words last night. I failed you."

"They ring in my head, Hannah. But you must not blame yourself when I avenge my brother against Montgomery. When it is done, I will be at peace."

"You still do not understand. Hatred grows and feeds on itself. Once Montgomery is dead, the cycle will continue. You must give it to God, Birch. You are not strong enough to bear it. The Good Book says, 'Vengeance is mine; I will repay, saith the Lord.'"

"If I really believed that, I might be able

to do it. But I have seen no evidence of God repaying evil. Montgomery still walks the earth while my brother's bones molder in his grave." The word picture made him shudder. He had not been back to visit Charlie's grave since he was buried. He couldn't bear the thought of what lay beneath the gentle swell of green.

She shook her head. "Not necessarily in this world, my love. We may not see it until eternity."

"I would see it in this life. I will see it in this life because he will die by my hand." He pushed the plate of bread toward her. "Eat, love. Your concern does you justice, but you will not sway me from my purpose."

Tears filled her eyes. "You would throw our future away on mere vengeance? Am I so unimportant to you? You say God is more important than you are to me. Well, I say revenge is your mistress, and I'll not share you with her!" She rose and rushed from the room.

His stomach churning, Birch stared after her. Was she right? Was his vengeance more important? He shook his head. Who could argue with a woman? Hannah just left his head spinning with doubts. The sooner he left the better. Action would keep the thoughts at bay. He gulped his tea and went to check on the baby.

"Mama." Her tiny voice chattered gibberish, but her call for her mother was easily understood. He pushed open the door and went to get her.

She stood clinging to the rails of the crib, her dark eyes fixed on the doorway. When she saw Birch instead of her mother, her face puckered to cry.

"There now, darling," he said soothingly. "Come to Papa." As soon as the thoughtless words were out of his mouth, he flushed at what they revealed. He thought of Charlotte as his daughter. His and Hannah's.

He picked her up and made a noise of disgust. "Faith, but you are soaked." She smelled too. Holding her at arm's length, he looked around for clean clothes, and she would have to be bathed first.

He picked up a gown and nappy from the dresser and tucked it under his arm. Then still holding the squirming mite away from his body, he carried her downstairs. He poured hot water from the kettle into a bowl and undressed her. After setting her in it, he washed her with the bar of soap. She kicked and squirmed so hard, he had trouble holding on to her wet little body. Finally, she was clean, and he managed to get the nappy and gown on her.

She held her chubby arms up to him and chattered her incomprehensible sounds again. "You are a charmer. I hope you know that," he said with a smile. "Come here, sweet one." He picked her up and snuggled her against his chest. She smelled clean and fresh again. "You are going to get a new cousin today. Will you like having a playmate?"

As if the words had an impact on what was happening upstairs, Lydia cried out. His heart dropped, and he hurried up the steps with the baby in his arms. Dry mouthed, he paused at the door to Lydia's room. He could hear murmurs but could not make out any intelligible sounds. Tapping his knuckles on the door, he called out, "Can I do anything to help?"

"Just take care of Charlotte." Hannah's voice sounded strained. "Things are speeding up, and I cannot come out right now. Oh, and pray."

Pray? Not since Charlie's death had shattered his faith.

He paced back and forth in the hall. Charlotte squeaked a bit and gnawed on her fist. Shamed, he hugged her. "You are hungry. I should have realized." He carried her downstairs and plopped her in her chair.

Charlotte reached eagerly for the bread

and jam he offered and crammed half of it in her mouth at once. He laughed at her antics and watched to make sure she didn't choke. With half an ear listening for sounds from upstairs, he paced across the kitchen floor. How would he bear it if that were Hannah in such pain? He could hear the moans and screams from down here.

He sank weakly into a chair beside her. "I think having a baby the way we had you is much better." She seemed to be finished and raised her arms for him to pick her up. "You need another wash." Taking the still-wet cloth, he wiped the jam from her face and fingers, then took her from the chair and went into the parlor.

More noises erupted from upstairs, and he paced the floor some more. He should take Charlotte outside where they didn't have to listen to Lydia, but he wanted to be here if Hannah needed him. The morning trickled by like sand through an hourglass.

Finally, just before lunch, the thin, reedy cry of a newborn squeaked out. He released a huge grin and tossed Charlotte in the air. "Sounds like your new cousin is here."

She gurgled with joy and patted his face with her hands. He kissed her cheek and carried her upstairs again. Standing outside Lydia's door, he heard her voice. She was all right. Mother and baby were both all right. He didn't realize quite how worried he was until he knew that. Hannah had brought them through.

He rapped on the door. "We want to see the new baby."

"Just a minute." Hannah's voice sounded tired but happy. A few minutes later she opened the door with a weary smile. Her smile widened when she saw her daughter. "Want to see your new cousin, Charlotte? His name is John Galen."

The baby immediately put up a fuss. "Mama." She reached out for Hannah.

Birch handed her over, his gaze meeting Hannah's. This was life, real life. Sharing the raising of their daughter together and a houseful more. All he had to do was give up his vengeance and leave it to God. It sounded so simple. But so impossible. He dropped his gaze. He would leave in the morning.

Chapter 28

Galen slipped through the throng of soldiers and into his tent. He needed to gather his things and get away before the Continental Army engaged the British, even now massing across the field near Bemis Heights, New York. He'd had all he could take of General Benedict Arnold. The intrigue of the spying game had been fun, but not enough fun to stick around for the battle. He would especially be glad to get out of this vile northern countryside.

He stuffed his belongings in his haversack and slung it over his back. Poking his head out of the tent, he saw the army rushing to form their ranks. Mayhap it would be better to simply wait in his tent for them to leave, then sneak away under cover of darkness.

He pulled his head back inside before anyone could see him and debated about what he should do. It was all that stupid cow Lydia's fault he was even here. If not for her, he would be in New York attending winter balls and fetes and sleeping with the woman Major Hugh Montgomery desired. That had been a fine time. He had enjoyed laughing up his sleeve at the cocky major.

He released a heavy sigh. Now he was here in the dangerous countryside outside Albany, New York. He was hungry nearly all the time with a ragged uniform, holes in his boots, and fleas. He could have borne the first two, but the fleas nearly drove him mad. He felt like a peasant, scratching all the time. But soon he would be back in the British camp with hot food and fresh clothes. General Howe had promised him a promotion and a new position of authority in New York. He could thumb his nose at Montgomery. He smiled at the thought.

Finally the sounds of the departing army faded, and Galen peeked outside once again. The camp looked deserted. Now was his chance. He stepped outside and faded into the forest. Avoiding the well-traveled paths, he slipped away and made his way to the British camp at Fort Edward. It was deserted too, as the two armies formed battle lines, but he would wait. He was in no hurry to get shot for the British either.

It was already October — 1778 would be here soon. Galen never would have imagined Washington's ragged army could hold on for so long. But now that the French were in the war on the side of the Americans, he had high hopes the British would take this opportunity to crush both the fledgling country and their hated enemy, France. British honor would be at stake.

The sounds of battle drifted over the meadow. Shrieks of anger and pain, the clash of bayonets, the boom of the cannons and muskets echoed for over four hours. Galen paced the deserted camp. Why hadn't the British army squashed the American forces immediately?

The first soldiers who returned came bolting across the fields in full rout. Galen frowned and stopped the red-faced soldier who reached him first. "Hold, soldier. What has happened in the battle?"

"Total defeat," the man panted. "The Americans surrounded us. They may be here any moment. Take cover if you value your life." The man shook off Galen's hand and dashed away.

Defeat? That was simply not possible. Clinton's army was on the move this way too, and would bring reinforcements. All the men had to do was hold firm. But the panic of the returning men proved the seriousness of the situation.

After a wretched night Galen resolved to try to slip away as soon as he could. He didn't intend to be taken captive. He walked the length of the camp to decide how he might escape. On his way back to his cabin, he heard a familiar voice.

"Wright? What are you doing here?"

Galen rotated in a slow turn and stared into Montgomery's face. "Major Montgomery."

"I asked you a question. I heard you had defected to the Americans." His eyes narrowed. "You're spying for them, aren't you?" He grabbed Galen's arm. "You're under arrest, Lieutenant."

"No! I have been in the American camp spying for General Howe. I have important information for him." Galen tried to pull his arm out of Montgomery's grip.

"Likely story." Montgomery sneered. "Do you think I would believe anything you told me? We shall see what the commander has to say of this."

He propelled Galen through the camp to the commander's tent, and an hour later Galen found himself tossed into the brig, a small windowless cabin with a dirt floor. Over the next few days, he cursed Montgomery heartily and vowed vengeance. But heavily guarded, there was no opportunity to escape. Within a week he was sailing down the Hudson in chains to face charges of treason. It might take weeks to get in touch with Howe.

Birch tried to put Hannah's face from his mind. The hurt in her eyes when she'd told him good-bye had nearly broken his resolve. But she could have stopped him with a word. If she had told him she would marry him, he would have stayed at the lighthouse on the cliff with her and let Montgomery live. She had no one to blame but herself.

Her words kept echoing through his mind. *"I cannot save you, my love. You must look to Jesus for that."* He pushed them away. He didn't want to think about it. She was wrong. That power had been in her hands, but she had refused to exercise it. It was better this way. Once Montgomery was dead, he would be able to sleep at night.

New York City had not changed in the months he'd been gone. The busy streets and sidewalks were filled with people, many of them British. He would have to be careful. Too many people knew his face. If he was caught, he would hang.

He rented a room and positioned himself at the window to watch the comings and goings of the English troops. He was there

383

nearly a week before he saw Montgomery. As irate as ever, the officer looked as though he had come from the war field. His uniform showed smears of mud, as did his boots.

Montgomery prodded forward another man in chains. Birch peered through the dirty glass. Was that Galen Wright? What was he doing in chains? Birch frowned. The man deserved it, but Lydia would be quite upset. He thought of Lydia's fatherless baby boy. Should he try to save Galen? The thought stuck in his craw. There was no guarantee the man would even stand by Lydia now.

Over the next few days, Birch made his plans to capture Montgomery. He purchased a white wig and a larger British uniform, then went to the harbor and looked over the ships. He was shocked to see his *Mermaid* still floating in the tide. He had assumed she would be confiscated into the navy. Skirting the thugs guarding the harbor, he stole a dinghy and rowed out to the ship and climbed aboard. Though deserted, she appeared to be in fine condition. She was larger than what he'd had in mind, but he knew her well. With just a few crew members, he might be able to use her.

He went back to the quay and spent the next few nights hiring crew. Two of them were members of his original crew, including Riley, and they promised to find six more willing men who knew how to keep their mouths shut and were loyal to America. Now he just had to get Montgomery aboard.

The next morning he dressed in the uniform and stuffed padding inside. With the wig on he looked like a portly British colonel. Montgomery had only seen him once, and Birch thought he would not see through his disguise. He took a silver-tipped walking stick and affected a limp. Perfect.

He limped down the stairs and across the street. Entering the British offices, he approached the soldier on duty. "I wish to see Major Hugh Montgomery. Tell him Colonel Marsh wishes to see him."

The soldier jumped up immediately. "Yes, sir." He disappeared down a hall and came back just moments later. "Follow me, sir. The major is in."

Keeping his face impassive, Birch limped after him.

Montgomery stood as he entered the room. He saluted. "Colonel, sir, I am at your disposal."

"I won't beat around the bush, Major. I have heard you captured a dangerous American spy single-handedly. Very impressive."

Montgomery almost swelled with pride. "Yes, sir. As soon as I saw him, I knew he was up to no good. I had other dealings with him and knew he would betray us sooner or later."

"Excellent. I have need of such a sharp man as you for a special assignment."

Montgomery raised a brow. "Assignment? How may I help you, Colonel?"

"I need a man who is astute about matters such as these to take over the intelligence division in the South. I've already arranged for a fine home at one of the plantations in North Carolina for you. You'll have every comfort while you organize the activities of our various spies and couriers. Think you can handle it?"

"Oh yes, sir!" Montgomery's eyes were shining with excitement. "When do I leave?"

"I have a ship waiting in the harbor now. Gather your things and be aboard the *Mermaid* at six in the morning, where we shall discuss the particulars of your duties on the voyage. Glad to have you aboard my team, Major." He turned to go but stopped at a call from Montgomery.

"Colonel, would it be permissible to bring the prisoner, Galen Wright? I wish to see to his punishment personally."

Birch suppressed a grim smile. So he

wasn't the only one who sought revenge. How ironic. He hesitated a moment. Galen would surely see through his disguise, but by that time, it would be too late. "That would be fine, Major." He nodded. "Until the morrow."

He could see Montgomery practically rubbing his hands together. Limping out the door, Birch felt like doing the same thing. Would the man beg for mercy when he realized what awaited him? He hoped not. He hated a coward.

Birch collected his belongings and made his way to the harbor. He boarded the ship and checked to see that all was in readiness for the morrow. He couldn't afford to have anything go wrong. This was his one and only chance to avenge his brother's murder. The crew was all aboard and knew what they were to do. They seemed as eager for the confrontation as he.

The long night seemed endless as Birch waited for the morning. The cold November gale bit through his coat as he waited on the deck. Finally, he saw three figures hurrying up the gangway.

Another soldier had come along to guard Galen. Birch frowned. He didn't want any more British soldiers aboard than necessary. But with eight of his own crew, surely one more soldier would be all right. He stepped farther back into the shadows. Galen mustn't see his face until they were away from the harbor. Nothing must go wrong.

Riley, his first mate, greeted Montgomery. "Sir, welcome aboard. The colonel will be along shortly. Step away from the rail, and we'll raise the gangplank for departure."

Birch watched the men. Why wasn't he more elated at the success of his plan? He felt dead inside, not joyous at the thought of his vengeance. What was wrong with him?

Let it go.

Shaking away the inner voice, he stared at Montgomery and remembered the butchery of his brother's body. This man had done it, and he must pay.

The crew hoisted anchor and raised the small sail. Slowly, the ship glided away from shore. Only then did Birch step out of the shadows. He still wore the disguise and was curious to see how long it would take Galen to recognize him.

As soon as Galen set eyes on him, his eyes narrowed, then suddenly widened. He began to laugh. "Montgomery, you are a fool. This is no British colonel."

Montgomery jerked around and stared at Birch, then back to Galen. "Shut up, traitor." He cuffed him. "If you speak against your betters again, I shall throw you to the sharks."

Galen growled and charged Montgomery, but the guard jerked his chain, and he fell to the deck. "Look at him again," he growled. " 'Tis Captain Birch Meredith whose head is wanted by the Crown for treason. He has played you for a bloody fool."

While Montgomery stared, Birch casually removed his wig and pulled the stuffing from the uniform. One of his crew plucked the weapons from the major and the guard. Montgomery's face suffused with scarlet.

Birch grinned. "I have to admit it was easier to fool you than I expected." He held up his flintlock pistol to check Montgomery's charge. "You should not give me an excuse to shoot you too quickly, Major."

Montgomery stopped and glared at him. "What is the meaning of this charade?"

"I should have thought it was obvious, Major. You are my prisoner." Birch motioned to the stairs behind the British soldiers. "Let us go to the salon where I shall explain all this out of the wind." He motioned for them to go first.

They filed down the steps into the captain's salon, and Birch had them all sit down. "Do you remember asking me if I was related to any southern Merediths?"

The major frowned. "I remember."

"What if I told you the answer was aye?"

Fear flashed into Montgomery's eyes. "Frightened are you, Major? You have good reason to be."

"What are you talking about?" Galen asked. "What does having relatives in the South have to do with anything?"

"Explain it to him, Major." Birch propped a foot on a chair and stared at him.

Montgomery cut his gaze from side to side and wet his lips. "Ah, well . . ." He looked down at the floor.

Birch's lip curled, contempt burning in his belly. "Ashamed, Major? Ashamed of your little fox chase? Ashamed that you hung a young boy of fifteen by his heels and slaughtered him as you would an animal?" He raised his voice. "I have waited for the best time to exact my vengeance all these years, Major, but the wait is over. You will die in the sea. The frigid waters will claim you, and as you struggle to stay afloat, you'll have time to think about what you did to my brother!" He shouted the last word in Montgomery's face, and he flinched.

"He was a spy!"

Birch thrust his face closer to Montgomery. "He was *fifteen!*"

Galen made a sound of disgust, and Birch whirled around to face him. "And you are no better, Wright. You used a sweet, innocent girl then discarded her when she became pregnant. Have you even wondered what has become of her? If you have a child?"

Galen ran his tongue over his lips. "Have I a child?"

"A fine son, whom you do not deserve." He was full of rage at both men. Why could they not see where their actions had led them?

"Where are Lydia and the child?" Galen asked.

"You almost sound as if you care," Birch said. "She is far from your reach. Hannah cares for her and the babe, and methinks she would kill you if you dared harm her sister again."

Galen blanched. "Hannah knows it is my babe?"

"Of course. Did you think Lydia would hide it? The poor fool still pines for you."

"I could wed her, give the child a name," Galen muttered. "I had nothing to do with your brother. Kill Montgomery, by all means, but not me."

What a coward. Birch felt a shaft of utter

disdain for the man. What had Lydia ever seen in him? Still, if this poor excuse for a man would truly give the babe a name, Lydia might be able to weather the shame and have some sort of life. Right now the best she could hope for was a life of prostitution or the charity of her sister. "I might consider that offer," he told Galen. No need to let him know he wouldn't kill him anyway.

Hope brightened Galen's dull eyes. "You know 'tis what Lydia wants. And the babe will need a father."

Birch nodded with reluctance. "Now I must ask you to go to your cabins." He indicated the lower hold and marched them down to the tiny cabins in the lower deck where he put them in separate cabins and locked them in.

Before he shut the door to Montgomery's cabin, he stared at his hated enemy. "We set sail for Gurnet, Major, but you shall not live to see its shores."

CHAPTER 29

Hannah expelled a weary sigh and trudged up the steps to the first light tower. Between keeping the lights and caring for Lydia and both babies, she was plumb worn out. She held her hands over the meager warmth of the wicks and rubbed them. Winter had come early this year. It was not yet December, and already ice chunks floated offshore. The first blizzard of the season had blown through last week, and ten-foot drifts covered the walls of her house. Her wool cloak did little to keep out the piercing cold.

She stared out over the black sea. Much as she wanted to sail away, she wouldn't want to be out on a night like this. She shivered and went back to her tasks. The children would want feeding in a few hours, and she hoped to get some sleep before then. When she'd come out this morning at two, she'd checked on young John and found him sleeping peacefully. It must be nearly three now, and he was often up at five demanding his breakfast.

She sighed again at the thought of Lydia. She was pining. Hidden away in Hannah's house lest the town elders see her and her babe, she talked incessantly of Galen. But then Lydia's mind seemed to have no bearing in reality lately. She rambled as though Galen was coming back to her.

If Hannah heard that name once more, she would scream. She shook her head and went down the winding staircase. It did no good to argue with Lydia. Galen would never be less than perfect in her eyes.

Exiting the tower, she saw a shape flit past the side of the house. The moon caught golden hair. Lydia. Where was she going? Hannah hurried after her sister. Rounding the corner of the house, she saw the white flash of Lydia's shift disappearing down the cliff path.

Her heart in her throat, Hannah hurried as fast as she dared through the snowdrifts. What was Lydia doing out in just her shift? Hannah glanced down to see where she was going, and a shaft of moonlight revealed bare footprints in the snow. No shoes!

Giving up all pretense of watching where she walked herself, she struggled through the snow. She had to find Lydia before she caught a cold. She almost appeared to be asleep.

At the top of the cliff, she scanned the windswept beach below and saw Lydia standing beside a patch of frozen marsh grass. Staring out to sea, the wind whipped her hair and shift straight back. She looked like the figurehead on a ship.

Should she call out to her? Hannah started down the path. What if she became startled or disoriented? She might run right into the icy waves and drown. No, she had best simply reach her sister and physically take her back to the house. They would be fortunate if Lydia didn't come down with winter fever.

Lydia seemed not to hear her approach but just gazed out to sea. She didn't seem to feel the cold or the wind. Standing like a statue, she didn't so much as move her head. Hannah felt as though she moved through mud or quicksand. Her heart pounded with exertion and fear. Finally, she was close enough to touch her.

Hannah took Lydia's arm in a firm grip. "Sister, you should be inside. Come, let me get you to bed." She kept her voice gentle and turned Lydia away from the wind.

"Why is Galen not here?" Lydia's voice was a haunted whisper. "He still loves me. I know he does, Hannah."

The eyes that gazed into Hannah's were not familiar. She could see no trace of the lighthearted girl who had come to stay with her nearly a year and a half year ago. "Of course, he does," she said soothingly. "Come along, Lydia. You are like a block of ice." She propelled her firmly back the way they'd come, but it was like propelling a rag doll. Lydia moved without resistance.

At the top of the cliff, Lydia paused and looked back out over the frigid sea. "I should like to walk into the ocean and let the waves carry me to Galen. Do you think they would know where to take me?" Her voice was faraway and almost singsong.

Terror gripped Hannah. "No, you must not, Lydia. Galen is not on the sea. He is fighting in the war, remember? You must not think of such things. Galen needs you to care for his child until he comes back from the war." The mention of Galen calmed Lydia immediately, as Hannah had hoped, and she followed Hannah back to the house.

Once inside, she put her sister in a chair with a quilt around her and a hot brick at her feet. Lydia stared listlessly into the dancing flames. Finally her head bobbed, and she fell asleep in the chair. Hannah sank into the chair beside her and buried her face in her hands. What was she to do? How could she deal with this on top of the children and the lighthouse?

She was so very tired. She'd tried as hard as she knew to meet the needs of her loved ones, but she felt as though she'd failed. Birch had left her to carry out his retribution, and her sister had borne a bastard child and would likely be punished by the town elders once they heard of it. Neither of them had listened to her.

They have the right to choose, as you did.

The voice was in her heart, but it soothed her as much as if it had been audible. She was trying to take too much responsibility for those she loved. She couldn't make them do right — they had to make their own decisions. Praying for them to seek God's wisdom, she sat with her head bowed for a long time.

When young John's thin, reedy cry came, she rose stiffly. She glanced at Lydia, hating to waken her, but the babe would need nursing. She went up the steps and picked up the baby. He already was beginning to look like his father. The same blue eyes and blond hair, the same chin and stubborn mouth. The image of Galen in a far more innocent time. They would need wisdom from God to raise this one to channel that stubbornness in the right ways.

She cuddled him, changed his nappy, and carried him to his mother. Lydia was already awake. Hannah was glad to see the bright light of awareness in her eyes.

"Why am I sleeping in the chair?" she asked Hannah.

"You do not remember awakening in the night?"

"No. And my feet hurt as though they've been burned."

"Let me see." Hannah handed her the baby and knelt to examine Lydia's feet. They were fiery red, but she saw no evidence of frostbite. "I found you outside in your shift and bare feet about three this morning. Methinks you were walking in your sleep." That was all she needed to know.

"Outside?" Bewildered, Lydia's lovely face was creased with a frown.

"No harm done. Your son thinks he shall starve if you don't feed him."

Distracted from her questions, Lydia looked down and smiled at the crying babe. She unbuttoned her shift and began to nurse him. "He looks much like Galen, does he not?"

"I was thinking that myself when I picked him up this morning. Galen will never be able to deny his paternity."

"Galen would never try to deny it!" Lydia smoothed a hand over his downy hair. "He will love the babe when he sees him."

"Of course not, Lydia. I only meant that he would be proud to see himself so clearly in his son."

"Methinks John and I shall go find him as soon as I am well again."

"You cannot." Hannah couldn't keep the words back though she knew it would just make her sister more resolved to have her own way. "John is much too young to be traveling about the countryside in the middle of a war."

Lydia surprised her by nodding. "You are right, Sister. I may have to wait a bit. I shall write him a letter and tell him of his son. He will find us."

Hannah breathed a sigh of relief. There was not much chance of that. If Galen wanted Lydia and his son, he would not have sent her away like he did. He doubtless thought he was well rid of them both. They had likely seen the last of the man.

Two days out of Gurnet, the nor'easter struck. Birch stayed with the crew on deck battling the wind and waves. The cold wind lashed the ship with fury, and the men took turns warming up in the cabin below. The wind drove them off course, and by the time the storm had ended, they were another day's distance from their goal.

The first clear morning after the storm, Birch woke with a sense of purpose. This was the day. He would have his vengeance today. They were far from shore, an ideal place to drop the major overboard. He dressed with haste, took his sword and his pistol, and went to the hold.

He unlocked the door to Montgomery's cabin. "Come with me."

Montgomery took one look at his stony face and backed away. "No, you cannot do it, Captain." He put his hands up as a shield. "Take me to the authorities and charge me with murder, but don't just leave me in the sea. What about sharks?"

Birch gave a bark of laughter. "Sharks would be fast, Major. Face your death like a man."

Montgomery gave him a disdainful glance. "What do you know about being a man? If you were a real man, you would face me in an honest fight."

"The way you killed my brother in an honest fight?" Birch's voice was low, but his remark hit home. The major flushed and his eyes went flat.

"Fine. But my demise will be on your conscience, Captain." He pulled on his coat and stood waiting.

"I can handle it." But could he? He was beginning to wonder. Could he even do it? He felt a shaft of shame at his feeble determination. Where had his resolve for vengeance gone? Montgomery should have been dead already.

Birch motioned for the major to come out of the cabin, then unlocked Galen's cabin as well. He should witness the execution so he would be too afraid to back out on his promise to Lydia.

Galen eased to his feet and smiled at Montgomery. "So your death warrant is about to be served, eh, Major?" He slipped his arms into his coat sleeves and picked up his tricorn hat. "I shall enjoy seeing you flailing in the waves."

"Just remember you shall suffer the same fate if you double-cross me." Birch felt as though he'd made a bargain with the devil. Galen was a slippery villain.

Galen's face darkened. "I will remember."

Birch marched them to the deck. A pale sun shone weakly from a light-blue sky. Cold gray waves battered the hull of the ship. He remembered the feel of the ocean's cold grip himself. He'd fallen overboard in the winter once, and only the quick response of his crew had saved him. He'd been near death in only moments. The crew had put the plank out for Montgomery.

"Get on the plank," Birch said, his heart pounding so hard he found it hard to think. The Scripture Hannah quoted to him floated in his mind. *"Vengeance is mine; I shall repay, saith the Lord."* Hannah's now-familiar words pestered him again. *"Jesus must save you. I cannot."* He willed all those words away. He'd waited years for this moment. Years to watch Montgomery pay. He would not let soft words from Hannah deter him from his purpose.

But no matter how hard he tried, he couldn't still God's voice in his head. Turning to look into his enemy's face, he saw the fear in Montgomery's eyes. In that moment Birch knew killing him would solve nothing. It wouldn't bring back his brother, and it wouldn't satisfy that place in his heart that wanted an end. No ending would ever come, even if Montgomery died. Birch would still have to live without his brother and without his Hannah.

He couldn't do it. His shoulders slumped, and he stumbled to the other side of the deck. Falling onto his knees he released his bitterness and hatred.

" 'Tis yours, Lord," he whispered. "Forgive me for my hard-heartedness."

The astonished murmurs of his crew broke through his introspection as though from a great distance, and he rose to his feet. Light. He felt light and free. The heaviness he'd carried since Charlie's death was gone.

He spun around and faced Montgomery, still standing on the end of the plank. "Get down. God has convinced me to leave you in his hands."

An astounded smile dawned on the major's face. He stepped toward the deck.

"No!" Galen howled. He threw himself forward on his knees before any of the crew could stop him. "He must die." He shoved at Montgomery's legs, and the major teetered on the gangplank.

The major stepped back and lost his footing. With a scream he pitched over the edge and into the icy water below. A crew member wrestled Galen to the deck.

"Montgomery!" Birch flung himself to the rail and saw him floundering in the gray waves. He seized a cask tied to a rope beside the rail and heaved it overboard. "Grab the cask!"

Swimming awkwardly, the major struck out for the cask, but it bobbed out of his reach. He made another try and managed to get an arm around it. His face was as white as the foam striking it.

The man was weakening fast. "Hang on! We'll haul you in." Birch motioned for his first mate and another sailor to help him, and they pulled on the rope.

Birch leaned over the side and shouted at Montgomery, "Hold tight. You're almost here."

Montgomery was barely keeping his head above the water. Waves splashed in his face, and sputtering, he went under several times. When they had him positioned at the ship's ladder, Birch scrambled over the side to help him.

"Let me, Cap'n," Riley said. " 'Tis too dangerous."

Birch shook his head. "I want to do it." He felt responsible since he had forced Montgomery to get on the plank. The major was barely hanging on to consciousness. A wave struck him and pushed him out of Birch's reach. Then a fin sliced through the water. Birch felt pure terror at the sight of the shark.

"Montgomery! Swim to me! Shark!" Birch yelled the words into the sea. "Shark!"

The major's half-closed eyes opened wide, and he turned to see the fin coming toward him. He screamed and cursed, but he wouldn't let go of the cask and swim to the ship.

"Swim, Major!" Birch leaned out as far as he dared with his arm outreached. "You have to swim!" He shouted to his men on deck, "Pull, men! We have to get him."

The men were yanking on the rope, but the pitch of the ship and the white-capped waves jerked the cask back out nearly as fast as they pulled it in. The major screamed again, and the shark reached him. He gave a choking shriek and was yanked beneath the water. Waves of red bubbled up to replace him, but whitecaps soon replaced them.

Birch hid his face against the rough wood of the ship and shuddered. He made a slow climb back to the deck. God had truly had his vengeance this day. Montgomery had almost been safe. Birch swung his legs over the railing and stood on the deck on shaking legs.

"Good riddance!" Galen writhed in the grip of the two sailors, and a wild exultation shone from his eyes. "I said I would have my revenge on him, but he did not believe me."

Galen laughed, and the malevolent sound made Birch cringe inside. Was that how

Hannah had felt when he had vowed he would have his vengeance? He understood now.

"Take him below," he told his men. He couldn't bear to look upon his face.

He stared out over the empty sea. No trace of Montgomery remained. Now Birch could go to Hannah with a clear conscience. In three days he would see her green eyes again and tell her the past's shackles on him were gone.

Chapter 30

Hannah felt as though she had not slept in months, though in truth it had been only a few days. She often found Lydia wandering the house at night. Her eyes would be vacant, and she remembered nothing the next morning. Hannah didn't know what to do. She couldn't go to Mother Thomas for help, and Olive was far away in Boston.

December had come, but the weather had been unusually mild the past few days. The pale-blue sky and sunshine brightened her mood, and she decided to go for a walk while Lydia stayed with the children. She wouldn't be gone long, and Lydia was always fine during the day.

She strolled along the path at the top of the cliff overlooking the sea. The choppy waves splashed noisily on the rocks below. Mingled with the sound of the surf, she thought she heard voices. She hurried to the edge of the cliff, then looked down into the cove.

Two men got out of a ship's boat and started up the path to the lighthouse. When they were within ten feet of her, her heart jumped. She knew that confident stride. Birch had come back. Joy nearly choked her. He looked up and saw her. Lifting a hand in greeting, their eyes connected as never before, and somehow Hannah realized what that meant. He'd let the past go.

The other man noticed Birch's distraction and reacted instantly, pulling the pistol from Birch's belt. Birch made a move as if to attack him, but the man gestured toward her.

"I shall shoot her, Captain. Stay where you are!"

Galen's voice. Hannah put a hand to her throat and glanced behind her. She hoped Lydia still slept.

Birch's hand dropped, and he glanced at Hannah with an apology in his eyes. She looked around for a weapon, but the heavy snowfall had covered any branches she might have used for a club.

Galen prodded Birch with the pistol and forced him to Hannah's side. He waved the pistol in her face and laughed as though at a fine joke. His eyes shone with a strange light, and Hannah shuddered.

"We meet again, sweet Hannah." His gaze

raked over her, and he smiled again. "Just as lovely as ever." He glanced at Birch. "We shall see who is married to Lydia this day, shall we not, Captain?"

His cryptic words puzzled Hannah. She glanced at Birch, but he just shrugged. She sensed a coiled power in his bunched muscles and knew Galen would not have the upper hand for long.

"Hello, my love." Birch made a move as though to take her in his arms, but Galen jabbed him with the pistol again.

"She is not for you, Captain. Haven't you realized that yet?" Galen motioned toward the house. "Let us go to the house and discuss this like civilized folks, shall we?"

They had no choice, so Hannah led the way back to the house. She just prayed Lydia would realize something was amiss and get John's sword from the bedroom. A vain hope, she knew. Lydia would never believe evil of Galen.

The warmth of the crackling fire welcomed them. Galen sighed. He settled in the chair next to the fire and waved the pistol in Hannah's direction. "Fix me some hot food, Hannah. That fare aboard ship was not fit for man or beast." He shoved a stool at Birch. "Have a seat, Captain."

His eyes on the pistol, Birch sat slowly on

the stool. Hannah hesitated a moment. She hated to leave them alone. Galen was so unpredictable.

He saw her still standing in the doorway. "Now!" he roared. "Do not try my patience."

There were knives in the kitchen. Could she use one on Galen? She would if she had to, but she would rather get it to Birch. She was small and slight and would be no match for Galen's burly muscles. She slipped the largest and sharpest one in her pocket, then took another and quickly cut some of the roast pork on the skewer she'd been preparing for supper. She raked some potatoes from the coals and cut two slices of bread. After putting it on a plate, she carried it to Galen.

His eyes brightened at the food. "You shall make someone a good wife, Hannah. Birch thinks it will be him." He laughed again.

Hannah glanced at Birch. She could see her own puzzlement reflected in his eyes. What was Galen planning?

"Cut my meat for me. I cannot do it one-handed."

She'd hoped Galen would put down the pistol to eat, but he was too sly for that. She took the plate from him and cut up his food. Handing it back, her other hand went to her pocket, and she fondled the knife. If she had the courage to use it, now was the time, while Galen's head was bent over his plate. But she could not force her hand to pull out the knife and plunge it into his back. All the atrocities he'd committed against her family rose in her mind, and her hand trembled, but still she refused to move.

Lydia came down the stairs. Her eyes widened when she saw Galen. She started toward him with outstretched arms. "My love, my Galen, you have found me."

He looked up from his plate. "Stay back, Lydia. Can you not see I am eating?"

She stopped. "Of course, Galen. But I am so happy to see you. Would you like to see your son?"

He nodded without looking up from his plate. "Fetch him."

Lydia practically ran up the steps. At the top of the stairs, she looked back down, and Hannah felt a pang at the joy on her face. Poor Lydia. Poor, poor Lydia. So blind, so deceived.

Within moments she came flying back down the steps with young John in her arms. She held him out proudly for Galen's inspection. "He looks just like his papa."

Galen pushed his empty plate away and stared at his son. "So he does." A trace of awe tinged his voice. "A fine boy, Lydia. Now give him to Hannah."

Lydia stared at Hannah with a question in her eyes. Hannah shrugged. She had no idea what Galen intended. Lydia walked to her sister and handed her the baby.

"Now tie up the good Captain." He held the pistol to Hannah's head. "If you value her life, Captain, you will make no move."

"I-I have no rope." Lydia held her hands out.

"Well, find some!"

Lydia flinched at his roar. "Yes, Galen."

She went to the kitchen, and Hannah heard her rummaging in the storeroom. Hannah's heart sank. They stowed rope in there. She stared at Birch, and his eyes told her to have courage. She took heart from the peace and determination in his gaze.

A few minutes later Lydia returned carrying a length of rope. "Here is some." She bounced on her toes.

"Tie him tight." Galen's eyes watched her every move with a slight smile. "And stuff a rag in his mouth. I have heard enough of his preaching about forgiveness to last a lifetime."

Hannah must make a move or it would be too late. She shifted young John to her left arm and reached into her pocket with her right hand. No one saw her furtive movement except Lydia. In an instant she discerned her sister's intention.

"No!" she screamed. She fought Hannah for the knife.

Hampered as she was by the baby, Hannah couldn't put up much of a fight, and Lydia succeeded in wresting it from her.

"Very good, Lydia." Galen's smile widened. He gestured to Lydia again. "Tie him up and make it tight. I don't want him to get away."

Lydia slipped the knife into her pocket and tied Birch's hands behind him, then wrapped the rope around the chair legs.

Hannah thought Birch might have managed to bulk his muscles as he was being tied to allow him some slack to work with. Given time, he might work his way free. But she didn't think they would have much time.

Testing it for strength, she stepped back and turned to Galen. "Where are we going when we leave here?"

Galen didn't answer at first. He just surveyed the scene with a satisfied expression. He stood and strolled around Birch. "I intend to kill you, Captain."

Hannah trembled, an awful feeling roiling through her.

Galen turned to Hannah. "Beg me for his

life, Hannah," he said with a smirk. "If you ask prettily, I might spare him."

"Please, Galen, he has done nothing to you."

"Oh, but he has. He stole what belonged to me, what I took for myself when you were sixteen. For that he deserves the severest penalty."

"You were the one who stole by force what should have been for my husband alone." Hannah couldn't still the hot words.

Lydia frowned. "What do you mean, Hannah? Galen would not force a woman. He is an honorable man." She turned to Galen. "Is that not so, my love?"

He snorted. "You were ever a fool, Lydia. She has always belonged to me. When she would not come to me willingly, I had no choice but to take what belonged to me."

Lydia's eyes widened in horror. "It-it is true?"

Hannah lowered her head and whispered, "It's true."

The horror in Lydia's eyes bled out into serenity. "No matter. That is past. We shall leave this place with our son and sail to England."

Galen scowled. "You still do not understand, do you, wench? You were nothing but a pretty face to pass the time until Hannah could be mine again. Hannah knows she and I were destined to be together. Your usefulness has come to an end."

He took the baby in one arm, still keeping the pistol trained on Hannah. "Put your cloak on, Hannah, and fetch a blanket for the babe. We shall take him with us. I would not leave my son in the care of a doxy like Lydia. Do as I say, and I will let your captain live." He smiled cruelly. "This time."

"No!" Lydia wailed. "You cannot take my baby."

Galen pressed his lips together, and Hannah could see he was holding on to his temper by the merest whisker. "If you do not stop your ceaseless haranguing, I shall tie you to the chair and stuff a rag in your mouth too. I have had enough of your nagging." He pointed the gun at Birch's head. "Do what I say, Hannah, or I shall shoot him now."

Her heart full of dread, Hannah hurried to obey. Her hands trembled as she tied her cloak about her shoulders and picked up a wool blanket in which to wrap John. Glancing at Birch, she could see his bonds were nearly loose. She averted her eyes quickly before she drew Galen's attention to it as well.

Galen handed her the baby. "Come

along." He pulled his own coat on, took her arm, and propelled her toward the door. "By the time your captain is free, we shall be to Plymouth and duly married. He will be able to do nothing."

Birch strained against his bonds, his eyes pleading with Hannah to refuse to go. But she could not stand by and see Galen shoot him. She had no doubt he would do it.

Lydia wrung her hands. "Take me with you, Galen. Surely this is a jest. You would not be so cruel. I birthed your son. Hannah cannot love you as I do." She had no cloak around her, but she followed them out the door and toward the cliff path.

At the top of the cliff, Galen turned to face her. "I have had enough, Lydia! Go away, or I shall shoot you and be done with it." His face dark with rage, he waved the pistol at her. "You have been a thorn in my side this past year. I have what I came for!"

As the awful truth of what was happening finally sank in, she blanched. "You don't love me, Galen? You truly do not?"

"How many times must I say it? I have never loved you. Now leave us be!" He faced Hannah and gestured to the path that led to the beach. "You go first, my dear."

Hannah could see Lydia's face. Her eyes were sunken, her mouth scrunched up in pain. As though in a dream, Lydia slipped her hand in her pocket and drew out the knife. She looked down at her hand, then at Galen. Her face changed and became ferocious. With a cry she flew at his back, and the pistol fell to the ground.

He turned to meet her and grappled for the knife as Birch, free of his bonds, burst out of the house and started to close the distance between them. He snatched up the pistol, but there was no opportunity to use it.

Lydia was like a wild woman. She clung to the knife, biting and scratching. She and Galen were as one person, with no chance for Birch to shoot Galen without risking Lydia. Birch moved forward to try to separate them, but before he reached them, they teetered on the edge of the cliff.

Hannah's breath caught in her throat. "Lydia, be careful," she cried.

Lydia seemed to realize the danger. She turned her gaze and met Hannah's for a moment. Then she smiled a sad smile and turned her attention back to Galen. She threw her body against him in a final frenzied attack and forced him even closer to the brink.

"No!" Galen rolled his eyes in terror as one foot slipped over the edge. His arms windmilled frantically, then with a final despairing cry, he and Lydia pitched over the precipice.

Hannah screamed and rushed to the edge of the cliff and looked down. Two crumpled bodies lay on the rocks below, the sea lapping blood away with every wave. The waves were already trying to carry them out to sea. Tears stung her eyes, and she buried her face in John's blanket and wept.

Moments later, Birch called her name. More sobs burst from her throat, and she stumbled into his waiting arms. "Dead. They went over the cliff," she babbled.

"I saw." Birch drew her close, and she clung to him as to a rock in a storm. They stood there for several minutes as Hannah sobbed. She didn't see how she could bear this devastating blow.

His arm still around her, Birch stepped to the edge. "The sea has taken them."

Hannah buried her face in his coat. Visions of Lydia as a child tumbled through her mind. Such a bright and happy child, ruined by Galen.

Birch seemed to know what she was thinking. "She had to make her own choices, my love. Just as you and I have to. Come inside. We must get the babe out of the cold. And check on Charlotte too. She may be awake and frightened." He guided her toward the house, and she leaned into his strength.

Inside the house she hurried up the stairs. She put John in his bed and smoothed the soft cap of hair. He would know the bright spirit who had been his mother. She would tell him. He was all she had left of her sister. Tears pooled in her eyes, and she choked back a sob. Crying wouldn't change anything, but it was all she could do to hold back the tears.

Straightening her shoulders, she brushed the tears from her cheeks and went down the hall to check on Charlotte. The babe was just beginning to awaken. "Would you like to see Papa, darling girl?" Hannah whispered. She picked her up and carried her downstairs.

Birch turned to stare at her when she came into the parlor. The love in his eyes brought a lump to her throat.

He held out his arms for Charlotte. "Hello, sweet girl. Will you come to Papa?"

Charlotte stared at him gravely for a moment, then held out her chubby arms for him. He directed a joyous smile to Hannah and took their daughter in his arms.

After a few moments he kissed the top of Charlotte's curly head. "I must see if I can recover the bodies, my love." He handed the baby back to Hannah. "I may not be back till the morrow. I have much to tell you."

"I shall be here."

The rest of the afternoon dragged by. Hannah finally put Charlotte to bed and retired herself. Thinking of Lydia and her ruined life, it was a long time before Hannah slept, and then only after many tears.

The sun had hardly begun to pinken the horizon when she heard pounding on the door. Her feet still bare, she rushed down the steps and threw open the door. Birch stood there, his pirate eyes boring into her. He held out his arms, and she rushed into them.

"Did you find them?" Her words were muffled against the wool of his uniform.

His arms tightened, and he kissed the top of her head. "No, my love. The sea did not want to give them up."

Tears sprang to her eyes, and she nodded. " 'Tis better this way. I would rather remember Lydia as the laughing maid she was."

He guided her inside and shut the door behind them. Sitting on the sofa, he pulled her into his lap. "I am free, Hannah. Free of vengeance and hatred."

"I knew as soon as I saw you." Her heart was near bursting with joy.

He smiled tenderly. "You will wed me now?" Putting his hands on her shoulders, he stared into her face. "It will not be easy these first years, my mermaid. I shall have to go back to war. The fight for liberty rages on."

"I know." For some reason, she was unafraid.

He traced her jaw with his finger. The touch brought shivers to her spine. She turned her face into his hand and kissed the palm. He took her mobcap off and gently took the pins from her hair. The dark locks tumbled from her head, and he thrust his hands into the mass of curls. She quivered at the touch of his hands in her hair.

"I thought I might never get to do this," he murmured. He buried his face in her neck. "You smell like the sea after a rain, fresh and sweet."

Hannah put her arms around his waist. He gathered her closer and left a trail of kisses up her neck and across her cheek until his lips found hers. As their breath mingled, he pulled her closer, and she was lost in the wonder of his kiss.

EPILOGUE

As she did every day at sunrise and sunset, Hannah stood on the lonely hillside in the fading light of day and looked out over the water for her husband's ship. The babe in her womb kicked, and she rubbed at her belly. "Peace, little one. Your father promised to be home in time for your birth, and I know it will be so."

Charlotte looked up at her. "Papa?" Little John echoed his big sister's query with a questioning look.

"Soon, my loves." She took each child by the hand. Birch needed to hurry though. The babe was due next week, and she grew impatient to see him.

As she turned to retreat to the house, over her shoulder she caught sight of a white sail. Her heart thumped in her chest, and she turned back to face the sea. From the shape of the ship, it could be the *Mermaid.*

As the ship grew nearer, a boat was lowered, and a lone figure waved at her. Birch! She picked up both children, and they waved at their father as he rowed to shore.

"Let us go meet Papa." She led the children down the rocky slope to the beach.

She felt as light as the clouds floating in the sky as she waited for her husband. It seemed forever until he leapt over the side of the boat and pulled it the last few feet to shore in the waves.

His fierce embrace told her everything she needed to know.

"The treaty is ready to be signed. I shall not leave you again." He pressed a final kiss on her head, then swung Charlotte into his arms and tossed her up in the air. She squealed with delight, but John hung back with his thumb in his mouth.

Hannah pressed a hand to her chest, and tears sprang to her eyes. "Oh, Birch! I could expire from joy."

The light in his pirate eyes was a blaze of love and devotion. "What say you to the notion of letting someone else keep the light, my love?"

"I would say I have my eye on a suitable gentleman." A young man from the village had been helping her as her belly grew ponderous and she grew awkward. "We shall to go to Boston?"

His grin spread across his face. "I have a yen to see China when the babe is old enough. The *Mermaid* is well equipped for the journey, and I have already outfitted the captain's quarters to hold our brood of children."

The breath left her lungs as visions of Shanghai, silk, and exotic teas flooded her mind.

He put down Charlotte and embraced Hannah again. "Your light led me to freedom, my love. What need have I of a lighthouse when you are by my side?"

With his arm around her shoulders, he turned her to face the sea and his ship. "Together we will embark on adventures beyond comprehension, Hannah. What say you to that?"

Her heart was so full she found it hard to speak, so she turned and threw her arms around his neck. " 'Twas a momentous day when I pulled you from the sea, Captain. I don't think I shall throw you back."

A NOTE FROM THE AUTHOR

Dear Reader,

To say I'm thrilled to deliver this book to you is an understatement. *Freedom's Light* has languished in my virtual drawer for eighteen years, but it's been a precious story to me from the first moment I came up with the idea.

This is the novel that landed me my wonderful agent Karen Solem, and this is the book I've always regretted not publishing. The Revolutionary War period was a tough sell back when I wrote it, and I wasn't sure this novel would ever be in your hands. I'm so thankful my terrific editor Amanda Bostic loved it as much as I do and wanted to bring it to life.

Please let me know what you think of Hannah and Birch's story!

Colleen Coble
colleen@colleencoble.com
colleencoble.com

ACKNOWLEDGMENTS

I'm so blessed to belong to the terrific HarperCollins Christian Publishing dream team! I've been with my great fiction team for fifteen years, and they are like family to me. I learn something new with every book, which makes writing so much fun for me!

Our fiction publisher and editor, Amanda Bostic, is as dear to me as a daughter. She really gets suspense and has been my friend from the moment I met her all those years ago. Fabulous cover guru Kristen Ingebretson works hard to create the perfect cover — and does. And, of course, I can't forget the other friends in my amazing fiction family: Becky Monds, Kristen Golden, Allison Carter, Jodi Hughes, Paul Fisher, Matt Bray, Kimberly Carlton, Laura Wheeler, and Kayleigh Hines. You are all such a big part of my life. I wish I could name all the great folks at HCCP who work on selling my books through different venues. I'm truly blessed!

Julee Schwarzburg is a dream editor to work with. She totally gets fiction, and our partnership is pure joy. This book was a special challenge with such historical detail, and her eye on making sure it was right was a tremendous help!

My agent, Karen Solem, has helped shape my career in many ways, and that includes kicking an idea to the curb when necessary. We are about to celebrate eighteen years together! And my critique partner of twenty years, Denise Hunter, is the best sounding board ever. Thanks, friends!

I'm so grateful for my husband, Dave, who carts me around from city to city, washes towels, and chases down dinner without complaint. My kids — Dave, Kara (and now Donna and Mark) — love and support me in every way possible, and my little granddaughter, Alexa, makes every day a joy. She's talking like a grown-up now, and having her spend the night is more fun than I can tell you. Our little grandson, Elijah, is seventeen months old now, and we are expecting a new baby in May. Exciting times!

Most important, I give my thanks to God,

who has opened such amazing doors for me and makes the journey a golden one.

DISCUSSION QUESTIONS

1. Arranged marriages were common in this era. What do you think about that idea?

2. I sometimes wonder which side of the conflict I would have been on. Have you ever thought about our struggle for freedom and how you would have reacted? Would you have sided with England and tried to keep the status quo or would you have fought hard for autonomy?

3. Lydia's willfulness seems all too common these days. Why do you think society seems to have gone in the direction of self?

4. A grudge can become all consuming. For me, it's harder to forgive something done against a loved one than against me personally. What do you struggle with?

5. The story dealt with obsession in several

different forms. Galen's obsession with Hannah, Lydia's obsession with Galen, Birch's obsession with revenge, and various obsessions with power. Which one is the hardest for you to understand?

6. The Puritan church of that era could focus on rules and not love. Have you ever experienced a church like that?

7. Jesus was Hannah's first love. That can be hard to maintain in the stresses of life. What anchors you?

8. Hannah always circled back to what Birch really needed — God. For me personally, I often seek to help someone in my own power, which is exactly the opposite of what I should be doing. How do you deal with this issue?

ABOUT THE AUTHOR

Colleen Coble is a *USA TODAY* bestselling author and RITA finalist best known for her romantic suspense novels, including *Tidewater Inn, Rosemary Cottage,* and the Mercy Falls, Lonestar, Rock Harbor, and Sunset Cove series.

Visit her website at www.colleencoble.com
Twitter: @colleencoble
Facebook: colleencoblebooks

The employees of Thorndike Press hope you have enjoyed this Large Print book. All our Thorndike, Wheeler, and Kennebec Large Print titles are designed for easy reading, and all our books are made to last. Other Thorndike Press Large Print books are available at your library, through selected bookstores, or directly from us.

For information about titles, please call:
  (800) 223-1244

or visit our website at:
  gale.com/thorndike

To share your comments, please write:
  Publisher
  Thorndike Press
  10 Water St., Suite 310
  Waterville, ME 04901